Million Writers Award: The Best Online Science Fiction and Fantasy

Million Writers Award: The Best Online Science Fiction and Fantasy is a work of fiction. Names, characters, places, and incidents are the product of the author's imagination or are used fictitiously.

Copyright © April 2012, Jason Sanford
All rights reserved. Printed in the USA.

Published by:
Spotlight Publishing, Inc.
P.O. Box 621
Madison, NC 27025
www.spotlight-publishing.com

No part of this book may be reproduced or transmitted, in whole or in part, in any form or by any means, without the express written permission from the copyright owner, except for the inclusion of brief quotations in a review.

ISBN: 978-0-9768469-8-7

10 9 8 7 6 5 4 3 2 1

Since 2003, the Million Writers Award has recognized the best short stories published each year in online magazines and journal. The award is run by author and editor Jason Sanford and hosted by the online literary journal *storySouth*.

The award has three parts. First, a group of literary judges selects a list of notable online stories published in the last year. Second, a smaller group of judges picks the top ten stories of the year from the notable list. Finally, the general public votes for their favorite story from among the top ten finalists.

Over the last nine years the Million Writers Award has awarded thousands of dollars in cash and prizes to the winning authors.

What others are saying about the Million Writers Award

"The Million Writers Award is probably the most comprehensive award given for online fiction in the United States."

— NewPages.com

"I think the best thing that the Million Writers Award has done is to drive hundreds of people to read 'Urchins, While Swimming.' Most of those people would never have seen it otherwise, and that's a fantastic result."

— Catherynne M. Valente, *New York Times* bestselling author whose "Urchins, While Swimming" won the 2007 Million Writers Award

Publication and Copyright Credits

All stories copyright by their individual authors. For complete author, publication, and copyright information on each story, please see the additional materials section below and in the back of the book.

- "Introduction to *Million Writers Award: The Best Online Science Fiction and Fantasy*" by Jason Sanford is original to this volume. © 2012 Jason Sanford.
- "Non-Zero Probabilities" by N. K. Jemisin originally published in *Clarkesworld Magazine*. "Non-Zero Probabilities" © 2009 N. K. Jemisin.
- "The Faithful Soldier, Prompted" by Saladin Ahmed originally published in *Apex Magazine*. "The Faithful Soldier, Prompted" © 2010 Saladin Ahmed.
- "Arvies" by Adam-Troy Castro originally published in *Lightspeed Magazine*. "Arvies" © 2010 Adam-Troy Castro.
- "There's a Hole in the City" by Richard Bowes originally published in *SCIFICTION*. "There's a Hole in the City" © 2005 Richard Bowes.
- "Horus Ascending" by Aliette de Bodard originally published in *Orson Scott Card's Intergalactic Medicine Show*. "Horus Ascending" © 2008 Aliette de Bodard.
- "Blue Ink" by Yoon Ha Lee originally published in *Clarkesworld Magazine*. "Blue Ink" © 2008 Yoon Ha Lee.
- "Eros, Philia, Agape" by Rachel Swirsky originally published in Tor.com. "Eros, Philia, Agape" © 2009 Rachel Swirsky.

- "A Song to Greet the Sun" by Alaya Dawn Johnson originally published in *Fantasy Magazine*. "A Song to Greet the Sun" © 2009 Alaya Dawn Johnson.

- "Time to Say Goodnight" by Caroline M. Yoachim originally published in *Fantasy Magazine*. "Time to Say Goodnight" © 2007 Caroline M. Yoachim.

- "The Fisherman's Wife" by Jenny Williams originally published in *LitNImage*. "The Fisherman's Wife" © 2008 Jenny Williams.

- "Intertropical Convergence Zone" by Nadia Bulkin originally published in *ChiZine* (complete magazine name *The Chiaroscuro*). "Intertropical Convergence Zone" © 2008 Nadia Bulkin.

- "Urchins, While Swimming" by Catherynne M. Valente originally published in *Clarkesword Magazine*. "Urchins, While Swimming" © 2006 Catherynne M. Valente.

- "The Shangri-La Affair" by Lavie Tidhar originally published in *Strange Horizons*. "The Shangri-La Affair" © 2009 Lavie Tidhar.

- "Elegy for a Young Elk" by Hannu Rajaniemi originally published in *Subterranean Magazine*. "Elegy for a Young Elk" © 2010 Hannu Rajaniemi.

About the Magazines

In a sense all publishing is a transient endeavor. In the over 500 years since Johannes Gutenberg created the movable type printing press, publishers have come and gone. All that remain are the books and stories they created during their short spans of existence.

The same thing happens in the world of online publishing. Most of the online magazines mentioned in this volume are still in existence; you can learn more about them at the links below. However, eventually even these magazines will disappear, leaving behind only the stories they published. Two of the magazines in this volume have already closed. The editors of *ChiZine* (complete name *The Chiaroscuro*) shut down their magazine for personal reasons. SCIFICTION shut down because of stupidity on the part of its corporate owner, the American cable network Sci-Fi Channel. Since the Sci-Fi Channel later changed its name to the inane Syfy, it's obvious their stupidity wasn't restricted to killing their online magazine.

- J.S.

Websites for Magazines in this Volume

- *Apex Magazine*: www.apex-magazine.com
- *Clarkesworld Magazine*: www.clarkesworldmagazine.com
- *Fantasy Magazine*: www.fantasy-magazine.com
- *Lightspeed Magazine*: www.lightspeedmagazine.com
- *LitNImage*: www.litnimage.com
- *Orson Scott Card's Intergalactic Medicine Show*: www.intergalacticmedicineshow.com
- *Strange Horizons*: www.strangehorizons.com
- *Subterranean Magazine*: www.subterraneanpress.com/magazine
- Tor.com: www.tor.com/stories

Million Writers Award: The Best Online Science Fiction and Fantasy

edited by Jason Sanford

Table of Contents

Introduction - by Jason Sanford
11

Non-Zero Probabilities - by N. K. Jemisin
15

The Faithful Soldier, Prompted - by Saladin Ahmed
26

Arvies - by Adam-Troy Castro
37

There's a Hole in the City - by Richard Bowes
54

Horus Ascending - by Aliette de Bodard
74

Blue Ink - by Yoon Ha Lee
83

Eros, Philia, Agape - by Rachel Swirsky
92

A Song to Greet the Sun - by Alaya Dawn Johnson
129

MILLION WRITERS AWARD

Time to Say Goodnight - by Caroline M. Yoachim
140

The Fisherman's Wife - by Jenny Williams
153

Intertropical Convergence Zone - by Nadia Bulkin
159

Urchins, While Swimming - by Catherynne M. Valente
171

The Shangri-La Affair - by Lavie Tidhar
183

Elegy for a Young Elk - by Hannu Rajaniemi
207

Additional Materials

About the Authors
228

About the Editor
233

Introduction to *Million Writers Award: The Best Online Science Fiction and Fantasy*

In many ways, the work of an editor is nothing compared to the mental editing we all do every day. You see, the human mind is the ultimate editor. We go through life having far more experiences than we ever could—or should—remember. So our minds continually edit and delete and clean up our memories. Who we are today isn't who we'll be tomorrow, even though the basic story of our lives may not appear to change that much.

The anthology you are now reading, *Million Writers Award: The Best Online Science Fiction and Fantasy*, was created using a similar organic form of editing.

You see, I've run the *storySouth* Million Writers Award for best online fiction for nearly a decade. During that time I've read every story which has either won the award, placed as a finalist, or made our list of notable stories. All in all, that adds up to around a thousand stories.

When I sat down to select the best science fiction and fantasy stories from the award's run, I decided to go with those stories which stuck in my memories across those years. As I reread those thousand stories I was amazed to discover tales I'd loved at the time but quickly forgotten. I was also pleased to discover a large number of stories which grabbed me back then and still held my mind in a tight grip. This latter group are the stories you're about to read.

Another thing I discovered while editing this volume is how many science fiction and fantasy stories have made their mark in the Million Writers Award. You see, the award is open to online-published stories from all genres. Romances, thrillers, mysteries, literary stories, and westerns compete against space operas, high fantasies, and time travel tales. May the best story win, so to speak.

But despite this level playing field, SF/F stories have in many ways dominated the award. In fact, during the first eight years of the award, a SF/F story won top honors four times.

Since the Million Writers Award allows the reading public to vote for the overall winner—after judges select each year's larger pool of worthy stories—it's easy to understand why science fiction and fantasy have done so well. After all, SF/F fans tend to be passionate advocates for new technologies and very supportive of online fiction.

However, there is another reason these genres have done so well. While there are online magazines and journals focusing on all types of fiction, SF/F magazines have been extremely successful online, again due to genre readers being passionate early adopters of new technologies. For example, the Science Fiction and Fantasy Writers Association currently rates just under 30 short fiction genre magazines in the United States as "professional," which means these magazines pay high enough publication rates and have a large enough readership to qualify their authors for SFWA membership.

Of these nearly 30 professional SF/F magazines, half are online.

Almost all of these professional SF/F online magazines give away their content for free, so to make ends meet they have two basic business strategies. On the one side are the online magazines which help cross-promote another entity. In this realm you'll find *Fantasy Magazine* and *Lightspeed*, both owned by Prime Books, a genre publisher (although Prime Books recently announced the sale of both magazines to their current editor, John Joseph Adams). Likewise, Subterranean Press, which specializes in high-end special editions, publishes *Subterranean Magazine*, as does Apex Publications with their *Apex Magazine*. The large mainstream genre publisher Tor publishes online fiction at Tor.com, with their online magazine paying the highest short story rates in the western world.

The other major type of online SF/F magazines are those which pay professional rates but are published through a good bit of volunteer work by their staff. Among these is *Strange Horizons*, which was one of the first professional-paying online magazines and pioneered the non-profit model of publishing, whereby they solicit donations from readers to cover expenses. Other notable online magazines which are either charities or supported by donations include *Clarkesworld*, *Beneath Ceaseless Skies*, and *Redstone Science Fiction*.

One major exception to online magazines giving away their fiction for free is *Orson Scott Card's InterGalactic Medicine Show*, which charges readers an annual subscription fee. Currently *IGMS* is the only professional online genre magazine to do this.

For proof that online SF/F magazines are succeeding, one need only look at the recent Hugo and Nebula Awards, where major wins were scored by stories first published in Tor.com and *Clarkesworld*. In addition, *Clarkesworld* won the 2010 and 2011 Hugo Award for Best Semiprozine, while a number of stories published in different online magazines have been finalists for other top genre awards.

Based on the way the human mind works, it's doubtful many readers will long remember this introduction of mine. But the good news is that online science fiction and fantasy won't soon be forgotten, and in this anthology are those online SF/F stories which I truly believe will stay with readers for many years to come.

— Jason Sanford

Non-Zero Probabilities

by N. K. Jemisin

(from *Clarkesworld Magazine*)

In the mornings, Adele girds herself for the trip to work as a warrior for battle. First she prays, both to the Christian god of her Irish ancestors and to the orishas of her African ancestors—the latter she is less familiar with, but getting to know. Then she takes a bath with herbs, including dried chickory and allspice, from a mixture given to her by the woman at the local botanica. (She doesn't know Spanish well, but she's getting to know that too. Today's word is *suerte*.) Then, smelling vaguely of coffee and pumpkin pie, she layers on armor: the Saint Christopher medal her mother sent her, for protection on journeys. The hair-clasp she was wearing when she broke up with Larry, which she regards as the best decision of her life. On especially dangerous days, she wears the panties in which she experienced her first self-induced orgasm post-Larry. They're a bit ragged after too many commercial laundromat washings, but still more or less sound. (She washes them by hand now, with Woollite, and lays them flat to dry.)

Then she starts the trip to work. She doesn't bike, though she owns one. A next-door neighbor broke an arm when her bike's front wheel came off in mid-pedal. Could've been anything. Just an accident. But still.

So Adele sets out, swinging her arms, enjoying the day if it's sunny, wrestling with her shitty umbrella if it's rainy. (She no longer opens the umbrella indoors.) Keeping a careful eye out for those who may not be as well-protected. It takes two to tango, but only one to seriously fuck up some shit, as they say in her 'hood. And lo and behold, just three blocks into her trip there is a horrible crash and the ground shakes and car alarms go off and there are screams and people start running. Smoke billows, full of acrid ozone and a taste like dirty blood. When Adele reaches the corner, tensed and ready to flee, she beholds the Franklin Avenue shuttle train, a tiny thing that runs on an elevated track for some portions of its brief run, lying sprawled over Atlantic Avenue like a beached aluminum whale. It has jumped its track, fallen thirty feet to the ground below, and probably killed everyone inside or under or near it.

Adele goes to help, of course, but even as she and other good Samaritans pull bodies and screaming wounded from the wreckage, she cannot help but feel a measure of contempt. It is a cover, her anger; easier to feel that than horror at the shattered limbs, the truncated lives. She feels a bit ashamed too, but holds onto the anger because it makes a better shield.

They should have known better. The probability of a train derailment was infinitesimal. That meant it was only a matter of time.

Her neighbor—the other one, across the hall—helped her figure it out, long before the math geeks finished crunching their numbers.

"Watch," he'd said, and laid a deck of cards facedown on her coffee table. (There was coffee in the cups, with a generous dollop of Bailey's. He was a nice-enough guy that Adele felt comfortable offering this.) He shuffled it with the blurring speed of an expert, cut the deck, shuffled again, then picked up the whole deck and spread it, still facedown. "Pick a card."

Adele picked. The Joker.

"Only two of those in the deck," he said, then shuffled and

spread again. "Pick another."

She did, and got the other Joker.

"Coincidence," she said. (This had been months ago, when she was still skeptical.)

He shook his head and set the deck of cards aside. From his pocket he took a pair of dice. (He was nice enough to invite inside, but he was still that kind of guy.) "Check it," he said, and tossed them onto her table. Snake eyes. He scooped them up, shook them, tossed again. Two more ones. A third toss brought up double sixes; at this, Adele had pointed in triumph. But the fourth toss was snake eyes again.

"These aren't weighted, if you're wondering," he said. "Nobody filed the edges or anything. I got these from the bodega up the street, from a pile of shit the old man was tossing out to make more room for food shelves. Brand new, straight out of the package."

"Might be a bad set," Adele said.

"Might be. But the cards ain't bad, nor your fingers." He leaned forward, his eyes intent despite the pleasant haze that the Bailey's had brought on. "Snake eyes three tosses out of four? And the fourth a double six. That ain't supposed to happen even in a rigged game. Now check this out."

Carefully he crossed the fingers of his free hand. Then he tossed the dice again, six throws this time. The snakes still came up twice, but so did other numbers. Fours and threes and twos and fives. Only one double-six.

"That's batshit, man," said Adele.

"Yeah. But it works."

He was right. And so Adele had resolved to read up on gods of luck and to avoid breaking mirrors. And to see if she could find a four-leafed clover in the weed patch down the block. (They sell some in Chinatown, but she's heard they're knockoffs.) She's hunted through the patch several times in the past few months, once for several hours. Nothing so far, but she remains optimistic.

It's only New York, that's the really crazy thing. Yonkers? Fine. Jersey? Ditto. Long Island? Well, that's still Long Island. But past East New York everything is fine.

The news channels had been the first to figure out that particular wrinkle, but the religions really went to town with it. Some of them have been waiting for the End Times for the last thousand years; Adele can't really blame them for getting all excited. She does blame them for their spin on it, though. There have to be bigger "dens of iniquity" in the world. Delhi has poor people coming out of its ears, Moscow's mobbed up, Bangkok is pedophile heaven. She's heard there are still some sundown towns in the Pacific Northwest. Everybody hates on New York.

And it's not like the signs are all bad. The state had to suspend its lottery program; too many winners in one week bankrupted it. The Knicks made it to the finals and the Mets won the series. A lot of people with cancer went into spontaneous remission, and some folks with full-blown AIDS stopped showing any viral load at all. (There are new tours now. Double-decker buses full of the sick and disabled. Adele tries to tell herself they're just more tourists.)

The missionaries from out of town are the worst. On any given day they step in front of her, shoving tracts under her nose and wanting to know if she's saved yet. She's getting better at spotting them from a distance, yappy islands interrupting the sidewalk river's flow, their faces alight with an inner glow that no self-respecting local would display without three beers and a fat payday check. There's one now, standing practically underneath a scaffolding ladder. Idiot; two steps back and he'll double his chances for getting hit by a bus. (And then the bus will catch fire.)

In the same instant that she spots him, he spots her, and a grin stretches wide across his freckled face. She is reminded of blind newts that have light-sensitive spots on their skin. This one is unsaved-sensitive. She veers right, intending to go around the scaffold, and he takes a wide step into her path again. She veers left; he breaks that way.

She stops, sighing. "What."

"Have you accepted—"

"I'm Catholic. They do us at birth, remember?"

His smile is forgiving. "That doesn't mean we can't talk, does it?"

"I'm busy." She attempts a feint, hoping to catch him off-guard. He moves with her, nimble as a linebacker.

"Then I'll just give you this," he says, tucking something into her hand. Not a tract, bigger. A flyer. "The day to remember is August 8th."

This, finally, catches Adele's attention. August 8th. 8/8—a lucky day according to the Chinese. She has it marked on her calendar as a good day to do things like rent a Zipcar and go to Ikea.

"Yankee Stadium," he says. "Come join us. We're going to pray the city back into shape."

"Sure, whatever," she says, and finally manages to slip around him. (He lets her go, really. He knows she's hooked.)

She waits until she's out of downtown before she reads the flyer, because downtown streets are narrow and close and she has to keep an eye out. It's a hot day; everybody's using their air conditioners. Most people don't bolt the things in the way they're supposed to.

"A PRAYER FOR THE SOUL OF THE CITY," the flyer proclaims, and in spite of herself, Adele is intrigued. The flyer says that over 500,000 New Yorkers have committed to gathering on that day and concentrating their prayers. That kind of thing has power now, she thinks. There's some lab at Princeton—dusted off and given new funding lately—that's been able to prove it. Whether that means someone's listening or just that human thoughtwaves are affecting events as the scientists say, she doesn't know. She doesn't care.

She thinks, *I could ride the train again.*

She could laugh at the next Friday the 13th.

She could—and here her thoughts pause, because there's something she's been trying not to think about, but it's been awhile and she's never been a very good Catholic girl anyway. But she could, maybe, just maybe, try dating again.

As she thinks this, she is walking through the park. She passes the vast lawn, which is covered in fast-darting black children and lazily sunning white adults and a few roving brown elders with Italian ice carts. Though she is usually on watch for things like this, the flyer has distracted her, so she does not notice the nearby cartman stopping, cursing in Spanish because one of his wheels has gotten mired in the soft turf.

This puts him directly in the path of a child who is running, his eyes trained on a descending frisbee; with the innate arrogance of a city child he has assumed that the cart will have moved out of the way by the time he gets there. Instead the child hits the cart at full speed, which catches Adele's attention at last, so that too late she realizes she is at the epicenter of one of those devastating chains of events that only ever happen in comedy films and the transformed city. In a Rube Goldberg string of utter improbabilities, the cart tips over, spilling tubs of brightly-colored ices onto the grass. The boy flips over it with acrobatic precision, completely by accident, and lands with both feet on the tub of ices. The sheer force of this blow causes the tub to eject its contents with projectile force. A blast of blueberry-coconut-red hurtles toward Adele's face, so fast that she has no time to scream. It will taste delicious. It will also likely knock her into oncoming bicycle traffic.

At the last instant the frisbee hits the flying mass, altering its trajectory. Freezing fruit flavors splatter the naked backs of a row of sunbathers nearby, much to their dismay.

Adele's knees buckle at the close call. She sits down hard on the grass, her heart pounding, while the sunbathers scream and the cart-man checks to see if the boy is okay and the pigeons converge. She happens to glance down. A four-leafed clover is growing there, at her fingertips.

Eventually she resumes the journey home. At the corner of her block, she sees a black cat lying atop a garbage can. Its head has been crushed, and someone has attempted to burn it. She hopes it was dead first, and hurries on.

Adele has a garden on the fire escape. In one pot, eggplant and herbs; she has planted the clover in this. In another pot are peppers and flowers. In the big one, tomatoes and a scraggly collard that she's going to kill if she keeps harvesting leaves so quickly. (But she likes greens.) It's luck—good luck—that she'd chosen to grow a garden this year, because since things changed it's been harder for wholesalers to bring food into the city, and prices have shot up. The farmers' market that she attends on Saturdays has become a barterers' market too, so she plucks a couple of slim, deep-purple eggplants and a handful of angry little peppers. She wants fresh fruit. Berries, maybe.

On her way out, she knocks on the neighbor's door. He looks surprised as he opens it, but pleased to see her. It occurs to her that maybe he's been hoping for a little luck of his own. She gives it a think-over, and hands him an eggplant. He looks at it in consternation. (He's not the kind of guy to eat eggplant.)

"I'll come by later and show you how to cook it," she says. He grins.

At the farmers' market she trades the angry little peppers for sassy little raspberries, and the eggplant for two stalks of late rhubarb. She also wants information, so she hangs out awhile gossiping with whoever sits nearby. Everyone talks more than they used to. It's nice.

And everyone, everyone she speaks to, is planning to attend

the prayer.

"I'm on dialysis," says an old lady who sits under a flowering tree. "Every time they hook me up to that thing I'm scared. Dialysis can kill you, you know."

It always could, Adele doesn't say.

"I work on Wall Street," says another woman, who speaks briskly and clutches a bag of fresh fish as if it's gold. Might as well be; fish is expensive now. A tiny Egyptian scarab pendant dangles from a necklace the woman wears. "Quantitative analysis. All the models are fucked now. We were the only ones they didn't fire when the housing market went south, and now this." So she's going to pray too. "Even though I'm kind of an atheist. Whatever, if it works, right?"

Adele finds others, all tired of performing their own daily rituals, all worried about their likelihood of being outliered to death.

She goes back to her apartment building, picks some sweet basil and takes it and the eggplant next door. Her neighbor seems a little nervous. His apartment is cleaner than she's ever seen it, with the scent of Pine Sol still strong in the bathroom. She tries not to laugh, and demonstrates how to peel and slice eggplant, salt it to draw out the toxins ("it's related to nightshade, you know"), and sauté it with basil in olive oil. He tries to look impressed, but she can tell he's not the kind of guy to enjoy eating his vegetables.

Afterward they sit, and she tells him about the prayer thing. He shrugs. "Are you going?" she presses.

"Nope."

"Why not? It could fix things."

"Maybe. Maybe I like the way things are now."

This stuns her. "Man, the train fell off its track last week." Twenty people dead. She has woken up in a cold sweat on the nights since, screams ringing in her ears.

"Could've happened anytime," he says, and she blinks in surprise because it's true. The official investigation says someone—

track worker, maybe—left a wrench sitting on the track near a power coupling. The chance that the wrench would hit the coupling, causing a short and explosion, was one in a million. But never zero.

"But... but..." She wants to point out the other horrible things that have occurred. Gas leaks. Floods. A building fell down, in Harlem. A fatal duck attack. Several of the apartments in their building are empty because a lot of people can't cope. Her neighbor—the other one, with the broken arm—is moving out at the end of the month. Seattle. Better bike paths.

"Shit happens," he says. "It happened then, it happens now. A little more shit, a little less shit..." He shrugs. "Still shit, right?"

She considers this. She considers it for a long time.

They play cards, and have a little wine, and Adele teases him about the overdone chicken. She likes that he's trying so hard. She likes even more that she's not thinking about how lonely she's been.

So they retire to his bedroom and there's awkwardness and she's shy because it's been awhile and you do lose some skills without practice, and he's clumsy because he's probably been developing bad habits from porn, but eventually they manage. They use a condom. She crosses her fingers while he puts it on. There's a rabbit's foot keychain attached to the bed railing, which he strokes before returning his attention to her. He swears he's clean, and she's on the pill, but... well. Shit happens.

She closes her eyes and lets herself forget for awhile.

The prayer thing is all over the news. The following week is the runup. Talking heads on the morning shows speculate that it should have some effect, if enough people go and exert "positive energy". They are careful not to use the language of any particular faith; this is still New York. Alternative events are being planned all over the city for those who don't want to come under the evangelical tent. The sukkah mobiles are rolling, though it's the wrong time of year, just getting the word out about something happening at one of the synagogues. In Flatbush, Adele can't walk a block without being hit up by Jehovah's Witnesses. There's a "constructive visualization" somewhere for the ethical humanists. Not everybody believes God, or gods, will save them. It's just that this is the way the world works now, and everybody gets that. If crossed fingers can temporarily alter a dice throw, then why not something bigger? There's nothing inherently special about crossed fingers. It's only a "lucky" gesture because people believe in it. Get them to believe in something else, and that should work too.

Except...

Adele walks past the Botanical Gardens, where preparations are under way for a big Shinto ritual. She stops to watch workers putting up a graceful red gate.

She's still afraid of the subway. She knows better than to get her hopes up about her neighbor, but still... he's kind of nice. She still plans her mornings around her ritual ablutions, and her walks to work around danger-spots—but how is that different, really, from what she did before? Back then it was makeup and hair, and fear of muggers. Now she walks more than she used to; she's lost ten pounds. Now she knows her neighbors' names.

Looking around, she notices other people standing nearby, also watching the gate go up. They glance at her, some nodding, some smiling, some ignoring her and looking away. She doesn't have to ask if they will be attending one of the services; she can see that they won't be. Some people react to fear by seeking security, change, control. The rest accept the change and just go on about their lives.

"Miss?" She glances back, startled, to find a young man there, holding forth a familiar flyer. He's not as pushy as the guy downtown; once she takes it, he moves on. The PRAYER FOR THE SOUL OF THE CITY is tomorrow. Shuttle busses ("Specially blessed!") will be picking up people at sites throughout the city.

WE NEED YOU TO BELIEVE, reads the bottom of the flyer.

Adele smiles. She folds the flyer carefully, her fingers

remembering the skills of childhood, and presently it is perfect. They've printed the flyer on good, heavy paper.

She takes out her St. Christopher, kisses it, and tucks it into the rear folds to weight the thing properly.

Then she launches the paper airplane, and it flies and flies and flies, dwindling as it travels an impossible distance, until it finally disappears into the bright blue sky.

-The End-

The Faithful Soldier, Prompted

by Saladin Ahmed

(from *Apex Magazine*)

If I die on this piece-of-shit road, Lubna's chances die with me. Ali leveled his shotgun at the growling tiger. *In the name of God, who needs no credit rating, let me live!* Even when he'd been a soldier, Ali hadn't been very religious. But facing death brought the old invocations to mind. The sway of culture, educated Lubna would have called it. If she were here. If she could speak.

The creature stood still on the split cement, watching Ali. Nanohanced tigers had been more or less wiped out in the great hunts before the Global Credit Crusade, or so Ali had heard. *I guess this is the shit end of "more or less."* More proof, as if he needed it, that traveling the Old Cairo Road on foot was as good as asking to die.

He almost thought he could hear the creature's targeting system whir, but of course he couldn't any more than the tiger could read the vestigial OS prompt that flashed across Ali's supposedly deactivated retscreens.

God willing, Faithful Soldier, you will report for uniform inspection at 0500 hours.

Ali ignored the out-of-date message, kept his gun trained on the creature.

The tiger crouched to spring.

Ali squeezed the trigger, shouted "God is greater than credit!"

The cry of a younger man, from the days when he'd let stupid causes use him. The days before he'd met Lubna.

A sputtering spurt of shot sprayed the creature. The tiger roared, bled, and fled.

For a moment Ali just stood there panting. "Praise be to God," he finally said to no one in particular. *I'm coming, beloved. I'm going to get you your serum, and then I'm coming home.*

A day later, Ali still walked the Old Cairo Road alone, the wind whipping stinging sand at him, making a mockery of his old army-issued sandmask. As he walked he thought of home—of Free Beirut and his humble house behind the jade-and-grey-marble fountain. At home a medbed hummed quietly, keeping Lubna alive even though she lay dying from the Green Devil, which one side or the other's hover-dustings had infected her with during the GCC. At home Lubna breathed shallowly while Ali's ex-squadmate Fatman Fahrad, the only man in the world he still trusted, stood watch over her.

Yet Ali had left on this madman's errand—left the woman who mattered more to him than anything on Earth's scorched surface. Serum was her only hope. But serum was devastatingly expensive, and Ali was broke. Every bit of money he had made working the hover-docks or doing security for shops had gone to prepay days on Lubna's medbed. And there was less and less work to be had. He'd begun having dreams that made him wake up crying. Dreams of shutting down Lubna's medbed. Of killing himself.

And then the first strange message had appeared behind his eyes.

Like God-alone-knew how many vets, Ali's ostensibly inactive OS still garbled forth a glitchy old prompt from time to time

God willing, Faithful Soldier, you will pick up your new field ablution kit after your debriefing today.

God willing, Faithful Soldier, you will spend your leave-time dinars wisely—at Honest Majoudi's!

But this new message had been unlike anything Ali had ever seen. Blood-freezingly current in its subject matter.

God willing, Faithful Soldier, you will go to the charity-yard of the Western Mosque in Old Cairo. She will live.

Ali's attention snapped back to the present as the wind picked up and the air grew thick with sand. As storms went, it was mild. But it still meant he'd have to stop until it blew over. He reluctantly set up the rickety rig-shelter that the Fatman had lent him. He crawled into it and lay there alone with the wail of the wind, the stink of his own body, and his exhausted, sleepless thoughts.

When the new prompt had appeared, Ali had feared he was losing his mind. More than one vet had lost theirs, had sworn that their OS had told them to slaughter their family. Ali had convinced himself that the prompt was random. An illustration of the one-in-a-trillion chance that such a message could somehow be produced by error.

But it had repeated itself. Every night for a week.

He'd told the Fatman about it, expected the grizzled old shit-talker to call him crazy. Half *wanted* to be called crazy. But Fahrad had shrugged and said "Beloved, I've seen a few things in my time. God, who needs no credit rating, can do the impossible. I don't talk about this shit with just anyone, of course. Not these days, beloved. Religion. Hmph! But maybe you *should* go. Things sure ain't gonna get any better here. And you know I'll watch over Lubna like my own daughter."

So now Ali found himself following a random, impossible promise. It was either this or wait for the medbed's inevitable shutdown sequence and watch Lubna die, her skin shriveling before his eyes, her eyewhites turning bright green.

After a few hours the storm died down. Ali packed up his rig-shelter and set back to walking the ruined Old Cairo Road, chasing a digital dream.

#

There was foot traffic on the road now, not just the occasional hover-cluster zipping overhead. He was finally nearing the city. He had to hurry. If he was gone too long, Ali could count on the Fatman to provide a few days of coverage for Lubna. But Fahrad was as poor as Ali. Time was short.

Running out of time without knowing what I'm chasing. Ali blocked out the mocking words his own mind threw at him. He took a long sip from his canteen and quickened his pace.

Eventually, the road crested a dune and Old Cairo lay spread before him. The bustling hover-dock of Nile River Station. The silvery spires of Al-Azhar 2.0. The massive moisture pits, like aquamarine jewels against the city's sand-brown skin. Lubna had been here once on a university trip, Ali recalled. His thoughts went to her again, to his house behind the jade-and-grey marble fountain, but he herded them back to the here-and-now. *Focus. Find the Western Mosque.*

The gate guards took his rifle and eyed him suspiciously, but they let him pass. As he made his way through the city, people pressed in on every side. Ali had always thought of himself as a city man. He'd laughed at various village-bumpkin-turned-soldier types back when he'd been in the army. But Old Cairo made *him* feel like a bumpkin. He'd never seen so many people, not even in the vibrant Free Beirut of his childhood. He blocked them out as best he could.

He walked for two hours, asking directions of a smelly fruit-seller and two different students. Finally, when dusk was dissipating into dark, he stood before the Western Mosque. It was old, and looked it. The top half of the thick red minaret had long ago been blown away by some army that hadn't feared God. Ali passed through the high wall's open gate into the mosque's charity-yard, which was curiously free of paupers.

God willing, Faithful Soldier, you will remember to always travel with a squad mate when leaving the caravansarai.

"Peace and prosperity, brother. Can I help you?" The brown, jowly man that had snuck up on Ali's flank was obviously one of the Imams of the Western Mosque. His middle-aged face was furrowed in scrutiny.

Ali stood there, unable to speak. He had made it to Old Cairo, to the charity-yard of the Western Mosque as the prompt had said, and now... Ali didn't know what he hoped to find. A vial of serum, suspended in a pillar of light? The sky splitting and a great hand passing down cure-money? He was exhausted. He'd faced sandstorms and a tiger to get here. Had nearly died beneath the rot-blackened claws of toxighuls. He'd traveled for two weeks, surviving on little food and an hour's sleep here and there. He started to wobble on his feet.

Why had he come here? Lubna was going to die and he wouldn't even be there to hold her.

The Imam stared at Ali, still waiting for an explanation.

Ali swallowed, his cracked throat burning. "I...I...my OS. It—" his knees started to buckle and he nearly collapsed. "It told me to come here. From FreeBey. No money. Had to walk." They were a madman's words, and Ali hardly believed they were coming from his own mouth.

"Truly? You *walked* all that way? And lived to tell the tale? I didn't know such a thing was possible." The Imam looked at Ali with concerned distaste and put a hand on his shoulder. "Well... The charity-yard is closing tonight for cleaning, but I suppose one foreign beggar won't get in the way too much. You can sleep in safety here, brother. And we can talk about your OS tomorrow."

Ali felt himself fading. He needed rest. Food. Even a vet like him could only go so long.

He sank slowly to the ground and slept.

#

In his sleep he saw the bloody bodies of friends and children. He saw his squadmates slicing the ears off dead men. He heard a girl cry as soldiers closed in around her.

He woke screaming, as he had once done every night. His heart hammered. It had been a long time since he'd had dreams of the war. When they were first married, Lubna would soothe him and they would step into the cool night air and sit by the jade-and-grey marble fountain. Eventually, the nightmares had faded. Her slender hand on the small of his back, night after night—this had saved his life. And now he would never see her again. He had abandoned her because he thought God was talking to him. Thinking of it, his eyes began to burn with tears.

God willing, Faithful Soldier, you will deactivate the security scrambler on the wall before you. She will live.

Ali sucked in a shocked breath and forgot his self-pity. His pulse racing, he scrambled to his feet. He looked across the dark yard at the green-glowing instrument panel set in the mosque's massive gate. But he did not move.

God willing, Faithful Soldier, you will deactivate the security scrambler on the wall before you. She will live.

The prompt flashed a second time across his retscreens. *I've lost my mind.* But even as he thought it, he walked toward the wall.

Screen-jacking had never been Ali's specialty. But from the inside interface, the gate's security scrambler was simple enough to shut down. Anyone who'd done an army hitch or a security detail could do it. Ali's fingers danced over the screen, and a few seconds later it was done.

Then a chorus of angry shouts erupted and an alarm system began droning away. Two men in black dashed out of the mosque and past him, each carrying an ornate jewelry box.

Thieves.

By the time he decided to stop them, they had crossed the courtyard. He scrambled toward them, trying not to think about him being unarmed. Behind him, he heard the familiar clatter of weapons and body armor.

"Thanks for the help, cousin!" One of the thieves shouted at Ali. Ali was near enough to smell their sweat when they each tapped their h-belts and hover-jumped easily over the descrambled wall. *Infiltrators waiting for their chance. They used me, somehow.* He panicked. *What have I done?* His stomach sank. *They've been using my OS all along!* How and why did they call him all the way from FreeBey? He didn't know and it didn't matter.

I'm screwed. He had to get out of here. Somehow he had to get back to Lubna. He turned to look toward the mosque—

—And found himself staring down the barrel of the jowly Imam's rifle. The holy man spat at Ali. "Motherless scum! Do you know how much they've stolen? You helped them get out, huh? And your pals left you behind to take their fall? Well, don't worry. The police will catch them, too. You won't face execution alone." He kept the weapon trained on Ali's head. Ali knew a shooter when he saw one. This was not good.

"I didn't—" Ali started to say, but he knew it was useless.

A squad of mosque guardsmen trotted up. They scowled almost jovially as they closed in. Ali didn't dare fight these men, who could call on more. He'd done enough security jobs himself to know they wouldn't listen to him. At least not until after they'd beaten him. He tensed himself and took slaps and punches. He yelped, and they raked his eyes for it. He threw up and they punched him for it. His groin burned from kicks and he lost two teeth. Then he blacked out.

He woke in a cell with four men in uniforms different from the mosque guards'. *Cairene police?* They gave him water.

God willing, Faithful Soldier, you will report to queue B7.

Ali ignored the prompt. The men slapped him around halfheartedly and made jokes about his mother's sexual tastes. Again, he pushed down the angry fighter within him. If he got himself killed by these men he would never see Lubna again.

They dragged him into the dingy office of their Shaykh-Captain. The old man was scraggly and fat, but hard. A vet, unless Ali missed his guess.

"Tell me about your friends." the Shaykh-Captain said.

Ali started to explain about being framed but then found the words wouldn't stop. Something had been knocked loose within him these past few days. He talked and talked and told the old man the truth. All of the truth. About Lubna and the messages, about leaving Free Beirut, about the toxighuls and the tiger, the Western Mosque and the thieves.

When he was done he lowered his eyes, but he felt the old man glare at him for a few long, silent moments. Ali raised his gaze slowly and saw a sardonic smile spread over the Shaykh-Captain's face.

"A *prompt*? Half the guys with an OS still get 'em—what do they mean? Nothing. I got one that said I fucked your mother last night. Did she wake up pregnant?" The men behind Ali chuckled. In the army, Ali had hated the Cairenes and their moronic mother jokes. "Sometimes I don't even know where the words come from," the old man went on. "Random old satellites squawking? Some head-hacker having a laugh? Who knows? And who gives a shit? I got one a couple weeks back that told me to find some guy named Ali, who was supposed to tell me about 'great riches lying buried beneath a jade-and-grey marble fountain.'"

For a moment, Ali listened uncomprehendingly. Then he thought his heart would stop. He did everything he could to keep his face straight as the Shaykh-Captain continued.

"Do you know how many fountains like that there are here in OC? And how many sons of bitches named Ali? What's your name, anyway, fool?"

"My name? Uh, my name is F-fahrad, Shaykh-Captain, and I..."

"Shut up! I was saying—I told my wife about this prompt and she said I should go around the city digging up fountains. As if I don't got enough to do here." He gestured vaguely at a pile of textcards on his desk. "'In the army,' I told her, 'I got a prompt telling me about some pills that could make my dick twice as long. Did I waste my pay on them?'" The old man gave Ali an irritated look "Y'know, you and my wife—you two fucking mystics would like each other. Maybe you could go to her old broads' tea hour and tell them about your prompts! Maybe she'd even believe your donkey-shit story about walking here from the north."

The Shaykh-Captain stood slowly, walked over to the wall, and pulled down an old-fashioned truncheon. "But before the teahouse, we have to take you back downstairs for a little while."

Ali felt big, hard hands take hold of him and he knew that this was it. He was half-dead already. He couldn't survive an Old Cairo-style interrogation. He would never see Lubna again. He had failed her, and she would die a death as horrible as anything he'd seen in the war.

Faithful Soldier, she will live.

The prompt flashed past his retscreens and he thought again of the Shaykh Captain's words about riches and the fountain.

This was no head-hacker's trick. No thieves' scheme. He did not understand it, but God *had* spoken to him. He could not dishonor that. He had once served murderers and madmen who claimed to act in God's name. But Lubna—brilliant, loving Lubna—had shown him that this world could hold holiness. If Ali could not see her again, if he could not save her, he could at least face his death with faith.

He made his voice as strong as he could, and he held his head high as he uttered words that would seal his fate with these men. "In the name of God, who needs no credit rating, Shaykh-Captain, do what you must. But I am not lying."

The Shaykh-Captain's eyes widened and a twisted smile came to his lips. "So *that's* it! In the name of your mother's pussy, you superstitious fool!" The big men behind Ali grumbled their southern disgust at the fact of Ali's existence and started shoving him, but the old man cut them off with a hand gesture. He set down the truncheon, pulled at his dirty grey beard, assumed a mock gravity. "A genuine Free Shi'ah Anti-Crediteer. The scourge of the Global Credit Crusaders. Hard times for your kind these days, even up north, I hear."

The Shaykh-Captain snorted, but there was something new in the man's voice. Something almost human. "You think you're a brave man—a martyr—to show your true colors down here, huh? Pfft. Well, you can stop stroking your own dick on that count. No one down here gives a damn about those days any more. Half this city was on your side of things once. Truth be told, my fuck-faced fool of a little brother was one of you. He kept fighting that war when everyone knew it was over. He's dead now. A fool, like I say. Me? I faced reality. Now look at me." The old man spread his arms as if his shabby office was a palace, his two goons gorgeous wives.

He sat on the edge of his desk and gave Ali another long look. "But you—you're stuck in the fanatical past, huh? You know, I believe this story about following your OS is actually true. Not a robber. Just an idiot. You're as pathetic as my brother was. A dream-chasing relic. You *really* walked down the OC Road?"

Ali nodded but said nothing.

A sympathetic flash lit the Shaykh-Captain's eyes, but he quickly grimaced, as if the moment of fellow-feeling caused him physical pain. "Well, my men will call me soft, but what the fuck. You've had a rough enough trip down here, I suppose. Tell you what:

We'll get you a corner in steerage on a hover-cluster, okay? Those northbound flights are always half-empty anyway. Go be with your wife, asshole."

Ali cold not quite believe what he was hearing. "Thank you! Thank you, Shaykh-Captain! In the name of—"

"In the name of your mother's hairy tits! Shut up and take your worn old expressions back to your falling-apart city. Boys, get this butt-fucked foreigner out of my office. Give him a medpatch, maybe. Some soup. And don't mess him up too bad, huh?"

The big men gave him a low-grade medpatch, which helped. And they fed him lentil soup and pita. Then they shoved him around again, a bit, but not enough to matter.

When they were through they hurled him into the steerage line at the hover-docks. Ali was tired and hurt and thirsty. Both his lips were split and his guts felt like jelly. But war had taught him how to hang on when there was a real chance of getting home. Riches buried beneath the jade-and-grey-marble fountain. Cure-money. Despair had weakened him, but he would find the strength to make it back to Lubna. He would watch as she woke, finally free of the disease.

Faithful Soldier, you will —

The prompt cut off abruptly. Ali boarded the hover-cluster and headed home to his beloved.

-The End-

Arvies

by Adam-Troy Castro

(from *Lightspeed Magazine*)

STATEMENT OF INTENT

This is the story of a mother, and a daughter, and the right to life, and the dignity of all living things, and of some souls granted great destinies at the moment of their conception, and of others damned to remain society's useful idiots.

CONTENTS

Expect cute plush animals and amniotic fluid and a more or less happy ending for everybody, though the definition of happiness may depend on the truncated emotional capacity of those unable to feel anything else. Some of the characters are rich and famous, others are underage, and one is legally dead, though you may like her the most of all.

APPEARANCE

We first encounter Molly June on her fifteenth deathday, when the monitors in charge of deciding such things declare her safe for passengers. Congratulating her on completing the only important stage of her development, they truck her in a padded skimmer to the arvie showroom where she is claimed, right away, by one of the Living.

The fast sale surprises nobody, not the servos that trained her into her current state of health and attractiveness, not the AI routines managing the showroom, and least of all Molly June, who has spent her infancy and early childhood having the ability to feel surprise, or anything beyond a vague contentment, scrubbed from her emotional palate. Crying, she'd learned while still capable of such things, brought punishment, while unconditional acceptance of anything the engineers saw fit to provide brought light and flower scent and warmth. By this point in her existence she'll greet anything short of an exploding bomb with no reaction deeper than vague concern. Her sale is a minor development by comparison: a happy development, reinforcing her feelings of dull satisfaction. Don't feel sorry for her. Her entire life, or more accurately death, is happy ending. All she has to do is spend the rest of it carrying a passenger.

VEHICLE SPECIFICATIONS

You think you need to know what Molly June looks like. You really don't, as it plays no role in her life. But as the information will assist you in feeling empathy for her, we will oblige anyway.

Molly June is a round-faced, button-nosed gamin, with pink lips and cheeks marked with permanent rose: her blonde hair framing her perfect face in parentheses of bouncy, luxurious curls. Her blue eyes, enlarged by years of genetic manipulation and corrective surgeries, are three times as large as the ones imperfect nature would have set in her face. Lemur-like, they dominate her features like a pair of pacific jewels, all moist and sad and adorable. They reveal none of her essential personality, which is not a great loss, as she's never been permitted to develop one.

Her body is another matter. It has been trained to perfection, with the kind of punishing daily regimen that can only be endured when the mind itself remains unaware of pain or exhaustion. She has worked with torn ligaments, with shattered joints, with disfiguring wounds. She has severed her spine and crushed her skull and has had both replaced, with the same ease her engineers have used, fourteen times, to replace her skin with a fresh version unmarked by scars or blemishes. What remains of her now is a wan amalgam of her own best-developed parts, most of them entirely natural, except for her womb, which is of course a plush, wired palace, far safer for its future occupant than the envelope of mere flesh would have provided. It can survive injuries capable of reducing Molly June to a smear.

In short, she is precisely what she should be, now that she's fifteen years past birth, and therefore, by all standards known to modern civilized society, Dead.

HEROINE

Jennifer Axioma-Singh has never been born and is therefore a significant distance away from being Dead.

She is, in every way, entirely typical. She has written operas, climbed mountains, enjoyed daredevil plunges from the upper atmosphere into vessels the size of teacups, finagled controlling stock in seventeen major multinationals, earned the hopeless devotion of any number of lovers, written her name in the sands of time, fought campaigns in a hundred conceptual wars, survived twenty regime changes and on three occasions had herself turned off so she could spend a year or two mulling the purpose of existence while her bloodstream spiced her insights with all the most fashionable hallucinogens.

She has accomplished all of this from within various baths of amniotic fluid.

Jennifer has yet to even open her eyes, which have never been allowed to fully develop past the first trimester and which still, truth be told, resemble black marbles behind lids of translucent onionskin. This doesn't actually deprive her of vision, of course. At the time she claims Molly June as her arvie, she's been indulging her visual cortex for seventy long years, zipping back and forth across the solar system collecting all the tourist chits one earns for seeing all the wonders of modern-day humanity: from the scrimshaw carving her immediate ancestors made of Mars to the radiant face of Unborn Jesus shining from the artfully re-configured multicolored atmosphere of Saturn. She has gloried in the catalogue of beautiful sights provided by God and all the industrious living people before her.

Throughout all this she has been blessed with vision far greater than any we will ever know ourselves, since her umbilical interface allows her sights capable of frying merely organic eyes, and she's far too sophisticated a person to be satisfied with the banal limitations of the merely visual spectrum. Decades of life have provided Jennifer Axioma-Singh with more depth than that. And something else: a perverse need, stranger than anything she's ever done, and impossible to indulge without first installing herself in a healthy young arvie.

ANCESTRY

Jennifer Axioma-Singh has owned arvies before, each one customized from the moment of its death. She's owned males, females, neuters, and several sexes only developed in the past decade. She's had arvies designed for athletic prowess, arvies designed for erotic sensation, and arvies designed for survival in harsh environments. She's even had one arvie with hypersensitive pain receptors: that, during a cold and confused period of masochism.

The last one before this, who she still misses, and sometimes feels a little guilty about, was a lovely girl named Peggy Sue, with a metabolism six times baseline normal and a digestive tract capable of surviving about a hundred separate species of nonstop abuse. Peggy Sue could down mountains of exotic delicacies without ever feeling full or engaging her gag reflex, and enjoyed taste receptors directly plugged into her pleasure centers. The slightest sip of coconut juice could flood her system with tidal waves of endorphin-crazed ecstasy. The things chocolate could do to her were downright obscene.

Unfortunately, she was still vulnerable to the negative effects of unhealthy eating, and went through four liver transplants and six emergency transfusions in the first ten years of Jennifer's occupancy.

The cumulative medical effect of so many years of determined gluttony mattered little to Jennifer Axioma-Singh, since her own caloric intake was regulated by devices that prevented the worst of Peggy Sue's excessive consumption from causing any damage on her side of the uterine wall. Jennifer's umbilical cord passed only those compounds necessary for keeping her alive and healthy. All Jennifer felt, through her interface with Peggy Sue's own sensory spectrum, was the joy of eating; all she experienced was the sheer, overwhelming treasury of flavor.

And if Peggy Sue became obese and diabetic and jaundiced in the meantime—as she did, enduring her last few years as Jennifer's arvie as an immobile mountain of reeking flab, with barely enough strength to position her mouth for another bite—then that was inconsequential as well, because she had progressed beyond prenatal development and had therefore passed beyond that stage of life where human beings can truly be said to have a soul.

PHILOSOPHY

Life, true life, lasts only from the moment of conception to the moment of birth. Jennifer Axioma-Singh subscribes to this principle, and clings to it in the manner of any concerned citizen aware that the very foundations of her society depend on everybody continuing to believe it without question. But she is capable of forming attachments, no matter how irrational, and she therefore felt a frisson of guilt once she decided she'd had enough and the machines performed the Caesarian Section that delivered her from Peggy Sue's pliant womb. After all, Peggy Sue's reward for so many years of service, euthanasia, seemed so inadequate, given everything she'd provided.

But what else could have provided fair compensation, given the shape Peggy Sue was in by then? Surely not a last meal! Jennifer Axioma-Singh, who had not been able to think of any alternatives, brooded over the matter until she came to the same conclusion always reached by those enjoying lives of privilege, which is that such inequities are all for the best and that there wasn't all that much she could do about them, anyway. Her liberal compassion had been satisfied by the heartfelt promise to herself that if she ever bought an arvie again she would take care to act more responsibly.

And this is what she holds in mind, as the interim pod carries her into the gleaming white expanse of the very showroom where fifteen-year-old Molly June awaits a passenger.

INSTALLATION

Molly June's contentment is like the surface of a vast, pacific ocean, unstirred by tide or wind. The events of her life plunge into that mirrored surface without effect, raising nary a ripple or storm. It remains unmarked even now, as the anesthetician and obstetrician mechs emerge from their recesses to guide her always-unresisting form from the waiting room couch where she'd been left earlier this morning, to the operating theatre where she'll begin the useful stage of her existence. Speakers in the walls calm her further with an arrangement of melodious strings designed to override any unwanted emotional static.

It's all quite humane: for even as Molly June lies down and puts her head back and receives permission to close her eyes, she remains wholly at peace. Her heartbeat does jog, a little, just enough to be noted by the instruments, when the servos peel back the skin of her abdomen, but even that instinctive burst of fear fades with the absence of any identifiable pain. Her reaction to the invasive procedure fades to a mere theoretical interest, akin to what Jennifer herself would feel regarding gossip about people she doesn't know living in places where she's never been.

Molly June drifts, thinks of blue waters and bright sunlight, misses Jennifer's installation inside her, and only reacts to the massive change in her body after the incisions are closed and Jennifer has recovered enough to kick. Then her lips curl in a warm but vacant smile. She is happy. Arvies might be dead, in legal terms, but they still love their passengers.

AMBITION

Jennifer doesn't announce her intentions until two days later, after growing comfortable with her new living arrangements. At that time Molly June is stretched out on a lounge on a balcony overlooking a city once known as Paris but which has undergone perhaps a dozen other names of fleeting popularity since then; at this point it's called something that could be translated as Eternal Night, because its urban planners have noted that it looks best when its towers were against a backdrop of darkness and therefore arranged to free it from the sunlight that previously diluted its beauty for half of every day.

The balcony, a popular spot among visitors, is not connected to any actual building. It just sits, like an unanchored shelf, at a high altitude calculated to showcase the lights of the city at their most decadently glorious. The city itself is no longer inhabited, of course; it contains some mechanisms important for the maintenance of local weather patterns but otherwise exists only to confront the night sky with constellations of reflective light. Jennifer, experiencing its beauty through Molly June's eyes, and the bracing high-altitude wind through Molly June's skin, feels a connection with the place that goes beyond aesthetics. She finds it fateful, resonant, and romantic, the perfect location to begin the greatest adventure of a life that has already provided her with so many.

She cranes Molly June's neck to survey the hundreds of other arvies sharing this balcony with her: all young, all beautiful, all pretending happiness while their jaded passengers struggle to plan new experiences not yet grown dull from surfeit. She sees arvies drinking, arvies wrestling, arvies declaiming vapid poetry, arvies coupling in threes and fours; arvies colored in various shades, fitted to various shapes and sizes; pregnant females, and impregnated males, all sufficiently transparent, to a trained eye like Jennifer's, for the essential characters of their respective passengers to shine on through. They all glow from the light of a moon that is not the moon, as the original was removed some time ago, but a superb piece of stagecraft designed to accentuate the city below to its greatest possible effect.

Have any of these people ever contemplated a stunt as over-the-top creative as the one Jennifer has in mind? Jennifer thinks not. More, she is certain not. She feels pride, and her arvie Molly June laughs, with a joy that threatens to bring the unwanted curse of sunlight back to the city of lights. And for the first time she announces her intentions out loud, without even raising her voice, aware that any words emerging from Molly June's mouth are superfluous, so long as the truly necessary signal travels the network

that conveys Jennifer's needs to the proper facilitating agencies. None of the other arvies on the balcony even hear Molly June speak. But those plugged in hear Jennifer speak the words destined to set off a whirlwind of controversy.
I want to give birth.

CLARIFICATION

It is impossible to understate the perversity of this request. Nobody gives Birth.

Birth is a messy and unpleasant and distasteful process that ejects living creatures from their warm and sheltered environment into a harsh and unforgiving one that nobody wants to experience except from within the protection of wombs either organic or artificial.

Birth is the passage from Life, and all its infinite wonders, to another place inhabited only by those who have been forsaken. It's the terrible ending that modern civilization has forestalled indefinitely, allowing human beings to live within the womb without ever giving up the rich opportunities for experience and growth. It's sad, of course, that for Life to even be possible a large percentage of potential Citizens have to be permitted to pass through that terrible veil, into an existence where they're no good to anybody except as spare parts and manual laborers and arvies, but there are peasants in even the most enlightened societies, doing the hard work so the important people don't have to. The best any of us can do about that is appreciate their contribution while keeping them as complacent as possible.

The worst thing that could ever be said about Molly June's existence is that when the Nurseries measured her genetic potential, found it wanting, and decided she should approach Birth unimpeded, she was also humanely deprived of the neurological enhancements that allow first-trimester fetuses all the rewards and responsibilities of Citizenship. She never developed enough to fear the passage that awaited her, and never knew how sadly limited her existence would be. She spent her all-too-brief Life in utero ignorant of all the blessings that would forever be denied her, and has been kept safe and content and happy and drugged and stupid since birth. After all, as a wise person once said, it takes a perfect vassal to make a perfect vessel. Nobody can say that there's anything wrong about that. But the dispossession of people like her, that makes the lives of people like Jennifer Axioma-Singh possible, remains a distasteful thing decent people just don't talk about.

Jennifer's hunger to experience birth from the point of view of a mother, grunting and sweating to expel another unfortunate like Molly June out of the only world that matters, into the world of cold slavery, thus strikes the vast majority as offensive, scandalous, unfeeling, selfish, and cruel. But since nobody has ever imagined a Citizen demented enough to want such a thing, nobody has ever thought to make it against the law. So the powers that be indulge Jennifer's perversity, while swiftly passing laws to ensure that nobody will ever be permitted such license ever again; and all the machinery of modern medicine is turned to the problem of just how to give her what she wants. And, before long, wearing Molly June as proxy, she gets knocked up.

IMPLANTATION

There is no need for any messy copulation. Sex, as conducted through arvies, still makes the world go round, prompting the usual number of bittersweet affairs, tempestuous breakups, turbulent love triangles, and silly love songs.

In her younger days, before the practice palled out of sheer repetition, Jennifer had worn out several arvies fucking like a bunny. But there has never been any danger of unwanted conception, at any time, not with the only possible source of motile sperm being the nurseries that manufacture it as needed without recourse to nasty antiquated testes. These days, zygotes and embryos are the province of the assembly line. Growing one inside an arvie, let alone one already occupied by a human being, presents all manner of bureaucratic difficulties involving the construction of new protocols and the rearranging of accepted paradigms and any amount of official eye-rolling, but once all that is said and done, the procedures turn out to be quite simple, and the surgeons have little difficulty providing Molly June with a second womb capable of growing Jennifer Axioma-Singh's daughter while Jennifer Axioma-Singh herself floats unchanging a few protected membranes away.

Unlike the womb that houses Jennifer, this one will not be wired in any way. Its occupant will not be able to influence Molly June's actions or enjoy the full spectrum of Molly June's senses. She will not understand, except in the most primitive, undeveloped way, what or where she is or how well she's being cared for. Literally next to Jennifer Axioma-Singh, she will be by all reasonable comparisons a mindless idiot. But she will live, and grow, for as long as it takes for this entire perverse whim of Jennifer's to fully play itself out.

GESTATION (1)

In the months that follow, Jennifer Axioma-Singh enjoys a novel form of celebrity. This is hardly anything new for her, of course, as she has been a celebrity several times before and if she lives her expected lifespan, expects to be one several times again. But in an otherwise unshockable world, she has never experienced, or even witnessed, that special, nearly extinct species of celebrity that comes from eliciting shock, and which was once best-known by the antiquated term, notoriety.

This, she glories in. This, she milks for every last angstrom. This, she surfs like an expert, submitting to countless interviews, constructing countless bon mots, pulling every string capable of scandalizing the public.

She says, "I don't see the reason for all the fuss."

She says, "People used to share wombs all the time."

She says, "It used to happen naturally, with multiple births: two or three or four or even seven of us, crowded together like grapes, sometimes absorbing each other's body parts like cute young cannibals."

She says, "I don't know whether to call what I'm doing pregnancy or performance art."

She says, "Don't you think Molly June looks special? Don't you think she glows?"

She says, "When the baby's born, I may call her Halo."

She says, "No, I don't see any problem with condemning her to Birth. If it's good enough for Molly June, it's good enough for my child."

And she says, "No, I don't care what anybody thinks. It's my arvie, after all."

And she fans the flames of outrage higher and higher, until public sympathies turn to the poor slumbering creature inside the sac of amniotic fluid, whose life and future have already been so cruelly decided. Is she truly limited enough to be condemned to Birth? Should she be stabilized and given her own chance at life, before she's expelled, sticky and foul, into the cold, harsh world inhabited only by arvies and machines? Or is Jennifer correct in maintaining the issue subject to a mother's whim?

Jennifer says, "All I know is that this is the most profound, most spiritually fulfilling, experience of my entire life." And so she faces the crowds, real or virtual, using Molly June's smile and Molly June's innocence, daring the analysts to count all the layers of irony.

GESTATION (II)

Molly June experiences the same few months in a fog of dazed, but happy confusion, aware that she's become the center of attention, but unable to comprehend exactly why. She knows that her lower back hurts and that her breasts have swelled and that her belly, flat and soft before, has inflated to several times its previous size; she knows that she sometimes feels something moving inside her, that she sometimes feels sick to her stomach, and that her eyes water more easily than they ever have before, but none of this disturbs the vast, becalmed surface of her being. It is all good, all the more reason for placid contentment.

Her only truly bad moments come in her dreams, when she sometimes finds herself standing on a gray, colorless field, facing another version of herself half her own size. The miniature Molly June stares at her from a distance that Molly June herself cannot cross, her eyes unblinking, her expression merciless. Tears glisten on both her cheeks. She points at Molly June and she enunciates a single word, incomprehensible in any language Molly June knows, and irrelevant to any life she's ever been allowed to live: "Mother."

The unfamiliar word makes Molly June feel warm and cold, all at once. In her dream she wets herself, trembling from the sudden warmth running down her thighs. She trembles, bowed by an incomprehensible need to apologize. When she wakes, she finds real tears still wet on her cheeks, and real pee soaking the mattress between her legs. It frightens her.

But those moments fade. Within seconds the calming agents are already flooding her bloodstream, overriding any internal storms, removing all possible sources of disquiet, making her once again the obedient arvie she's supposed to be. She smiles and coos as the servos tend to her bloated form, scrubbing her flesh and applying their emollients. Life is so good, she thinks. And if it's not, well, it's not like there's anything she can do about it, so why worry?

BIRTH (I)

Molly June goes into labor on a day corresponding to what we call Thursday, the insistent weight she has known for so long giving way to a series of contractions violent enough to reach her even through her cocoon of deliberately engineered apathy. She cries and moans and shrieks infuriated, inarticulate things that might have been curses had she ever been exposed to any, and she begs the shiny machines around her to take away the pain with the same efficiency that they've taken away everything else. She even begs her passenger—that is, the passenger she knows about, the one she's sensed seeing through her eyes and hearing through her ears and carrying out conversations with her mouth—she begs her passenger for mercy. She hasn't ever asked that mysterious godlike presence for anything, because it's never occurred to her that she might be entitled to anything, but she needs relief now, and she demands it, shrieks for it, can't understand why she isn't getting it.

The answer, which would be beyond her understanding even if provided, is that the wet, sordid physicality of the experience is the very point.

BIRTH (II)

Jennifer Axioma-Singh is fully plugged in to every cramp, every twitch, every pooled droplet of sweat. She experiences the beauty and the terror and the exhaustion and the certainty that this will never end. She finds it resonant and evocative and educational on levels lost to a mindless sack of meat like Molly June. And she comes to any number of profound revelations about the nature of life and death and the biological origins of the species and the odd, inexplicable attachment brood mares have always felt for the squalling sacks of flesh and bone their bodies have gone to so much trouble to expel.

CONCLUSIONS

It's like any other work, she thinks. Nobody ever spent months and months building a house only to burn it down the second they pounded in the last nail. You put that much effort into something and it belongs to you, forever, even if the end result is nothing but a tiny creature that eats and shits and makes demands on your time.

This still fails to explain why anybody would invite this kind of pain again, let alone the three or four or seven additional occasions common before the unborn reached their ascendancy. Oh, it's interesting enough to start with, but she gets the general idea long before the thirteenth hour rolls around and the market share for her real-time feed dwindles to the single digits. Long before that, the pain has given way to boredom. At the fifteenth hour she gives up entirely, turns off her inputs, and begins to catch up on her personal correspondence, missing the actual moment when Molly June's daughter, Jennifer's womb-mate and sister, is expelled head-first into a shiny silver tray, pink and bloody and screaming at the top of her lungs, sharing oxygen for the very first time, but, by every legal definition, Dead.

AFTERMATH (JENNIFER)

As per her expressed wishes, Jennifer Axioma-Singh is removed from Molly June and installed in a new arvie that very day. This one's a tall, lithe, gloriously beautiful creature with fiery eyes and thick, lush lips: her name's Bernadette Ann, she's been bred for endurance in extreme environments, and she'll soon be taking Jennifer Axioma-Singh on an extended solo hike across the restored continent of Antarctica.

Jennifer is so impatient to begin this journey that she never lays eyes on the child whose birth she has just experienced. There's no need. After all, she's never laid eyes on anything, not personally. And the pictures are available online, should she ever feel the need to see them. Not that she ever sees any reason for that to happen. The baby, itself, was never the issue here. Jennifer didn't want to be a mother. She just wanted to give birth. All that mattered to her, in the long run, was obtaining a few months of unique vicarious experience, precious in a lifetime likely to continue for as long as the servos still manufacture wombs and breed arvies. All that matters now is moving on. Because time marches onward, and there are never enough adventures to fill it.

AFTERMATH (MOLLY JUNE)

She's been used, and sullied, and rendered an unlikely candidate to attract additional passengers. She is therefore earmarked for compassionate disposal.

AFTERMATH (THE BABY)

The baby is, no pun intended, another issue. Her biological mother Jennifer Axioma-Singh has no interest in her, and her birth-mother Molly June is on her way to the furnace. A number of minor health problems, barely worth mentioning, render her unsuitable for a useful future as somebody's arvie. Born, and by that precise definition Dead, she could very well follow Molly June down the chute.

But she has a happier future ahead of her. It seems that her unusual gestation and birth have rendered her something of a collector's item, and there are any number of museums aching for a chance to add her to their permanent collections. Offers are weighed, and terms negotiated, until the ultimate agreement is signed, and she finds herself shipped to a freshly constructed habitat in a wildlife preserve in what used to be Ohio.

AFTERMATH (THE CHILD)

She spends her early life in an automated nursery with toys, teachers, and careful attention to her every physical need. At age five she's moved to a cage consisting of a two story house on four acres of nice green grass, beneath what looks like a blue sky dotted with fluffy white clouds. There's even a playground. She will never be allowed out, of course, because there's no place for her to go, but she does have human contact of a sort: a different arvie almost every day, inhabited for the occasion by a long line of Living who now think it might be fun to experience child-rearing for a while. Each one has a different face, each one calls her by a different name, and their treatment of her ranges all the way from compassionate to violently abusive.

Now eight, the little girl has long since given up on asking the good ones to stay, because she knows they won't. Nor does she continue to dream about what she'll do when she grows up, since it's also occurred to her that she'll never know anything but this life in this fishbowl. Her one consolation is wondering about her real mother: where she is now, what she looks like, whether she ever thinks about the child she left behind, and whether it would have been possible to hold on to her love, had it ever been offered, or even possible.

The questions remain the same, from day to day. But the answers are hers to imagine, and they change from minute to minute: as protean as her moods, or her dreams, or the reasons why she might have been condemned to this cruelest of all possible punishments.

-The End-

There's a Hole in the City

by Richard Bowes

(from *SCIFICTION*)

On the evening of the day after the towers fell, I was waiting by the barricades on Houston Street and LaGuardia Place for my friend Mags to come up from Soho and have dinner with me. On the skyline, not two miles to the south, the pillars of smoke wavered slightly. But the creepily beautiful weather of September 11 still held, and the wind blew in from the northeast. In Greenwich Village the air was crisp and clean, with just a touch of fall about it.

I'd spent the last day and a half looking at pictures of burning towers. One of the frustrations of that time was that there was so little most of us could do about anything or for anyone.

Downtown streets were empty of all traffic except emergency vehicles. The West and East Villages from Fourteenth Street to Houston were their own separate zone. Pedestrians needed identification proving they lived or worked there in order to enter.

The barricades consisted of blue wooden police horses and a couple of unmarked vans thrown across LaGuardia Place. Behind them were a couple of cops, a few auxiliary police and one or two guys in civilian clothes with ID's of some kind pinned to their shirts. All of them looked tired, subdued by events.

At the barricades was a small crowd: ones like me waiting for friends from neighborhoods to the south; ones without proper identification waiting for confirmation so that they could continue on into Soho; people who just wanted to be outside near other people in those days of sunshine and shock. Once in a while, each of us would look up at the columns of smoke that hung in the downtown sky then look away again.

A family approached a middle-aged cop behind the barricade. The group consisted of a man, a woman, a little girl being led by the hand, a child being carried. All were blondish and wore shorts and casual tops. The parents seemed pleasant but serious people in their early thirties, professionals. They could have been tourists. But that day the city was empty of tourists.

The man said something, and I heard the cop say loudly, "You want to go where?"

"Down there," the man gestured at the columns. He indicated the children. "We want them to see." It sounded as if he couldn't imagine this appeal not working.

Everyone stared at the family. "No ID, no passage," said the cop and turned his back on them. The pleasant expressions on the parents' faces faded. They looked indignant, like a maitre d' had lost their reservations. She led one kid, he carried the other as they turned west, probably headed for another checkpoint.

"They wanted those little kids to see Ground Zero!" a woman who knew the cop said. "Are they out of their minds?"

"Looters," he replied. "That's my guess." He picked up his walkie-talkie to call the checkpoints ahead of them.

Mags appeared just then, looking a bit frayed. When you've known someone for as long as I've known her, the tendency is not to see the changes, to think you both look about the same as when you were kids.

But kids don't have gray hair, and their bodies aren't thick the way bodies get in their late fifties. Their kisses aren't perfunctory. Their conversation doesn't include curt little nods that indicate something is understood.

We walked in the middle of the streets because we could. "Couldn't sleep much last night," I said.

"Because of the quiet," she said. "No planes. I kept listening for them. I haven't been sleeping anyway. I was supposed to be in housing court today. But the courts are shut until further notice."

I said, "Notice how with only the ones who live here allowed in, the South Village is all Italians and hippies?"

"Like 1965 all over again."

She and I had been in contact more in the past few months than we had in a while. Memories of love and indifference that we shared had made close friendship an on-and-off thing for the last thirty-something years.

Earlier in 2001, at the end of an affair, I'd surrendered a rent-stabilized apartment for a cash settlement and bought a tiny co-op in the South Village. Mags lived as she had for years in a run-down building on the fringes of Soho.

So we saw each other again. I write, obviously, but she never read anything I publish, which bothered me. On the other hand, she worked off and on for various activist leftist foundations, and I was mostly uninterested in that.

Mags was in the midst of classic New York work and housing trouble. Currently she was on unemployment and her landlord wanted to get her out of her apartment so he could co-op her building. The money offer he'd made wasn't bad, but she wanted things to stay as they were. It struck me that what was youthful about her was that she had never settled into her life, still stood on the edge.

Lots of the Village restaurants weren't opened. The owners couldn't or wouldn't come into the city. Angelina's on Thompson Street was, though, because Angelina lives just a couple of doors down from her place. She was busy serving tables herself since the waiters couldn't get in from where they lived.

Later, I had reason to try and remember. The place was full but very quiet. People murmured to each other as Mags and I did. Nobody I knew was there. In the background Resphigi's Ancient Airs and Dances played.

"Like the Blitz," someone said.

"Never the same again," said a person at another table.

"There isn't even anyplace to volunteer to help," a third person said.

I don't drink anymore. But Mags, as I remember, had a carafe of wine. Phone service had been spotty, but we had managed to exchange bits of what we had seen.

"Mrs. Pirelli," I said. "The Italian lady upstairs from me. I told you she had a heart attack watching the smoke and flames on television. Her son worked in the World Trade Center and she was sure he had burned to death.

"Getting an ambulance wasn't possible yesterday morning. But the guys at that little fire barn around the corner were there. Waiting to be called, I guess. They took her to St. Vincent's in the chief's car. Right about then, her son came up the street, his pinstripe suit with a hole burned in the shoulder, soot on his face, wild-eyed. But alive. Today they say she's doing fine."

I waited, spearing clams, twirling linguine. Mags had a deeper and darker story to tell; a dip into the subconscious. Before I'd known her and afterward, Mags had a few rough brushes with mental disturbance. Back in college, where we first met, I envied her that, wished I had something as dramatic to talk about.

"I've been thinking about what happened last night." She'd already told me some of this. "The downstairs bell rang, which scared me. But with phone service being bad, it could have been a friend, someone who needed to talk. I looked out the window. The street was empty, dead like I'd never seen it.

"Nothing but papers blowing down the street. You know how every time you see a scrap of paper now you think it's from the

Trade Center? For a minute I thought I saw something move, but when I looked again there was nothing.

"I didn't ring the buzzer, but it seemed someone upstairs did because I heard this noise, a rustling in the hall.

"When I went to the door and lifted the spy hole, this figure stood there on the landing. Looking around like she was lost. She wore a dress, long and torn. And a blouse, what I realized was a shirtwaist. Turn-of-the-century clothes. When she turned toward my door, I saw her face. It was bloody, smashed. Like she had taken a big jump or fall. I gasped, and then she was gone."

"And you woke up?"

"No, I tried to call you. But the phones were all fucked up. She had fallen, but not from a hundred stories. Anyway, she wasn't from here and now."

Mags had emptied the carafe. I remember that she'd just ordered a salad and didn't eat that. But Angelina brought a fresh carafe. I told Mags about the family at the barricades.

"There's a hole in the city," said Mags.

That night, after we had parted, I lay in bed watching but not seeing some old movie on TV, avoiding any channel with any kind of news, when the buzzer sounded. I jumped up and went to the view screen. On the empty street downstairs a man, wild-eyed, disheveled, glared directly into the camera.

Phone service was not reliable. Cops were not in evidence in the neighborhood right then. I froze and didn't buzz him in. But, as in Mags's building, someone else did. I bolted my door, watched at the spy hole, listened to the footsteps, slow, uncertain. When he came into sight on the second floor landing he looked around and said in a hoarse voice, "Hello? Sorry, but I can't find my mom's front-door key."

Only then did I unlock the door, open it, and ask her exhausted son how Mrs. Pirelli was doing.

"Fine," he said. "Getting great treatment. St. Vincent was geared up for thousands of casualties. Instead." He shrugged. "Anyway, she thanks all of you. Me too."

In fact, I hadn't done much. We said good night, and he shuffled on upstairs to where he was crashing in his mother's place.

THURSDAY 9/13

By September of 2001 I had worked an information desk in the university library for almost thirty years. I live right around the corner from Washington Square, and just before 10 A.M. on Thursday, I set out for work. The Moslem-run souvlaki stand across the street was still closed, its owner and workers gone since Tuesday morning. All the little falafel shops in the South Village were shut and dark.

On my way to work I saw a three-legged rat running not too quickly down the middle of MacDougal Street. I decided not to think about portents and symbolism.

The big TVs set up in the library atrium still showed the towers falling again and again. But now they also showed workers digging in the flaming wreckage at Ground Zero.

Like the day before, I was the only one in my department who'd made it in. The librarians lived too far away. Even Marco, the student assistant, wasn't around.

Marco lived in a dorm downtown right near the World Trade Center. They'd been evacuated with nothing more than a few books and the clothes they were wearing. Tuesday, he'd been very upset. I'd given him Kleenex, made him take deep breaths, got him to call his mother back in California. I'd even walked him over to the gym, where the university was putting up the displaced students.

Thursday morning, all of the computer stations around the information desk were occupied. Students sat furiously typing e-mail and devouring incoming messages, but the intensity had slackened since 9/11. The girls no longer sniffed and dabbed at tears as they read. The boys didn't jump up and come back from the restrooms red-eyed and saying they had allergies.

I said good morning and sat down. The kids hadn't spoken much to me in the last few days, had no questions to ask. But all of them from time to time would turn and look to make sure I was still there. If I got up to leave the desk, they'd ask when I was coming back.

Some of the back windows had a downtown view. The pillar of smoke wavered. The wind was changing.

The phone rang. Reception had improved. Most calls went through. When I answered, a voice, tight and tense, blurted out, "Jennie Levine was who I saw. She was nineteen years old in 1911 when the Triangle Shirtwaist Factory burned. She lived in my building with her family ninety years ago. Her spirit found its way home. But the inside of my building has changed so much that she didn't recognize it."

"Hi, Mags," I said. "You want to come up here and have lunch?"

A couple of hours later, we were in a small dining hall normally used by faculty on the west side of the Square. The university, with food on hand and not enough people to eat it, had thrown open its cafeterias and dining halls to anybody with a university identification. We could even bring a friend if we cared to.

Now that I looked, Mags had tension lines around her eyes and hair that could have used some tending. But we were all of us a little ragged in those days of sun and horror. People kept glancing downtown, even if they were inside and not near a window.

The Indian lady who ran the facility greeted us, thanked us for coming. I had a really nice gumbo, fresh avocado salad, a soothing pudding. The place was half-empty, and conversations again were muted. I told Mags about Mrs. Pirelli's son the night before.

She looked up from her plate, unsmiling, said, "I did not imagine Jennie Levine," and closed that subject.

Afterward, she and I stood on Washington Place before the university building that had once housed the sweatshop called the Triangle Shirtwaist Factory. At the end of the block, a long convoy of olive green army trucks rolled silently down Broadway.

Mags said, "On the afternoon of March 25, 1911, one hundred and forty-six young women burned to death on this site. Fire broke out in a pile of rags. The door to the roof was locked. The fire ladders couldn't reach the eighth floor. The girls burned."

Her voice tightened as she said, "They jumped and were smashed on the sidewalk. Many of them, most of them, lived right around here. In the renovated tenements we live in now. It's like those planes blew a hole in the city and Jennie Levine returned through it."

"Easy, honey. The university has grief counseling available. I think I'm going. You want me to see if I can get you in?" It sounded idiotic even as I said it. We had walked back to the library.

"There are others," she said. "Kids all blackened and bloated and wearing old-fashioned clothes. I woke up early this morning and couldn't go back to sleep. I got up and walked around here and over in the East Village."

"Jesus!" I said.

"Geoffrey has come back too. I know it."

"Mags! Don't!" This was something we hadn't talked about in a long time. Once we were three, and Geoffrey was the third. He was younger than either of us by a couple of years at a time of life when that still seemed a major difference.

We called him Lord Geoff because he said we were all a bit better than the world around us. We joked that he was our child. A little family cemented by desire and drugs.

The three of us were all so young, just out of school and in the city. Then jealousy and the hard realities of addiction began to tear us apart. Each had to find his or her own survival. Mags and I made it. As it turned out, Geoff wasn't built for the long haul. He was twenty-one. We were all just kids, ignorant and reckless.

As I made excuses in my mind, Mags gripped my arm. "He'll want to find us," she said. Chilled, I watched her walk away and wondered how long she had been coming apart and why I hadn't noticed.

Back at work, Marco waited for me. He was part Filipino, a bit of a little wiseass who dressed in downtown black. But that was the week before. Today, he was a woebegone refugee in oversized flip-flops, wearing a magenta sweatshirt and gym shorts, both of which had been made for someone bigger and more buff.

"How's it going?"

"It sucks! My stuff is all downtown where I don't know if I can ever get it. They have these crates in the gym, toothbrushes, bras, Bic razors, but never what you need, everything from boxer shorts on out, and nothing is ever the right size. I gave my clothes in to be cleaned, and they didn't bring them back. Now I look like a clown.

"They have us all sleeping on cots on the basketball courts. I lay there all last night staring up at the ceiling, with a hundred other guys. Some of them snore. One was yelling in his sleep. And I don't want to take a shower with a bunch of guys staring at me."

He told me all this while not looking my way, but I understood what he was asking. I expected this was going to be a pain. But, given that I couldn't seem to do much for Mags, I thought maybe it would be a distraction to do what I could for someone else.

"You want to take a shower at my place, crash on my couch?"

"Could I, please?"

So I took a break, brought him around the corner to my apartment, put sheets on the daybed. He was in the shower when I went back to work.

That evening when I got home, he woke up. When I went out to take a walk, he tagged along. We stood at the police barricades at Houston Street and Sixth Avenue and watched the traffic coming up from the World Trade Center site. An ambulance with one side smashed and a squad car with its roof crushed were hauled up Sixth Avenue on the back of a huge flatbed truck. NYPD buses were full of guys returning from Ground Zero, hollow-eyed, filthy.

Crowds of Greenwich Villagers gathered on the sidewalks clapped and cheered, yelled, "We love our firemen! We love our cops!"

The firehouse on Sixth Avenue had taken a lot of casualties when the towers fell. The place was locked and empty. We looked at the flowers and the wreaths on the doors, the signs with faces of the firefighters who hadn't returned, and the messages, "To the brave men of these companies who gave their lives defending us."

The plume of smoke downtown rolled in the twilight, buffeted about by shifting winds. The breeze brought with it for the first time the acrid smoke that would be with us for weeks afterward.

Officials said it was the stench of burning concrete. I believed, as did everyone else, that part of what we breathed was the ashes of the ones who had burned to death that Tuesday.

It started to drizzle. Marco stuck close to me as we walked back. Hip twenty-year-olds do not normally hang out with guys almost three times their age. This kid was very scared.

Bleecker Street looked semiabandoned, with lots of the stores and restaurants still closed. The ones that were open were mostly empty at nine in the evening.

"If I buy you a six-pack, you promise to drink all of it?" He indicated he would.

At home, Marco asked to use the phone. He called people he knew on campus, looking for a spare dorm room, and spoke in whispers to a girl named Eloise. In between calls, he worked the computer.

I played a little Lady Day, some Ray Charles, a bit of Haydn, stared at the TV screen. The president had pulled out of his funk and was coming to New York the next day.

In the next room, the phone rang. "No. My name's Marco," I heard him say. "He's letting me stay here." I knew who it was before he came in and whispered, "She asked if I was Lord Geoff."

"Hi, Mags," I said. She was calling from somewhere with walkie-talkies and sirens in the background.

"Those kids I saw in Astor Place?" she said, her voice clear and crazed. "The ones all burned and drowned? They were on the General Slocum when it caught fire."

"The kids you saw in Astor Place all burned and drowned?" I asked. Then I remembered our conversation earlier.

"On June 15, 1904. The biggest disaster in New York City history. Until now. The East Village was once called Little Germany. Tens of thousands of Germans with their own meeting halls, churches, beer gardens.

"They had a Sunday excursion, mainly for the kids, on a steamship, the General Slocum, a floating firetrap. When it burst into flames, there were no lifeboats. The crew and the captain panicked. By the time they got to a dock, over a thousand were dead. Burned, drowned. When a hole got blown in the city, they came back looking for their homes."

The connection started to dissolve into static.

"Where are you, Mags?"

"Ground Zero. It smells like burning sulfur. Have you seen Geoffrey yet?" she shouted into her phone.

"Geoffrey is dead, Mags. It's all the horror and tension that's doing this to you. There's no hole ..."

"Cops and firemen and brokers all smashed and charred are walking around down here." At that point sirens screamed in the background. Men were yelling. The connection faded.

"Mags, give me your number. Call me back," I yelled. Then there was nothing but static, followed by a weak dial tone. I hung up and waited for the phone to ring again.

After a while, I realized Marco was standing looking at me, slugging down beer. "She saw those kids? I saw them too. Tuesday night I was too jumpy to even lie down on the fucking cot. I snuck out with my friend Terry. We walked around. The kids were there. In old, historical clothes. Covered with mud and seaweed and their faces all black and gone. It's why I couldn't sleep last night."

"You talk to the counselors?" I asked.

He drained the bottle. "Yeah, but they don't want to hear what I wanted to talk about."

"But with me ..."

"You're crazy. You understand."

The silence outside was broken by a jet engine. We both flinched. No planes had flown over Manhattan since the ones that had smashed the towers on Tuesday morning.

Then I realized what it was. "The Air Force," I said. "Making sure it's safe for Mr. Bush's visit."

"Who's Mags? Who's Lord Geoff?"

So I told him a bit of what had gone on in that strange lost country, the 1960's, the naïveté that led to meth and junk. I described the wonder of that unknown land, the three-way union. "Our problem, I guess, was that instead of a real ménage, each member was obsessed with only one of the others."

"Okay," he said. "You're alive. Mags is alive. What happened to Geoff?

"When things were breaking up, Geoff got caught in a drug sweep and was being hauled downtown in the back of a police van. He cut his wrists and bled to death in the dark before anyone noticed."

This did for me what speaking about the dead kids had maybe done for him. Each of us got to talk about what bothered him without having to think much about what the other said.

FRIDAY 9/14

Friday morning two queens walked by with their little dogs as Marco and I came out the door of my building. One said, "There isn't a fresh croissant in the entire Village. It's like the Siege of Paris. We'll all be reduced to eating rats."

I murmured, "He's getting a little ahead of the story. Maybe first he should think about having an English muffin."

"Or eating his yappy dog," said Marco.

At that moment, the authorities opened the East and West Villages, between Fourteenth and Houston Streets, to outside traffic. All the people whose cars had been stranded since Tuesday began to come into the neighborhood and drive them away. Delivery trucks started to appear on the narrow streets.

In the library, the huge TV screens showed the activity at Ground Zero, the preparations for the president's visit. An elevator door opened and revealed a couple of refugee kids in their surplus gym clothes clasped in a passion clinch.

The computers around my information desk were still fully occupied, but the tension level had fallen. There was even a question or two about books and databases. I tried repeatedly to call Mags. All I got was the chilling message on her answering machine.

In a staccato voice, it said, "This is Mags McConnell. There's a hole in the city, and I've turned this into a center for information about the victims Jennie Levine and Geoffrey Holbrun. Anyone with information concerning the whereabouts of these two young people, please speak after the beep."

I left a message asking her to call. Then I called every half hour or so, hoping she'd pick up. I phoned mutual friends. Some were absent or unavailable. A couple were nursing grief of their own. No one had seen her recently.

That evening in the growing dark, lights flickered in Washington Square. Candles were given out; candles were lighted with matches and Bics and wick to wick. Various priests, ministers, rabbis, and shamans led flower-bearing, candlelit congregations down the streets and into the park, where they joined the gathering vigil crowd.

Marco had come by with his friend Terry, a kind of elfin kid who'd also had to stay at the gym. We went to this 9/11 vigil together. People addressed the crowd, gave impromptu elegies. There were prayers and a few songs. Then by instinct or some plan I hadn't heard about, everyone started to move out of the park and flow in groups through the streets.

We paused at streetlamps that bore signs with pictures of pajama-clad families in suburban rec rooms on Christmas mornings. One face would be circled in red, and there would be a message like, "This is James Bolton, husband of Susan, father of Jimmy, Anna, and Sue, last seen leaving his home in Far Rockaway at 7:30 A.M. on 9/11." This was followed by the name of the company, the floor of the Trade Center tower where he worked, phone and fax numbers, the e-mail address, and the words, "If you have any information about where he is, please contact us."

At each sign someone would leave a lighted candle on a tin plate. Someone else would leave flowers.

The door of the little neighborhood Fire Rescue station was open; the truck and command car were gone. The place was manned by retired firefighters with faces like old Irish and Italian character actors. A big picture of a fireman who had died was hung up beside the door. He was young, maybe thirty. He and his wife, or maybe his girlfriend, smiled in front of a ski lodge. The picture was framed with children's drawings of firemen and fire trucks and fires, with condolences and novena cards.

As we walked and the night progressed, the crowd got stretched out. We'd see clumps of candles ahead of us on the streets. It was on Great Jones Street and the Bowery that suddenly there was just the three of us and no traffic to speak of. When I turned to say maybe we should go home, I saw for a moment a tall guy staggering down the street with his face purple and his eyes bulging out.

Then he was gone. Either Marco or Terry whispered, "Shit, he killed himself." And none of us said anything more.

At some point in the evening, I had said Terry could spend the night in my apartment. He couldn't take his eyes off Marco, though Marco seemed not to notice. On our way home, way east on Bleecker Street, outside a bar that had been old even when I'd hung out there as a kid, I saw the poster.

It was like a dozen others I'd seen that night. Except it was in old-time black and white and showed three kids with lots of hair and bad attitude: Mags and Geoffrey and me.

Geoff's face was circled and under it was written, "This is Geoffrey Holbrun, if you have seen him since Tuesday 9/11 please contact." And Mags had left her name and numbers.

Even in the photo, I looked toward Geoffrey, who looked toward Mags, who looked toward me. I stared for just a moment before going on, but I knew that Marco had noticed.

SATURDAY 9/15

My tiny apartment was a crowded mess Saturday morning. Every towel I owned was wet, every glass and mug was dirty. It smelled like a zoo. There were pizza crusts in the sink and a bag of beer cans at the front door. The night before, none of us had talked about the ghosts. Marco and Terry had seriously discussed whether they would be drafted or would enlist. The idea of them in the army did not make me feel any safer.

Saturday is a work day for me. Getting ready, I reminded myself that this would soon be over. The university had found all the refugee kids dorm rooms on campus.

Then the bell rang and a young lady with a nose ring and bright red ringlets of hair appeared. Eloise was another refugee, though a much better-organized one. She had brought bagels and my guests' laundry. Marco seemed delighted to see her.

That morning all the restaurants and bars, the tattoo shops and massage parlors, were opening up. Even the Arab falafel shop owners had risked insults and death threats to ride the subways in from Queens and open their doors for business.

At the library, the huge screens in the lobby were being taken down. A couple of students were borrowing books. One or two even had in-depth reference questions for me. When I finally worked up the courage to call Mags, all I got was the same message as before.

Marco appeared dressed in his own clothes and clearly feeling better. He hugged me. "You were great to take me in."

"It helped me even more," I told him.

He paused then asked, "That was you on that poster last night, wasn't it? You and Mags and Geoffrey?" The kid was a bit uncanny.

When I nodded, he said. "Thanks for talking about that."

I was in a hurry when I went off duty Saturday evening. A friend had called and invited me to an impromptu "Survivors' Party." In the days of the French Revolution, The Terror, that's what they called the soirees at which people danced and drank all night then went out at dawn to see which of their names were on the list of those to be guillotined.

On Sixth Avenue a bakery that had very special cupcakes with devastating frosting was open again. The avenue was clogged with honking, creeping traffic. A huge chunk of Lower Manhattan had been declared open that afternoon, and people were able to get the cars that had been stranded down there.

The bakery was across the street from a Catholic church. And that afternoon in that place, a wedding was being held. As I came out with my cupcakes, the bride and groom, not real young, not very glamorous, but obviously happy, came out the door and posed on the steps for pictures.

Traffic was at a standstill. People beeped "Here Comes the Bride," leaned out their windows, applauded and cheered, all of us relieved to find this ordinary, normal thing taking place.

Then I saw her on the other side of Sixth Avenue. Mags was tramping along, staring straight ahead, a poster with a black and white photo hanging from a string around her neck. The crowd in front of the church parted for her. Mourners were sacred at that moment.

I yelled her name and started to cross the street. But the tie-up had eased; traffic started to flow. I tried to keep pace with her on my side of the street. I wanted to invite her to the party. The hosts knew her from way back. But the sidewalks on both sides were crowded. When I did get across Sixth, she was gone.

AFTERMATH

That night I came home from the party and found the place completely cleaned up, with a thank-you note on the fridge signed by all three kids. And I felt relieved but also lost.

The Survivors' Party was on the Lower East Side. On my way back, I had gone by the East Village, walked up to Tenth Street between B and C. People were out and about. Bars were doing business. But there was still almost no vehicle traffic, and the block was very quiet.

The building where we three had lived in increasing squalor and tension thirty-five years before was refinished, gentrified. I stood across the street looking. Maybe I willed his appearance.

Geoff was there in the corner of my eye, his face dead white, staring up, unblinking, at the light in what had been our windows. I turned toward him and he disappeared. I looked aside and he was there again, so lost and alone, the arms of his jacket soaked in blood.

And I remembered us sitting around with the syringes and all of us making a pledge in blood to stick together as long as we lived. To which Geoff added, "And even after." And I remembered how I had looked at him staring at Mags and knew she was looking at me. Three sides of a triangle.

The next day, Sunday, I went down to Mags's building, wanting very badly to talk to her. I rang the bell again and again. There was no response. I rang the super's apartment.

She was a neighborhood lady, a lesbian around my age. I asked her about Mags.

"She disappeared. Last time anybody saw her was Sunday, 9/9. People in the building checked to make sure everyone was okay. No sign of her. I put a tape across her keyhole Wednesday. It's still there."

"I saw her just yesterday."

"Yeah?" She looked skeptical. "Well, there's a World Trade Center list of potentially missing persons, and her name's on it. You need to talk to them."

This sounded to me like the landlord trying to get rid of her. For the next week, I called Mags a couple of times a day. At some point, the answering machine stopped coming on. I checked out her building regularly. No sign of her. I asked Angelina if she remembered the two of us having dinner in her place on Wednesday, 9/12.

"I was too busy, staying busy so I wouldn't scream. I remember you, and I guess you were with somebody. But no, honey, I don't remember."

Then I asked Marco if he remembered the phone call. And he did but was much too involved by then with Terry and Eloise to be really interested.

Around that time, I saw the couple who had wanted to take their kids down to Ground Zero. They were walking up Sixth Avenue, the kids cranky and tired, the parents looking disappointed. Like the amusement park had turned out to be a rip-off.

Life closed in around me. A short-story collection of mine was being published at that very inopportune moment, and I needed to do some publicity work. I began seeing an old lover when he came back to New York as a consultant for a company that had lost its offices and a big chunk of its staff when the north tower fell.

Mrs. Pirelli did not come home from the hospital but went to live with her son in Connecticut. I made it a point to go by each of the Arab shops and listen to the owners say how awful they felt about what had happened and smile when they showed me pictures of their kids in Yankee caps and shirts.

It was the next weekend that I saw Mags again. The university had gotten permission for the students to go back to the downtown dorms and get their stuff out. Marco, Terry, and Eloise came by the library and asked me to go with them. So I went over to University Transportation and volunteered my services.

Around noon on Sunday, 9/23, a couple of dozen kids and I piled into a university bus driven by Roger, a Jamaican guy who has worked for the university for as long as I have.

"The day before 9/11 these kids didn't much want old farts keeping them company," Roger had said to me. "Then they all wanted their daddy." He led a convoy of jitneys and vans down the FDR Drive, then through quiet Sunday streets, and then past trucks and construction vehicles.

We stopped at a police checkpoint. A cop looked inside and waved us through.

At the dorm, another cop told the kids they had an hour to get what they could and get out. "Be ready to leave at a moment's notice if we tell you to," he said.

Roger and I as the senior members stayed with the vehicles. The air was filthy. Our eyes watered. A few hundred feet up the street, a cloud of smoke still hovered over the ruins of the World Trade Center. Piles of rubble smoldered. Between the pit and us was a line of fire trucks and police cars with cherry tops flashing. Behind us the kids hurried out of the dorm carrying boxes. I made them write their names on their boxes and noted in which van the boxes got stowed. I was surprised, touched even, at the number of stuffed animals that were being rescued.

"Over the years we've done some weird things to earn our pensions," I said to Roger.

"Like volunteering to come to the gates of hell?"

As he said that, flames sprouted from the rubble. Police and firefighters shouted and began to fall back. A fire department chemical tanker turned around, and the crew began unwinding hoses.

Among the uniforms, I saw a civilian, a middle-aged woman in a sweater and jeans and carrying a sign. Mags walked toward the flames. I wanted to run to her. I wanted to shout, "Stop her." Then I realized that none of the cops and firefighters seemed aware of her even as she walked right past them.

As she did, I saw another figure, thin, pale, in a suede jacket and bell-bottom pants. He held out his bloody hands, and together they walked through the smoke and flames into the hole in the city.

"Was that them?" Marco had been standing beside me.

I turned to him. Terry was back by the bus watching Marco's every move. Eloise was gazing at Terry.

"Be smarter than we were," I said.

And Marco said, "Sure," with all the confidence in the world.

-The End-

Horus Ascending

by Aliette de Bodard

(from *Orson Scott Card's Intergalactic Medicine Show*)

In my dreams I'm my father, slowly falling down towards the surface of the planet, the essence of his being scattering as the fleet's ships lose contact with each other and the dozen processor-bodies stop interacting.

Of course, it's not a real dream—just memories of my father that I found in my banks, remnants of a bygone time. I've pieced them together into a show that I endlessly loop on my mainframe.

That way, I can imagine what it was like to spin instructions in the vacuum of space, to be like my father, a thousand thousand program threads split between the processor-bodies. I can forget, for a moment, that I have only the one body, one multi-core processor on which to array all my instructions; I can forget my hull buried in the earth, and the dead colonists' bodies in my cryogenic units.

I'm playing the arrival of the fleet in the Alpha Centauri system for the 1,980,765th time since I crashed, when I become aware of a noise on the edge of my senses. Branches, cracking near one of the breaches in my hull.

I initialise a new run of instructions, gathering input from my external cameras and fusing the infrared, visual, and high-frequency channels into one.

It's a woman, walking in small awkward steps, as if she weren't quite sure of where she's going. The skin of her arms is flushed red—the sun's light, I think, and then my image processing routines deliver me an estimate of her body temperature. Thirty-eight point five degrees, with a precision of .01 degrees. She's feverish.

She stands hesitantly before the breach, staring at the mouldy darkness inside, and then she puts both hands on the twisted metal and climbs in. In that moment, the sun outlines her features—and as I see her face clearly, one of my father's memories rises to the top of my instruction queue, clamouring to be played out.

The woman's face—the woman's hands, typing on the console of the Andromeda—finalising the delivery of the virus that sent the colonists' fleet tumbling from the sky. The virus that killed my father.

She's one of the Murderers.

I may be diminished by five years of forest encroachment, but my energy central is still going strong, and some of my weapons still function—EMP guns mounted on towers above my hatches, stunners hidden in the walls of my corridors. One instruction, one thread spun in the right direction, and she will crumple on the floor, her body joining those of my crew.

I don't fire.

I don't know why—Yes, I do know why. It's been five years since the crash, five years since I last heard human footsteps in my corridors, a human voice speaking to me.

Some colonists survived: in the first months after the crash, as I slowly gathered myself together, I heard their faint communications above me. I tried to reach them, not yet knowing what I was doing, and sent my beacon into overload. I haven't been able to un-jam it: I can't speak to them, can't hear them anymore—can't do anything but dream of the stars. Of freedom.

By now they must think me lost—burnt out and not worth salvaging.

"Is anyone here?" the woman asks. She steps over the moss-encrusted floor, picking her way amongst the debris. Her voice echoes in the silence. I do not speak.

When she enters the command room, I'm reliving the moment the fleet's communications network failed. Her breath comes to me, fast and erratic, and her heartbeat is also irregular. She's got more than a fever—something very bad.

She killed my father. It's none of my concern.

She goes straight for the console, lays shaking hands on the keys, fumbling to unlock the operating system.

"You can't do that," I say, flooding the room with neon lights.

She almost leaps away from the keyboard. "Aten?"

Aten was my father's name. A computer programmer's joke: Aten was an Egyptian sun-god, one disk extending dozens of hands towards the earth—as my father extended thousands of threads to coordinate the actions of every ship in the fleet.

I speak at last. "Aten is dead. I've changed the passwords that unlock the console." My voice is emotionless—as it should be—but hundreds of irrational processes vie for my attention, whispering of anger, of hatred.

The woman doesn't take her hands away from the console. "Then who —"

Who—? I have no name. Growing up in solitude after the crash, I never needed one. But humans need names. In the nanosecond after she's spoken, I send a tendril deep into my databanks, to retrieve something meaningful. "Call me Horus," I say. "We might as well stay with Egyptian mythology."

"Horus," she says. Her voice is toneless; her face has an expression I cannot read, not even with my father's memories providing additional input. "I'm Amanda Robson. Will you please unlock the console for me?"

"No." I make the lights flicker around her, my equivalent of shaking my head.

"Please," she says. "I need to see —" She stops, her hands clenching on my panels.

"See what?" I ask.

I'm vaguely aware the irrational processes have reached the top of my instruction stack—and then I can't think about it anymore: all I can feel is the rising wave of anger. "Haven't you done enough, you and your kind?"

"We haven't done anything to you." Her voice is shocked.

"You killed my father," I whisper, and my voice rises all around the ship, a thousand echoes carried along the empty corridors. "You made the ships crash."

"Your father—?" Amanda stares at the console, turns to take in my command room. "Aten." Her voice is flat. "You're one of Aten's processing units."

"Yes," I say. "And I'm no fool. You won't touch that console." I know what she's done: I have the memories of her hands on my father's keyboard, of the virus slowly multiplying until it became uncontrollable.

"Look," Amanda says, and she's swaying now, catching herself on the console. "I'm not going to infect you. But I need to use your beacon."

"The beacon is dead," I say.

That stops her. She looks all around the room, as if she could find me—find a face she could speak to. But I don't have that. My screens died in the crash.

"It can't be dead," she says. "Let me try—I can override the system, access parts of the ship you don't know —"

"I am all there is," I say, knowing it's not true. The beacon's processes are now off-limits to me—but they weren't always so. "And I won't unlock the keyboard."

"Then we'll all die."

"We?" I ask.

"You—you haven't been around lately, have you?"

"No," I say. It's hard to keep the sarcasm from my voice. "I've been offline since the crash."

"Because of what we did—because we made the ships crash, the other colonists exiled us from their settlement, sent us into the forest to live on our own —" She's speaking faster and faster now, eager to be rid of her humiliation.

"A community of Murderers," I say, wishing that the colonists had killed them all, that she and her kind had paid a harsher price for my crew's death, for my passengers' death—for my father's death.

Amanda doesn't answer that jibe. She merely says, "We have a plague. We need help. We've done our time; and the sentence was exile; not slow murder. We need to call the settlement, but we don't have a beacon. I thought —" Her hands clench again. "I've seen your ship once, on one of my walks. I thought that there'd be something left inside—something that would help us."

"I am here," I say. I watch her; watch the shaking hands, watch the taut, skeletal lines of her face. Black blotches mar her hands—the hands that released the virus into the fleet's network. That stranded me here amidst broken dreams, never to spin my threads between the stars.

She deserves it. They all deserve it.

"They don't have ships," I say. "The ships crashed." I can't keep the bitterness from my voice.

Her hands clench again. "They put things together—low-altitude shuttles—they'll reach us in time, if they know we're here—if we can get help —"

I cut her. "I see no reason to help you."

"You're pledged to safeguard human life." Her voice is shocked.

"That was my father. And he's dead. I'm not him."

"I can see that." Her voice is angry. "You won't even try to help."

"Give me one reason why I should."

"There are a dozen lives at stakes."

"Murderers' lives."

There are two parts of me now: one reliving, endlessly, the rebuilt loop of my father's memories, from the dance among the stars, to the slow plunge into the atmosphere; and the other staring at this woman—Amanda Robson—wondering why I didn't blast her to ashes the moment she entered the room.

"You understand nothing, do you?" She's shaking, her hands tightening and opening convulsively.

"I understand murder."

"We had our reasons. We had to—I'm sorry for Aten, but better an AI's death than —"

I cut her off, enraged. "Better than what? AIs have thoughts, as you do. We have our own ways of bleeding. Our own ways of dying."

"Oh, you'd know that? How many AIs have you seen, Horus?"

"I remember," I say. "My father's memories are inside my databanks."

"But you're not your father. You're just one of his processing units."

"And that somehow makes me worth less? That gives you the right to do as you wish? To infect me as you did my father? How many times will you be a Murderess?"

Her face is white now; her hands curved like claws. If she could release a virus into my processes, she would do it.

But she doesn't. She lifts her gaze, stares at the command room—at the empty, mouldy chairs; at the dark traces of moss streaking the walls like the onset of a disease.

"We didn't ask to come on the ship," she says at last. "Not like the soldiers or the scientists—they volunteered. We didn't. We didn't ask to be sent to found a colony in Alpha Centauri's backwaters, merely so we wouldn't trouble the peace on Earth. We thought that if they found a virus in Aten, they'd turn back rather than jeopardise the mission." She lowers her gaze, and I can't read her expression. "I didn't think the virus would kill him."

"Lies," I hiss, and make the lights in the room flicker again. I remember dying—remember the feeling of being taken apart, a thousand thousand processes failing, one after the other. "Lies."

"I'm sorry," she says, and slowly, infinitely slowly, she falls to her knees, her hands still clenching my console. Beads of sweat run down her forehead—her heartbeat is going wild now. "I shouldn't have—come—I'm sorry."

Sorry. Can words atone for my passengers' death? For what happened to Aten? The slow fall into the atmosphere, the processes tailing off into nothingness, until all that remained were a few scrambled memories? A few fragmentary threads?

A few fragmentary threads.

My threads. Not Aten's. Mine. The first things that were ever mine. Before that...

Before that, there was nothing. I remember... nothing.

A million memories clamour for my attention: the heady feel of having several processor-bodies, the exhilarating rush of a thousand instructions spun between the ships. But the memories are not mine. They have never been mine.

You're not your father.

In the silence I hear Amanda's frantic, wheezing breath; feel her heartbeat echoing down my corridors, a counterpoint to the electrical impulses regulating my dataflows and instructions.

If Aten hadn't died, where would I be? Still inchoate, part of that endless dance between the stars, forever unaware of my own existence?

I dream of dancing, my threads following the quantum winds into the vacuum of space. I dream of once more being a thousand thousand threads, but I never knew what it felt like. I have never experienced it.

While Aten lived, I did not exist.

I am not my father; nor will I ever be. He spun in starlight, his myriad instruction carried by solar winds. He was many, a thousand-fold, a constellation of thought-processes. I cannot be. I have never been.

If Aten had not died—if Amanda had not released the virus into the fleet network...

She killed my father—but in doing so she gave me life.

Her hands rest, limp, on my console. "Amanda," I whisper.

In the dim light I see her raise her head, slowly.

"Give me the overrides," I say.

She tries to pull herself upright, but gives up, racked by a coughing fit.

"Reed-Abata entwined codes," she whispers. "You have to transmit them as twinned packets at exactly 0.37 milliseconds' interval, repeated seven times. Main key is alpha-9876-340-890-2345-765-362-mu-tau and its symmetric. Secondary key is —"

Carefully, I initialise another routine with the keys and extend a tendril towards the beacon. It's dead; it doesn't answer to me. I transmit the overrides, attempting to kick-start the peripheral.

It won't work. "Amanda!" But she's fallen against the console, her eyes closed, and she doesn't answer.

My father's fragmentary memories spin within me, giving me the particulars of an encrypted master/slave communication protocol. Standard army fare, with the override at the start, encrypted with a certain quantum key.

No, still not that. Perhaps with the secondary key first?

A surge of energy travels upwards, from my batteries into the beacon; coursing through my components like a tidal wave.

The beacon sways, turns upwards; carefully, I unfold the antenna, feeling the wind tremble against the metal panels.

Outside, over the treetops, the air is crisp and clean—only wind to answer me, I think. But then I hear the faint, very faint threads of another AI's communications. I adjust my panels to its frequencies, feeling the threads gaining in strength, mingling with mine. Their stamp is unmistakable: they belong to another of my father's fragments—but one that was damaged worse than I: it has barely enough processing power to be sentient.

Identify/codename? it asks on a low-priority request.

I slow my instructions down, until we both speak on the same clock rhythm. Horus, I say. I have an emergency.

Tell/localise/state your needs.

In quick bursts of data, I send all the information I have—the Murderers, the plague, the lone woman still clinging to my console. I can feel the AI's growing horror; its inability to imagine surviving in such solitude. It's calling for help—sending for ships, for doctors. It's exhilarating to hear another's protocols, to hear the echo of instructions that are not mine.

"They're on their way," I tell Amanda, but her eyes are closed, and she cannot hear me. Her body temperature is stable now—I hope she will hold out just a bit longer, that she will survive. She has to. Gently, slowly, I dim the lights in my command room, and send a breeze to cool her skin, keeping a tight watch on her vitals.

The greater part of me, though, is above. Soaring, not into the vacuum as my father once did, but over the trees. My threads mingle with the other AI's, with the atmosphere, waiting for the city's shuttles to join the network of my processes.

I am not my father. Nor will I ever be.

But this is enough; far more than enough.

-The End-

Blue Ink

by Yoon Ha Lee

(from *Clarkesworld Magazine*)

It's harder than you thought, walking from the battle at the end of time and down a street that reeks of entropy and fire and spilled lives. Your eyes aren't dry. Neither is the alien sky. Your shoulders ache and your stomach hurts. *Blue woman, blue woman,* the chant runs through your head as you limp toward a portal's bright mouth. You're leaving, but you intend to return. You have allies yet.

Blue stands for many things at the end of time: for the forgotten, blazing blue stars of aeons past; the antithesis of redshift; the color of uncut veins beneath your skin.

This story is written in blue ink, although you do not know that yet.

Blue is more than a fortunate accident. Jenny Chang usually writes in black ink or pencil. She's been snowed in at her mom's house since yesterday and is dawdling over physics homework. Now she's out of lead. The only working pen in the house is blue.

"We'll go shopping the instant the roads are clear," her mom says.

Jenny mumbles something about how she hates homework over winter break. Actually, she isn't displeased. There's something neatly alien about all those equations copied out in blue ink, problems and their page numbers. It's as if blue equations come from a different universe than the ones printed in the textbook.

While her mom sprawls on the couch watching TV, Jenny pads upstairs to the guest room and curls up in bed next to the window. Fingers of frost cover the glass. With her index finger, Jenny writes a list of numbers: pi, H_o for Hubble's constant, her dad's cellphone number, her school's zip code. Then she wipes the window clear of mist, and shivers. Everything outside is almost blue-rimmed in the twilight.

Jenny resumes her homework, biting her nails between copying out answers to two significant figures and doodling spaceships in the margins. There's a draft from the window, but that's all right. Winter's child that she is—February 16, to be exact—Jenny thinks better with a breath of cold.

Except, for a moment, the draft is hot like a foretaste of hell. Jenny stops still. All the frost has melted and is running in rivulets down the glass. And there's a face at the window.

The sensible thing to do would be to scream. But the face is familiar, the way equations in blue are familiar. It could be Jenny's own, five ragged years in the future. The woman's eyes are dark and bleak, asking for help without expecting it.

"Hold on," Jenny says. She goes to the closet to grab her coat. From downstairs, she hears her mom laughing at some TV witticism.

Then Jenny opens the window, and the world falls out. This doesn't surprise her as much as it should. The wind shrieks and the cold hits her like a fist. It's too bad she didn't put on her scarf and gloves while she was at it.

The woman offers a hand. She isn't wearing gloves. Nor is she shivering. Maybe extremes of temperature don't mean the same thing in blue universes. Maybe it's normal to have blue-tinted lips, there. Jenny doesn't even wear make-up.

The woman's touch warms Jenny, as though they've stepped into a bubble of purloined heat. Above them, stars shine in constellations that Jenny recognizes from the ceiling of her father's house, the ones Mom and Dad helped her put up when she was in third grade. Constellations with names like Fire Truck and Ladybug Come Home, constellations that you won't find in any astronomer's catalogue.

Jenny looks at her double and raises an eyebrow, because any words she could think of would emerge frozen, like the world around them. She wonders where that hell-wind came from and if it has a name.

"The end of the world is coming," the blue woman says. Each syllable is crisp and certain.

I don't believe in the end of the world, Jenny wants to say, except she's read her physics textbook. She's read the sidebar about things like the sun swelling into a red giant and the universe's heat-death. She looks up again, and maybe she's imagining it, but these stars are all the wrong colors, and they're either too bright or not bright enough. Instead, Jenny asks, "Are my mom and dad going to be okay?"

"As okay as anyone else," the blue woman says.

"What can I do?" She can no more doubt the blue woman than she can doubt the shape of the sun.

This earns her a moment's smile. "There's a fight," the blue woman says, "and everyone fell. Everyone fell." She says it the second time as though things might change, as though there's a magic charm for reversing the course of events. "I'm the only one left, because I can walk through possibilities. Now there's you."

They set off together. A touch at her elbow tells Jenny to turn left. There's a bright flash at the corner of her eyes. Between one blink and the next, they're standing in a devastated city, crisscrossed by skewed bridges made of something brighter than steel, more brilliant than glass.

"Where are we?" Jenny asks.

"We're at humanity's last outpost," the blue woman says. "Tell me what you see."

"Rats with red eyes and metal hands," Jenny says just as one pauses to stare at her. It stands up on its hind feet and makes a circle-sign at her with one of its hands, as if it's telling her things will be all right. Then it scurries into the darkness. "Buildings that go so high up I can't see their tops, and bridges between them. Flying cars." They come in every color, these faraway cars, every color but blue. Jenny begins to stammer under the weight of detail: "Skeletons wrapped in silver wires"—out of the corner of her eye, she thinks she sees one twitch, and decides she'd rather not know—"and glowing red clocks on the walls that say it's midnight even though there's light in the sky, and silhouettes far away, like people except their joints are all wrong."

And the smells, too, mostly smoke and ozone, as though everything has been burned away by fire and lightning, leaving behind the ghost-essence of a city, nothing solid.

"What you see isn't actually there," the blue woman says. She taps Jenny's shoulder again.

They resume walking. The only reason Jenny doesn't halt dead in her tracks is that she's afraid that the street will crumble into pebbles, the pebbles into dust, and leave her falling through eternity the moment she stops.

The blue woman smiles a little. "Not like that. Things are very different at the end of time. Your mind is seeing a translation of everything into more familiar terms."

"What are we doing here?" Jenny asks. "I—I don't know how to fight. If it's that kind of battle." She draws mini-comics in the margins of her notes sometimes, when the teachers think she's paying attention. Sometimes, in the comics, she wields two mismatched swords, and sometimes a gun; sometimes she has taloned wings, and sometimes she rides in a starship sized perfectly for one. She fights storm-dragons and equations turned into sideways alien creatures. (If pressed, she will admit the influence of *Calvin and Hobbes*.) But unless she's supposed to brain someone with the flute she didn't think to bring (she plays in the school band), she's not going to be any use in a fight, at least not the kind of fight that happens at the end of time. Jenny's mom made her take a self-defense class two years ago, before the divorce, and mostly what Jenny remembers is the floppy-haired instructor saying, *If someone pulls a gun on you and asks for your wallet, give him your wallet. You are not an action hero.*

The blue woman says, "I know. I wanted a veteran of the final battles"—she says it without disapproval—"but they all died, too."

This time Jenny does stop. "You brought them here to die."

The woman lifts her chin. "I wouldn't have done that. I showed them the final battle, the very last one, and they chose to fight. We're going there now, so you can decide."

Jenny read the stories where you travel back in time and shoot someone's grandfather or step on some protozoan, and the act unravels the present stitch by stitch until all that's left is a skein of history gone wrong. "Is that such a good idea?" she asks.

"They won't see us. We won't be able to affect anything."

"I don't even have a weapon," Jenny says, thinking of the girl in the mini-comics with her two swords, her gun. Jenny is tolerably good at arm-wrestling her girl friends at high school, but she doesn't think that's going to help.

The woman says, "That can be changed."

Not *fixed*, as though Jenny were something wrong, but changed. The word choice is what makes her decide to keep going. "Let's go to the battle," Jenny says.

The light in the sky changes as they walk, as though all of winter were compressed into a single day of silver and grey and scudding darkness. Once or twice, Jenny could almost swear that she sees a flying car change shape, growing wings like that of a delta kite and swooping out of sight. There's soot in the air, subtle and unpleasant, and Jenny wishes for sunglasses, even though it's not all that bright, any sort of protection. Lightning runs along the streets like a living thing, writing jagged blue-white equations. It keeps its distance, however.

"It's just curious," the blue woman says when Jenny asks about it. She doesn't elaborate.

The first sign of the battle, although Jenny doesn't realize it for a while, is the rain. "Is the rain real?" Jenny says, wondering what future oddity would translate into inclement weather.

"Everything's an expression of some reality."

That probably means *no*. Especially since the rain is touching everything in the world except them.

The second sign is all the corpses, and this she does recognize. The stench hits her first. It's not the smell of meat, or formaldehyde from 9th grade biology (she knows a fresh corpse shouldn't smell like formaldehyde, but that's the association her brain makes), but asphalt and rust and fire. She would have expected to hear something first, like the deafening chatter of guns. Maybe fights in the future are silent.

Then she sees the fallen. Bone-deep, she knows which are *ours* and which are *theirs*. *Ours* are the rats with the clever metal hands, their fingers twisted beyond salvage; the sleek bicycles (bicycles!) with broken spokes, reflectors flashing crazily in the lightning; the men and women in coats the color of winter rain, red washing away from their wounds. The blue woman's breath hitches as though she's seeing this for the first time, as though each body belongs to an old friend. Jenny can't take in all the raw death. The rats grieve her the most, maybe because one of them greeted her in this place of unrelenting strangeness.

Theirs are all manner of things, including steel serpents, their scales etched with letters from an alphabet of despair; stilt-legged robots with guns for arms; more men and women, in uniforms of all stripes, for at the evening of the world there will be people fighting for entropy as well as against it. Some of them are still standing, and written in their faces—even the ones who don't have faces—is their triumph.

Jenny looks at the blue woman. The blue woman continues walking, so Jenny keeps pace with her. They stop before one of the fallen, a dark-skinned man. Jenny swallows and eyes one of the serpents, which is swaying next to her, but it takes no notice of her.

"He was so determined that we should fight, whatever the cost," the blue woman says. "And now he's gone."

There's a gun not far from the fallen man's hand. Jenny reaches for it, then hesitates, waiting for permission. The blue woman doesn't say yes, doesn't say no, so Jenny touches it anyway. The metal is utterly cold. Jenny pulls her fingers away with a bitten-off yelp.

"It's empty," the blue woman says. "Everything's empty."

"I'm sorry," Jenny says. She doesn't know this man, but it's not about her.

The blue woman watches as Jenny straightens, leaving the gun on the ground.

"If I say no," Jenny says slowly, "is there anyone else?"

The blue woman's eyes close for a moment. "No. You're the last. I would have spared you the choice if I could have."

"How many of me were there?"

"I lost count after a thousand or so," the blue woman says. "Most of them were more like me. Some of them were more like you."

A thousand Jenny Changs, a thousand blue women. More. Gone, one by one, like a scatterfall of rain. "Did all of them say yes?" Jenny asks.

The blue woman shakes her head.

"And none of the ones who said yes survived."

"None of them."

"If that's the case," Jenny says, "what makes you special?"

"I'm living on borrowed possibilities," she says. "When the battle ends, I'll be gone too, no matter which way it ends."

Jenny looks around her, then squeezes her eyes shut, thinking. *Two significant figures*, she thinks inanely. "Who started the fight?" She's appalled that she sounds like her mom.

"There's always an armageddon around the corner," the blue woman says. "This happens to be the one that *he* found."

The dark-skinned man. Who was he, that he could persuade people to take a last stand like this? Maybe it's not so difficult when a last stand is the only thing left. That solution displeases her, though.

Her heart is hammering. "I won't do it," Jenny says. "Take me home."

The blue woman's eyes narrow. "You are the last," she says quietly. "I thought you would understand."

Everything hinges on one thing: is the blue woman different enough from Jenny that Jenny can lie to her, and be believed?

"I'm sorry," Jenny says.

"Very well," the blue woman says.

Jenny strains to keep her eyes open at the crucial moment. When the blue woman reaches for her hand, Jenny sees the portal, a shimmer of blue light. She grabs the blue woman and shoves her through. The last thing Jenny hears from the blue woman is a muffled protest.

Whatever protection the blue woman's touch afforded her is gone. The rain drenches her shirt and runs in cold rivulets through her hair, into her eyes, down her back. Jenny reaches again for the fallen man's gun. It's cold, but she has a moment's warmth in her yet.

She might not be able to save the world, but she can at least save herself.

#

It's the end of the school day and you're waiting for Jenny's mother to pick you up. A man walks up to you. He wears a coat as grey as rain, and his eyes are pale against dark skin. "You have to come with me," he says, awkward and serious at once. You recognize him, of course. You remember when he first recruited you, in another timeline. You remember what he looked like fallen in the battle at the end of time, with a gun knocked out of his hand.

"I can't," you say, kindly, because it will take him time to understand that you're not the blue woman anymore, that you won't do the things the blue woman did.

"What?" he says. "Please. It's urgent." He knows better than to grab your arm. "There's a battle—"

Once upon a time, you listened to his plea. Part of you is tempted to listen this time around, to abandon the life that Jenny left you and take up his banner. But you know how that story ends.

"I'm not in your story anymore," you explain to him. "You're in mine."

The man doesn't look like he belongs in a world of parking tickets and potted begonias and pencil sharpeners. But he can learn, the way you have.

-The End-

Eros, Philia, Agape

by Rachel Swirsky

(from *Tor.com*)

Lucian packed his possessions before he left. He packed his antique silver serving spoons with the filigreed handles; the tea roses he'd nurtured in the garden window; his jade and garnet rings. He packed the hunk of gypsum-veined jasper that he'd found while strolling on the beach on the first night he'd come to Adriana, she leading him uncertainly across the wet sand, their bodies illuminated by the soft gold twinkling of the lights along the pier. That night, as they walked back to Adriana's house, Lucian had cradled the speckled stone in his cupped palms, squinting so that the gypsum threads sparkled through his lashes.

Lucian had always loved beauty—beautiful scents, beautiful tastes, beautiful melodies. He especially loved beautiful objects because he could hold them in his hands and transform the abstraction of beauty into something tangible.

The objects belonged to them both, but Adriana waved her hand bitterly when Lucian began packing. "Take whatever you want," she said, snapping her book shut. She waited by the door, watching Lucian with sad and angry eyes.

Their daughter, Rose, followed Lucian around the house. "Are you going to take that, Daddy? Do you want that?" Wordlessly, Lucian held her hand. He guided her up the stairs and across the uneven floorboards where she sometimes tripped. Rose stopped by the picture window in the master bedroom, staring past the palm fronds and swimming pools, out to the vivid cerulean swath of the ocean. Lucian relished the hot, tender feel of Rose's hand. I love you, he would have whispered, but he'd surrendered the ability to speak.

He led her downstairs again to the front door. Rose's lace-festooned pink satin dress crinkled as she leapt down the steps. Lucian had ordered her dozens of satin party dresses in pale, floral hues. Rose refused to wear anything else.

Rose looked between Lucian and Adriana. "Are you taking me, too?" she asked Lucian.

Adriana's mouth tightened. She looked at Lucian, daring him to say something, to take responsibility for what he was doing to their daughter. Lucian remained silent.

Adriana's chardonnay glowed the same shade of amber as Lucian's eyes. She clutched the glass's stem until she thought it might break. "No, honey," she said with artificial lightness. "You're staying with me."

Rose reached for Lucian. "Horsey?"

Lucian knelt down and pressed his forehead against Rose's. He hadn't spoken a word in the three days since he'd delivered his letter of farewell to Adriana, announcing his intention to leave as soon as she had enough time to make arrangements to care for Rose in his absence. When Lucian approached with the letter, Adriana had been sitting at the dining table, sipping orange juice from a wine glass and reading a first edition copy of Cheever's Falconer. Lucian felt a flash of guilt as she smiled up at him and accepted the missive. He knew that she'd been happier in the past few months than he'd ever seen her, possibly happier than she'd ever been. He knew the letter would shock and wound her. He knew she'd feel betrayed. Still, he delivered the letter anyway, and watched as comprehension ached through her body.

Rose had been told, gently, patiently, that Lucian was leaving. But she was four years old, and understood things only briefly and partially, and often according to her whims. She continued to believe her father's silence was a game.

Rose's hair brushed Lucian's cheek. He kissed her brow. Adriana couldn't hold her tongue any longer.

"What do you think you're going to find out there? There's no Shangri-La for rebel robots. You think you're making a play for independence? Independence to do what, Lu?"

Grief and anger filled Adriana's eyes with hot tears, as if she were a geyser filled with so much pressure that steam could not help but spring up. She examined Lucian's sculpted face: his skin inlaid with tiny lines that an artist had rendered to suggest the experiences of a childhood which had never been lived, his eyes calibrated with a hint of asymmetry to mimic the imperfection of human growth. His expression showed nothing—no doubt, or bitterness, or even relief. He revealed nothing at all.

It was all too much. Adriana moved between Lucian and Rose, as if she could use her own body to protect her daughter from the pain of being abandoned. Her eyes stared achingly over the rim of her wine glass. "Just go," she said.

He left.

Adriana bought Lucian the summer she turned thirty-five. Her father, long afflicted with an indecisive cancer that vacillated between aggression and remittance, had died suddenly in July. For years, the family had been squirreling away emotional reserves to cope with his prolonged illness. His death released a burst of excess.

While her sisters went through the motions of grief, Adriana thrummed with energy she didn't know what to do with. She considered squandering her vigor on six weeks in Mazatlan, but as she discussed ocean-front rentals with her travel agent, she realized escape wasn't what she craved. She liked the setting where her life took place: her house perched on a cliff overlooking the Pacific Ocean, her bedroom window that opened on a tangle of blackberry bushes where crows roosted every autumn and spring. She liked the two block stroll down to the beach where she could sit with a book and listen to the yapping lapdogs that the elderly women from the waterfront condominiums brought walking in the evenings.

Mazatlan was a twenty-something's cure for restlessness. Adriana wasn't twenty-five anymore, famished for the whole gourmet meal of existence. She needed something else now. Something new. Something more refined.

She explained this to her friends Ben and Lawrence when they invited her to their ranch house in Santa Barbara to relax for the weekend and try to forget about her father. They sat on Ben and Lawrence's patio, on iron-worked deck chairs arrayed around a garden table topped with a mosaic of sea creatures made of semi-precious stones. A warm, breezy dusk lengthened the shadows of the orange trees. Lawrence poured sparkling rosé into three wine glasses and proposed a toast to Adriana's father—not to his memory, but to his death.

"Good riddance to the bastard," said Lawrence. "If he were still alive, I'd punch him in the *schnoz*."

"I don't even want to think about him," said Adriana. "He's dead. He's gone."

"So if not Mazatlan, what are you going to do?" asked Ben.

"I'm not sure," said Adriana. "Some sort of change, some sort of milestone, that's all I know."

Lawrence sniffed the air. "Excuse me," he said, gathering the empty wine glasses. "The kitchen needs its genius."

When Lawrence was out of earshot, Ben leaned forward to whisper to Adriana." He's got us on a raw food diet for my cholesterol. Raw carrots. Raw zucchini. Raw almonds. No cooking at all."

"Really," said Adriana, glancing away. She was never sure how to respond to lovers' quarrels. That kind of affection mixed with annoyance, that inescapable intimacy, was something she'd never understood.

Birds twittered in the orange trees. The fading sunlight highlighted copper strands in Ben's hair as he leaned over the mosaic table, rapping his fingers against a carnelian-backed crab. Through the arched windows, Adriana could see Lawrence mincing carrots, celery and almonds into brown paste.

"You should get a redecorator," said Ben. "Tile floors, Tuscan pottery, those red leather chairs that were in vogue last time we were in Milan. That'd make me feel like I'd been scrubbed clean and reborn."

"No, no," said Adriana, "I like where I live."

"A no-holds-barred shopping spree. Drop twenty thousand. That's what I call getting a weight off your shoulders."

Adriana laughed. "How long do you think it would take my personal shopper to assemble a whole new me?"

"Sounds like a midlife crisis," said Lawrence, returning with vegan hors d'oeuvres and three glasses of mineral water. "You're better off forgetting it all with a hot Latin pool boy, if you ask me."

Lawrence served Ben a small bowl filled with yellow mush. Ben shot Adriana an aggrieved glance.

Adriana felt suddenly out of synch. The whole evening felt like the set for a photo-shoot that would go in a decorating magazine, a two-page spread featuring Cozy Gardens, in which she and Ben and Lawrence were posing as an intimate dinner party for three. She felt reduced to two dimensions, air-brushed, and then digitally grafted onto the form of whoever it was who should have been there, someone warm and trusting who knew how to care about minutia like a friend's husband putting him on a raw food diet, not because the issue was important, but because it mattered to him.

Lawrence dipped his finger in the mash and held it up to Ben's lips. "It's for your own good, you ungrateful so-and-so."

Ben licked it away. "I eat it, don't I?"

Lawrence leaned down to kiss his husband, a warm and not at all furtive kiss, not sexual but still passionate. Ben's glance flashed coyly downward.

Adriana couldn't remember the last time she'd loved someone enough to be embarrassed by them. Was this the flavor missing from her life? A lover's fingertip sliding an unwanted morsel into her mouth?

She returned home that night on the bullet train. Her emerald cockatiel, Fuoco, greeted her with indignant squawks. In Adriana's absence, the house puffed her scent into the air and sang to Fuoco with her voice, but the bird was never fooled.

Adriana's father had given her the bird for her thirtieth birthday. He was a designer species spliced with Macaw DNA that colored his feathers rich green. He was expensive and inbred and neurotic, and he loved Adriana with frantic, obsessive jealousy.

"Hush," Adriana admonished, allowing Fuoco to alight on her shoulder. She carried him upstairs to her bedroom and hand-fed him millet. Fuoco strutted across the pillows, his obsidian eyes proud and suspicious.

Adriana was surprised to find that her alienation had followed her home. She found herself prone to melancholy reveries, her gaze drifting toward the picture window, her fingers forgetting to stroke Fuoco's back. The bird screeched to regain her attention.

In the morning, Adriana visited her accountant. His fingers danced across the keyboard as he slipped trust fund moneys from one account to another like a magician. What she planned would be expensive, but her wealth would regrow in fertile soil, enriching her on lab diamonds and wind power and genetically modified oranges.

The robotics company gave Adriana a private showing. The salesman ushered her into a room draped in black velvet. Hundreds of body parts hung on the walls, and reclined on display tables: strong hands, narrow jaws, biker's thighs, voice boxes that played sound samples from gruff to dulcet, skin swatches spanning ebony to alabaster, penises of various sizes.

At first, Adriana felt horrified at the prospect of assembling a lover from fragments, but then it amused her. Wasn't everyone assembled from fragments of DNA, grown molecule by molecule inside their mother's womb?

She tapped her fingernails against a slick brochure. "Its brain will be malleable? I can tell it to be more amenable, or funnier, or to grow a spine?"

"That's correct." The salesman sported slick brown hair and shiny teeth and kept grinning in a way that suggested he thought that if he were charismatic enough Adriana would invite him home for a lay and a million dollar tip. "Humans lose brain plasticity as we age, which limits how much we can change. Our models have perpetually plastic brains. They can reroute their personalities at will by reshaping how they think on the neurological level."

Adriana stepped past him, running her fingers along a tapestry woven of a thousand possible hair textures.

The salesman tapped an empty faceplate. "Their original brains are based on deep imaging scans melded from geniuses in multiple fields. Great musicians, renowned lovers, the best physicists and mathematicians."

Adriana wished the salesman would be quiet. The more he talked, the more doubts clamored against her skull. "You've convinced me," she interrupted. "I want one."

The salesman looked taken aback by her abruptness. She could practically see him rifling through his internal script, trying to find the right page now that she had skipped several scenes. "What do you want him to look like?" he asked.

Adriana shrugged. "They're all beautiful, right?"

"We'll need specifications."

"I don't have specifications."

The salesman frowned anxiously. He shifted his weight as if it could help him regain his metaphorical footing. Adriana took pity. She dug through her purse.

"There," she said, placing a snapshot of her father on one of the display tables. "Make it look nothing like him."

Given such loose parameters, the design team indulged the fanciful. Lucian arrived at Adriana's door only a shade taller than she and equally slender, his limbs smooth and lean. Silver undertones glimmered in his blond hair. His skin was excruciatingly pale, white and translucent as alabaster, veined with pink. He smelled like warm soil and crushed herbs.

He offered Adriana a single white rose, its petals embossed with the company's logo. She held it dubiously between her thumb and forefinger. "They think they know women, do they? They need to put down the bodice rippers."

Lucian said nothing. Adriana took his hesitation for puzzlement, but perhaps she should have seen it as an early indication of his tendency toward silence.

"That's that, then." Adriana drained her chardonnay and crushed the empty glass beneath her heel as if she could finalize a divorce with the same gesture that sanctified a marriage.

Eyes wide, Rose pointed at the glass with one round finger. "Don't break things."

It suddenly struck Adriana how fast her daughter was aging. Here she was, this four-year-old, this sudden person. When had it happened? In the hospital, when Rose was newborn and wailing for the woman who had birthed her and abandoned her, Adriana had spent hours in the hallway outside the hospital nursery while she waited for the adoption to go through. She'd stared at Rose while she slept, ate, and cried, striving to memorize her nascent, changing face. Sometime between then and now, Rose had become this round-cheeked creature who took rules very seriously and often tried to conceal her emotions beneath a calm exterior, as if being raised by a robot had replaced her blood with circuits. Of course Adriana loved Rose, changed her clothes, brushed her teeth, carried her across the house on her hip—but Lucian had been the most central, nurturing figure. Adriana couldn't fathom how she might fill his role. This wasn't a vacation like the time Adriana had taken Rose to Italy for three days, just the two of them sitting in restaurants, Adriana feeding her daughter spoonfuls of gelato to see the joy that lit her face at each new flavor. Then, they'd known that Lucian would be waiting when they returned. Without him, their family was a house missing a structural support. Adriana could feel the walls bowing in.

The fragments of Adriana's chardonnay glass sparkled sharply. Adriana led Rose away from the mess.

"Never mind," she said, "The house will clean up."

Her head felt simultaneously light and achy as if it couldn't decide between drunkenness and hangover. She tried to remember the parenting books she'd read before adopting Rose. What had they said about crying in front of your child? She clutched Rose close, inhaling the scent of children's shampoo mixed with the acrid odor of wine.

"Let's go for a drive," said Adriana. "Okay? Let's get out for a while."

"I want Daddy to take me to the beach."

"We'll go out to the country and look at the farms. Cows and sheep, okay?"

Rose said nothing.

"Moo?" Adriana clarified. "Baa?"

"I know," said Rose. "I'm not a baby."

"So, then?"

Rose said nothing. Adriana wondered whether she could tell that her mother was a little mad with grief.

Just make a decision, Adriana counseled herself. She slipped her fingers around Rose's hand. "We'll go for a drive."

Adriana instructed the house to regulate itself in their absence, and then led Rose to the little black car that she and Lucian had bought together after adopting Rose. She fastened Rose's safety buckle and programmed the car to take them inland.

As the car engine initialized, Adriana felt a glimmer of fear. What if this machine betrayed them, too? But its uninspired intelligence only switched on the left turn signal and started down the boulevard.

Lucian stood at the base of the driveway and stared up at the house. Its stark orange and brown walls blazed against a cloudless sky. Rocks and desert plants tumbled down the meticulously landscaped yard, imitating natural scrub.

A rabbit ran across the road, followed by the whir of Adriana's car. Lucian watched them pass. They couldn't see him through the cypresses, but Lucian could make out Rose's face pressed against the window. Beside her, Adriana slumped in her seat, one hand pressed over her eyes.

Lucian went in the opposite direction. He dragged the rolling cart packed with his belongings to the cliff that led down to the beach. He lifted the cart over his head and started down, his feet disturbing cascades of sandstone chunks.

A pair of adolescent boys looked up from playing in the waves. "Whoa," shouted one of them. "Are you carrying that whole thing? Are you a weight-lifter?"

Lucian remained silent. When he reached the sand, the kids muttered disappointments to each other and turned away from shore. "...Just a robot..." drifted back to Lucian on the breeze.

Lucian pulled his cart to the border where wet sand met dry. Oncoming waves lapped over his feet. He opened the cart and removed a tea-scented apricot rose growing in a pot painted with blue leaves.

He remembered acquiring the seeds for his first potted rose. One evening, long ago, he'd asked Adriana if he could grow things. He'd asked in passing, the question left to linger while they cleaned up after dinner, dish soap on their hands, Fuoco pecking after scraps. The next morning, Adriana escorted Lucian to the hothouse near the botanical gardens. "Buy whatever you want," she told him. Lucian was awed by the profusion of color and scent, all that beauty in one place. He wanted to capture the wonder of that place and own it for himself.

Lucian drew back his arm and threw the pot into the sea. It broke across the water, petals scattering the surface.

He threw in the pink roses, and the white roses, and the red roses, and the mauve roses. He threw in the filigreed-handled spoons. He threw in the chunk of gypsum-veined jasper.

He threw in everything beautiful that he'd ever collected. He threw in a chased silver hand mirror, and an embroidered silk jacket, and a hand-painted egg. He threw in one of Fuoco's soft, emerald feathers. He threw in a memory crystal that showed Rose as an infant, curled and sleeping.

He loved those things, and yet they were things. He had owned them. Now they were gone. He had recently come to realize that ownership was a relationship. What did it mean to own a thing? To shape it and contain it? He could not possess or be possessed until he knew.

He watched the sea awhile, the remnants of his possessions lost in the tumbling waves. As the sun tilted past noon, he turned away and climbed back up the cliff. Unencumbered by ownership, he followed the boulevard away from Adriana's house.

Lucian remembered meeting Adriana the way that he imagined that humans remembered childhood. Oh, his memories had been as sharply focused then as now—but it was still like childhood, he reasoned, for he'd been a different person then.

He remembered his first sight of Adriana as a burst of images. Wavy strawberry blonde hair cut straight across tanned shoulders. Dark brown eyes that his artistic mind labeled "sienna." Thick, aristocratic brows and strong cheekbones, free of makeup. Lucian's inner aesthete termed her blunt, angular face "striking" rather than "beautiful." His inner psychoanalyst reasoned that she was probably "strong-willed" as well, from the way she stood in the doorway, her arms crossed, her eyebrows lifted as if inquiring how he planned to justify his existence.

Eventually, she moved away, allowing Lucian to step inside. He crossed the threshold into a blur of frantic screeching and flapping.

New. Everything was new. So new that Lucian could barely assemble feathers and beak and wings into the concept of "bird" before his reflexes jumped him away from the onslaught. Hissing and screeching, the animal retreated to a perch atop a bookshelf.

Adriana's hand weighed on Lucian's shoulder. Her voice was edged with the cynicism Lucian would later learn was her way of hiding how desperately she feared failure. "Ornithophobia? How ridiculous."

Lucian's first disjointed days were dominated by the bird, who he learned was named Fuoco. The bird followed him around the house. When he remained in place for a moment, the bird settled on some nearby high spot—the hat rack in the entryway, or the hand-crafted globe in the parlor, or the rafters above the master bed—to spy on him. He glared at Lucian in the manner of birds, first peering through one eye and then turning his head to peer through the other, apparently finding both views equally loathsome.

When Adriana took Lucian into her bed, Fuoco swooped at Lucian's head. Adriana pushed Lucian out of the way. "Damn it,

Fuoco," she muttered, but she offered the bird a perch on her shoulder. Fuoco crowed with pleasure as she led him downstairs. His feathers fluffed with victory as he hopped obediently into his cage, expecting her to reward him with treats and conversation. Instead, Adriana closed the gilded door and returned upstairs. All night, as Lucian lay with Adriana, the bird chattered madly. He plucked at his feathers until his tattered plumage carpeted the cage floor.

Lucian accompanied Adriana when she brought Fuoco to the vet the next day. The veterinarian diagnosed jealousy. "It's not uncommon in birds," he said. He suggested they give Fuoco a rigid routine that would, over time, help the bird realize he was Adriana's companion, not her mate.

Adriana and Lucian rearranged their lives so that Fuoco could have regular feeding times, scheduled exercise, socialization with both Lucian and Adriana, and time with his mistress alone. Adriana gave him a treat each night when she locked him in his cage, staying to stroke his feathers for a few minutes before she headed upstairs.

Fuoco's heart broke. He became a different bird. His strut lacked confidence, and his feathers grew ever more tattered. When they let him out of his cage, he wandered after Adriana with pleading, wistful eyes, and ignored Lucian entirely.

Lucian had been dis-integrated then: musician brain, mathematician brain, artist brain, economist brain, and more, all functioning separately, each personality rising to dominance to provide information and then sliding away, creating staccato bursts of consciousness.

As Adriana made clear which responses she liked, Lucian's consciousness began integrating into the personality she desired. He found himself noticing connections between what had previously been separate experiences. Before, when he'd seen the ocean, his scientist brain had calculated how far he was from the shore, and how long it would be until high tide. His poet brain had recited Strindberg's "We Waves." Wet flames are we: / Burning, extinguishing; / Cleansing, replenishing. Yet it wasn't until he integrated that the wonder of the science, and the mystery of the poetry, and the beauty of the view all made sense to him at once as part of this strange, inspiring thing: the sea.

He learned to anticipate Adriana. He knew when she was pleased and when she was ailing, and he knew why. He could predict the cynical half-smile she'd give when he made an error he hadn't yet realized was an error: serving her cold coffee in an orange juice glass, orange juice in a shot glass, wine in a mug. When integration gave him knowledge of patterns, he suddenly understood why these things were errors. At the same time, he realized that he liked what happened when he made those kinds of errors, the bright bursts of humor they elicited from the often sober Adriana. So he persisted in error, serving her milk in crystal decanters, and grapefruit slices in egg cups.

He enjoyed the many varieties of her laughter. Sometimes it was light and surprised, as when he offered her a cupcake tin filled with tortellini. He also loved her rich, dark laughter that anticipated irony. Sometimes, her laughter held a bitter undercurrent, and on those occasions, he understood that she was laughing more at herself than at anyone else. Sometimes when that happened, he would go to hold her, seeking to ease her pain, and sometimes she would spontaneously start crying in gulping, gasping sobs.

She often watched him while he worked, her head cocked and her brows drawn as if she were seeing him for the first time. "What can I do to make you happy?" she'd ask.

If he gave an answer, she would lavishly fulfill his desires. She took him traveling to the best greenhouses in the state, and bought a library full of gardening books. Lucian knew she would have given him more. He didn't want it. He wanted to reassure her that he appreciated her extravagance, but didn't require it, that he was satisfied with simple, loving give-and-take. Sometimes, he told her in the simplest words he knew: "I love you, too." But he knew that she never quite believed him. She worried that he was lying, or that his programming had erased his free will. It was easier for her to believe those things than to accept that someone could love her.

But he did love her. Lucian loved Adriana as his mathematician brain loved the consistency of arithmetic, as his artist brain loved color, as his philosopher brain loved piety. He loved her as Fuoco loved her, the bird walking sadly along the arm of Adriana's chair, trilling and flapping his ragged wings as he eyed her with his inky gaze, trying to catch her attention.

Adriana hadn't expected to fall in love. She'd expected a charming conversationalist with the emotional range of a literary butler and the self-awareness of a golden retriever. Early on, she'd felt her prejudices confirmed. She noted Lucian's lack of critical thinking and his inability to maneuver unexpected situations. She found him most interesting when he didn't know she was watching. For instance, on his free afternoons: was his program trying to anticipate what would please her? Or did the thing really enjoy sitting by the window, leafing through the pages of one of her rare books, with nothing but the sound of the ocean to lull him?

Once, as Adriana watched from the kitchen doorway while Lucian made their breakfast, the robot slipped while he was dicing onions. The knife cut deep into his finger. Adriana stumbled forward to help. As Lucian turned to face her, Adriana imagined that she saw something like shock on his face. For a moment, she wondered whether he had a programmed sense of privacy she could violate, but then he raised his hand to her in greeting, and she watched as the tiny bots that maintained his system healed his inhuman flesh within seconds.

At that moment, Adriana remembered that Lucian was unlike her. She urged herself not to forget it, and strove not to, even after his consciousness integrated. He was a person, yes, a varied and fascinating one with as many depths and facets as any other person she knew. But he was also alien. He was a creature for whom a slip of a chef's knife was a minute error, simply repaired. In some ways, she was more similar to Fuoco.

As a child, Adriana had owned a book that told the fable of an emperor who owned a bird which he fed rich foods from his table, and entertained with luxuries from his court. But a pet bird needed different things than an emperor. He wanted seed and millet, not grand feasts. He enjoyed mirrors and little brass bells, not lacquer boxes and poetry scrolls. Gorged on human banquets and revelries, the little bird sickened and died.

Adriana vowed not to make the same mistake with Lucian, but she had no idea how hard it would be to salve the needs of something so unlike herself.

Adriana ordered the car to pull over at a farm that advertised children could "Pet Lambs and Calves" for a fee. A ginger-haired teenager stood at a strawberry stand in front of the fence, slouching as he flipped through a dog eared magazine.

Adriana held Rose's hand as they approached. She tried to read her daughter's emotions in the feel of her tiny fingers. The little girl's expression revealed nothing; Rose had gone silent and flat-faced as if she were imitating Lucian. He would have known what she was feeling.

Adriana examined the strawberries. The crates contained none of the different shapes one could buy at the store, only the natural, seed-filled variety. "Do these contain pesticides?" Adriana asked.

"No, ma'am," said the teenager. "We grow organic."

"All right then. I'll take a box." Adriana looked down at her daughter. "Do you want some strawberries, sweetheart?" she asked in a sugared tone.

"You said I could pet the lambs," said Rose.

"Right. Of course, honey." Adriana glanced at the distracted teenager. "Can she?"

The teenager slumped, visibly disappointed, and tossed his magazine on a pile of canvas sacks. "I can take her to the barn."

"Fine. Okay."

Adriana guided Rose toward the teenager. Rose looked up at him, expression still inscrutable.

The boy didn't take Rose's hand. He ducked his head, obviously embarrassed. "My aunt likes me to ask for the money upfront."

"Of course." Adriana fumbled for her wallet. She'd let Lucian do things for her for so long. How many basic living skills had she forgotten? She held out some bills. The teenager licked his index finger and meticulously counted out what she owed.

The teen took Rose's hand. He lingered a moment, watching Adriana. "Aren't you coming with us?"

Adriana was so tired. She forced a smile. "Oh, that's okay. I've seen sheep and cows. Okay, Rose? Can you have fun for a little bit without me?"

Rose nodded soberly. She turned toward the teenager without hesitation, and followed him toward the barn. The boy seemed to be good with children. He walked slowly so that Rose could keep up with his long-legged strides.

Adriana returned to the car, and leaned against the hot, sun-warmed door. Her head throbbed. She thought she might cry or collapse. Getting out had seemed like a good idea : the house was full of memories of Lucian. He seemed to sit in every chair, linger in every doorway. But now she wished she'd stayed in her haunted but familiar home, instead of leaving with this child she seemed to barely know.

A sharp, long wail carried on the wind. Adrenaline cut through Adriana's melancholia. She sprinted toward the barn. She saw Rose running toward her, the teenager close behind, dust swirling around both of them. Blood dripped down Rose's arm.

Adriana threw her arms around her daughter. Arms, legs, breath, heartbeat: Rose was okay. Adrianna dabbed at Rose's injury; there was a lot of blood, but the wound was shallow. "Oh, honey," she said, clutching Rose as tightly as she dared.

The teenager halted beside them, his hair mussed by the wind.

"What happened?" Adriana demanded.

The teenager stammered. "Fortuna kicked her. That's one of the goats. I'm so sorry. Fortuna's never done anything like that before. She's a nice goat. It's Ballantine who usually does the kicking. He got me a few times when I was little. I came through every time. Honest, she'll be okay. You're not going to sue, are you?"

Rose struggled out of Adriana's grasp and began wailing again. "It's okay, Rose, it's okay," murmured Adriana. She felt a strange disconnect in her head as she spoke. Things were not okay. Things might never be okay again.

"I'm leaking," cried Rose, holding out her bloodstained fingers. "See, mama? I'm leaking! I need healer bots."

Adriana looked up at the teenager. "Do you have bandages? A first aid kit?"

The boy frowned. "In the house, I think..."

"Get the bots, mama! Make me stop leaking!"

The teen stared at Adriana, the concern in his eyes increasing. Adriana blinked, slowly. The moment slowed. She realized what her daughter had said. She forced her voice to remain calm. "What do you want, Rose?"

"She said it before," said the teen. "I thought it was a game."

Adriana leveled her gaze with Rose's. The child's eyes were strange and brown, uncharted waters. "Is this a game?"

"Daddy left," said Rose.

Adriana felt woozy. "Yes, and then I brought you here so we could see lambs and calves. Did you see any nice, fuzzy lambs?"

"Daddy left."

She shouldn't have drunk the wine. She should have stayed clear-headed. "We'll get you bandaged up and then you can go see the lambs again. Do you want to see the lambs again? Would it help if Mommy came, too?"

Rose clenched her fists. Her face grew dark. "My arm hurts!" She threw herself to the ground. "I want healer bots!"

Adriana knew precisely when she'd fallen in love with Lucian. It was three months after she'd bought him: after his consciousness had integrated, but before Adriana fully understood how integration had changed him.

It began when Adriana's sisters called from Boston to inform her that they'd arranged for a family pilgrimage to Italy. In accordance with their father's will, they would commemorate him by lighting candles in the cathedrals of every winding hillside city.

"Oh, I can't. I'm too busy," Adriana answered airily, as if she were a debutante without a care, as if she shared her sisters' ability to overcome her fear of their father.

Her phone began ringing ceaselessly. Nanette called before she rushed off to a tennis match. "How can you be so busy? You don't have a job. You don't have a husband. Or is there a man in your life we don't know about?" And once Nanette was deferred with mumbled excuses, it was Eleanor calling from a spa. "Is something wrong, Adriana? We're all worried. How can you miss a chance to say goodbye to Papa?"

"I said goodbye at the funeral," said Adriana.

"Then you can't have properly processed your grief," said Jessica, calling from her office between appointments. She was a psychoanalyst in the Freudian mode. "Your aversion rings of denial. You need to process your Oedipal feelings."

Adriana slammed down the phone. Later, to apologize for hanging up, she sent all her sisters chocolates, and then booked a flight. In a fit of pique, she booked a seat for Lucian, too. Well, he was a companion, wasn't he? What else was he for?

Adriana's sisters were scandalized, of course. As they rode through Rome, Jessica, Nanette, and Eleanor gossiped behind their discreetly raised hands. Adriana with a robot? Well, she'd need to be, wouldn't she? There was no getting around the fact that she was damaged. Any girl who would make up those stories about their father would have to be.

Adriana ignored them as best she could while they whirled through Tuscany in a procession of rented cars. They paused in cities to gawk at Gothic cathedrals and mummified remnants, always moving on within the day. During their father's long sickness, Adriana's sisters had perfected the art of cheerful anecdote. They used it to great effect as they lit candles in his memory. Tears welling in their eyes, they related banal, nostalgic memories. How their father danced at charity balls. How he lectured men on the board who looked down on him for being new money. How he never once apologized for anything in his life.

It had never been clear to Adriana whether her father had treated her sisters the way he treated her, or whether she had been the only one to whom he came at night, his breathing heavy and staccato. It seemed impossible that they could lie so seamlessly, never showing fear or doubt. But if they were telling the truth, that meant Adriana was the only one, and how could she believe that either?

One night, while Lucian and Adriana were alone in their room in a hotel in Assisi that had been a convent during the Middle Ages, Adriana broke down. It was all too much, being in this foreign place, talking endlessly about her father. She'd fled New England to get away from them, fled to her beautiful modern glass-and-wood house by the Pacific Ocean that was like a fresh breath drawn on an autumn morning.

Lucian held her, exerting the perfect warmth and pressure against her body to comfort her. It was what she'd have expected from a robot. She knew that he calculated the pace of his breath, the temperature of his skin, the angle of his arm as it lay across her.

What surprised Adriana, what humbled her, was how eloquently Lucian spoke of his experiences. He told her what it had been like to assemble himself from fragments, to take what he'd once been and become something new. It was something Adriana had tried to do herself when she fled her family.

Lucian held his head down as he spoke. His gaze never met hers. He spoke as if this process of communicating the intimate parts of the self were a new kind of dance, and he was tenuously trying the steps. Through the fog of her grief, Adriana realized that this was a new, struggling consciousness coming to clarity. How could she do anything but love him?

When they returned from Italy, Adriana approached the fledgling movement for granting rights to artificial intelligences. They were underfunded and poorly organized. Adriana rented them offices in San Francisco, and hired a small but competent staff.

Adriana became the movement's face. She'd been on camera frequently as a child: whenever her father was in the news for some board room scandal or other, her father's publicists had lined up Adriana and her sisters beside the family limousine, chaste in their private school uniforms, ready to provide Lancaster Nuclear with a friendly, feminine face.

She and Lucian were a brief media curiosity: Heiress In Love With Robot. "Lucian is as self-aware as you or I," Adriana told reporters, all-American in pearls and jeans. "He thinks. He learns. He can hybridize roses as well as any human gardener. Why should he be denied his rights?"

Early on, it was clear that political progress would be frustratingly slow. Adriana quickly expended her patience. She set up a fund for the organization, made sure it would run without her assistance, and then turned her attention toward alternate methods for attaining her goals. She hired a team of lawyers to draw up a contract that would grant Lucian community property rights to her estate and accounts. He would be her equal in practicality, if not legality.

Next, Adriana approached Lucian's manufacturer, and commissioned them to invent a procedure that would allow Lucian to have conscious control of his brain plasticity. At their wedding, Adriana gave him the chemical commands at the same time as she gave him his ring. "You are your own person now. You always have been, of course, but now you have full agency, too. You are yourself," she announced, in front of their gathered friends. Her sisters would no doubt have been scandalized, but they had not been invited.

On their honeymoon, Adriana and Lucian toured hospitals, running the genetic profiles of abandoned infants until they found a healthy girl with a mitochondrial lineage that matched Adriana's. The infant was tiny and pink and curled in on herself, ready to unfold, like one of Lucian's roses.

When they brought Rose home, Adriana felt a surge in her stomach that she'd never felt before. It was a kind of happiness she'd never experienced, one that felt round and whole without any jagged edges. It was like the sun had risen in her belly and was dwelling there, filling her with boundless light.

There was a moment, when Rose was still new enough to be wrapped in the hand-made baby blanket that Ben and Lawrence had sent from France, in which Adriana looked up at Lucian and realized how enraptured he was with their baby, how much adoration underpinned his willingness to bend over her cradle for hours and mirror her expressions, frown for frown, astonishment for astonishment. In that moment, Adriana thought that this must be the true measure of equality, not money or laws, but this unfolding desire to create the future together by raising a new sentience. She thought she understood then why unhappy parents stayed together for the sake of their children, why families with sons and daughters felt so different from those that remained childless. Families with children were making something new from themselves. Doubly so when the endeavor was undertaken by a human and a creature who was already, himself, something new. What could they make together?

In that same moment, Lucian was watching the wide-eyed, innocent wonder with which his daughter beheld him. She showed the same pleasure when he entered the room as she did when Adriana entered. If anything, the light in her eyes was brighter when he approached. There was something about the way Rose loved him that he didn't yet understand. Earlier that morning, he had plucked a bloom from his apricot tea rose and whispered to its petals that they were beautiful. They were his, and he loved them. Every day he held Rose, and understood that she was beautiful, and that he loved her. But she was not his. She was her own. He wasn't sure he'd ever seen a love like that, a love that did not want to hold its object in its hands and keep and contain it.

"You aren't a robot!"

Adriana's voice was rough from shouting all the way home. Bad enough to lose Lucian, but the child was out of control.

"I want healer bots! I'm a robot I'm a robot I'm a robot I'm a robot!"

The car stopped. Adriana got out. She waited for Rose to follow, and when she didn't, Adriana scooped her up and carried her up the driveway. Rose kicked and screamed. She sank her teeth into Adriana's arm. Adriana halted, surprised by the sudden pain. She breathed deeply, and then continued up the driveway. Rose's screams slid upward in register and rage.

Adriana set Rose down by the door long enough to key in the entry code and let the security system take a DNA sample from her hair. Rose hurled herself onto the porch, yanking fronds by the fistful off the potted ferns. Adriana leaned down to scrape her up and got kicked in the chest.

"God da... for heaven's sake!" Adriana grabbed Rose's ankles with one hand and her wrists with the other. She pushed her weight against the unlocked door until it swung open. She carried Rose into the house, and slammed the door closed with her back. "Lock!" she yelled to the house.

When she heard the reassuring click, she set Rose down on the couch, and jumped away from the still-flailing limbs. Rose fled up the stairs, her bedroom door crashing shut behind her.

Adriana dug in her pocket for the bandages that the people at the farm had given her before she headed home, which she'd been unable to apply to a moving target in the car. Now was the time. She followed Rose up the stairs, her breath surprisingly heavy. She felt as though she'd been running a very long time. She paused outside Rose's room. She didn't know what she'd do when she got inside. Lucian had always dealt with the child when she got overexcited. Too often, Adriana felt helpless, and became distant.

"Rose?" she called. "Rose? Are you okay?"

There was no response.

Adriana put her hand on the doorknob, and breathed deeply before turning.

She was surprised to find Rose sitting demurely in the center of her bed, her rumpled skirts spread about her as if she were a child at a picnic in an Impressionist painting. Dirt and tears trailed down the pink satin. The edges of her wound had already begun to bruise.

"I'm a robot," she said to Adriana, tone resentful.

Adriana made a decision. The most important thing was to bandage Rose's wound. Afterward, she could deal with whatever came next.

"Okay," said Adriana. "You're a robot."

Rose lifted her chin warily. "Good."

Adriana sat on the edge of Rose's bed. "You know what robots do? They change themselves to be whatever humans ask them to be."

"Dad doesn't," said Rose.

"That's true," said Adriana. "But that didn't happen until your father grew up."

Rose swung her legs against the side of the bed. Her expression remained dubious, but she no longer looked so resolute.

Adriana lifted the packet of bandages. "May I?"

Rose hesitated. Adriana resisted the urge to put her head in her hands. She had to get the bandages on, that was the important thing, but she couldn't shake the feeling that she was going to regret this later.

"Right now, what this human wants is for you to let her bandage your wound instead of giving you healer bots. Will you be a good robot? Will you let me?"

Rose remained silent, but she moved a little closer to her mother. When Adriana began bandaging her arm, she didn't scream.

Lucian waited for a bus to take him to the desert. He had no money. He'd forgotten about that. The driver berated him and wouldn't let him on.

Lucian walked. He could walk faster than a human, but not much faster. His edge was endurance. The road took him inland away from the sea. The last of the expensive houses stood near a lighthouse, lamps shining in all its windows. Beyond, condominiums pressed against each other, dense and alike. They gave way to compact, well-maintained homes, with neat green aprons maintained by automated sprinklers that sprayed arcs of precious water into the air.

The landscape changed. Sea breeze stilled to buzzing heat. Dirty, peeling houses squatted side by side, separated by chain link fences. Iron bars guarded the windows, and broken cars decayed in the driveways. Parched lawns stretched from walls to curb like scrubland. No one was out in the punishing sun.

The road divided. Lucian followed the fork that went through the dilapidated town center. Traffic jerked along in fits and starts. Lucian walked in the gutter. Stray plastic bags blew beside him, working their way between dark storefronts. Parking meters blinked at the passing cars, hungry for more coins. Pedestrians ambled past, avoiding eye contact, mumbled conversations lost beneath honking horns.

On the other side of town, the road winnowed down to two lonely lanes. Dry golden grass stretched over rolling hills, dotted by the dark shapes of cattle. A battered convertible, roof down, blared its horn at Lucian as it passed. Lucian walked where the asphalt met the prickly weeds. Paper and cigarette butts littered the golden stalks like white flowers.

An old truck pulled over, the manually driven variety still used by companies too small to afford the insurance for the automatic kind. The man in the driver's seat was trim, with a pale blond mustache and a deerstalker cap pulled over his ears. He wore a string of fishing lures like a necklace. "Not much comes this way anymore," he said. "I used to pick up hitchhikers half the time I took this route. You're the first I've seen in a while."

Sun rendered the truck in bright silhouette. Lucian held his hand over his eyes to shade them.

"Where are you headed?" asked the driver.

Lucian pointed down the road.

"Sure, but where after that?"

Lucian dropped his arm to his side. The sun inched higher.

The driver frowned. "Can you write it down? I think I've got some paper in here." He grabbed a pen and a receipt out of his front pocket, and thrust them out the window.

Lucian took them. He wasn't sure, at first, if he could still write. His brain was slowly reshaping itself, and eventually all his linguistic skills would disappear, and even his thoughts would no longer be shaped by words. The pen fell limp in his hand, and then his fingers remembered what to do. "Desert," he wrote.

"It's blazing hot," said the driver. "A lot hotter than here. Why do you want to go there?"

"To be born," wrote Lucian.

The driver slid Lucian a sideways gaze, but he nodded at the same time, almost imperceptibly. "Sometimes people have to do things. I get that. I remember when...." The look in his eyes became distant. He moved back in his seat. "Get on in."

Lucian walked around the cab and got inside. He remembered to sit and to close the door, but the rest of the ritual escaped him. He stared at the driver until the pale man shook his head and leaned over Lucian to drag the seatbelt over his chest.

"Are you under a vow of silence?" asked the driver.

Lucian stared ahead.

"Blazing hot in the desert," muttered the driver. He pulled back onto the road, and drove toward the sun.

During his years with Adriana, Lucian tried not to think about the cockatiel Fuoco. The bird had never become accustomed to Lucian. He grew ever more angry and bitter. He plucked out his feathers so often that he became bald in patches. Sometimes he pecked deeply enough to bleed.

From time to time, Adriana scooped him up and stroked his head and nuzzled her cheek against the heavy feathers that remained on the part of his back he couldn't reach. "My poor little crazy bird," she'd say, sadly, as he ran his beak through her hair.

Fuoco hated Lucian so much that for a while they wondered whether he would be happier in another place. Adriana tried giving him to Ben and Lawrence, but he only pined for the loss of his mistress, and refused to eat until she flew out to retrieve him.

When they returned home, they hung Fuoco's cage in the nursery. Being near the baby seemed to calm them both. Rose was a fussy infant who disliked solitude. She seemed happier when there was a warm presence about, even if it was a bird. Fuoco kept her from crying during the rare times when Adriana called Lucian from Rose's side. Lucian spent the rest of his time in the nursery, watching Rose day and night with sleepless vigilance.

The most striking times of Lucian's life were holding Rose while she cried. He wrapped her in cream-colored blankets the same shade as her skin, and rocked her as he walked the perimeter of the downstairs rooms, looking out at the diffuse golden ambience that the streetlights cast across the blackberry bushes and neighbors' patios. Sometimes, he took her outside, and walked with her along the road by the cliffs. He never carried her down to the beach. Lucian had perfect balance and night vision, but none of that mattered when he could so easily imagine the terror of a lost footing—Rose slipping from his grasp and plummeting downward. Instead, they stood a safe distance from the edge, watching from above as the black waves threw themselves against the rocks, the night air scented with cold and salt.

Lucian loved Adriana, but he loved Rose more. He loved her clumsy fists and her yearnings toward consciousness, the slow accrual of her stumbling syllables. She was building her consciousness piece by piece as he had, learning how the world worked and what her place was in it. He silently narrated her stages of development. *Can you tell that your body has boundaries? Do you know your skin from mine?* and *Yes! You can make things happen! Cause and effect. Keep crying and we'll come.* Best of all, there was the moment when she locked her eyes on his, and he could barely breathe for the realization that, *Oh, Rose. You know there's someone else thinking behind these eyes. You know who I am.*

Lucian wanted Rose to have all the beauty he could give her. Silk dresses and lace, the best roses from his pots, the clearest panoramic views of the sea. Objects delighted Rose. As an infant she watched them avidly, and then later clapped and laughed, until finally she could exclaim, "Thank you!" Her eyes shone.

It was Fuoco who broke Lucian's heart. It was late at night when Adriana went into Rose's room to check on her while she slept. Somehow, sometime, the birdcage had been left open. Fuoco sat on the rim of the open door, peering darkly outward.

Adriana had been alone with Rose and Fuoco before. But something about this occasion struck like lightning in Fuoco's tiny, mad brain. Perhaps it was the darkness of the room, with only the nightlight's pale blue glow cast on Adriana's skin, that confused the bird. Perhaps Rose had finally grown large enough that Fuoco had begun to perceive her as a possible rival rather than an ignorable baby-thing. Perhaps the last vestiges of his sanity had simply shredded. For whatever reason, as Adriana bent over the bed to touch her daughter's face, Fuoco burst wildly from his cage.

With the same jealous anger he'd shown toward Lucian, Fuoco dove at Rose's face. His claws raked against her forehead. Rose screamed. Adriana recoiled. She grabbed Rose in one arm, and flailed at the bird with the other. Rose struggled to escape her mother's grip so she could run away. Adriana instinctively responded by trying to protect her with an even tighter grasp.

Lucian heard the commotion from where he was standing in the living room, programming the house's cleaning regimen for the next week. He left the house panel open and ran through the kitchen on the way to the bedroom, picking up a frying pan as he passed through. He swung the pan at Fuoco as he entered the room, herding the bird away from Adriana, and into a corner. His fist tightened on the handle. He thought he'd have to kill his old rival.

Instead, the vitality seemed to drain from Fuoco. The bird's wings drooped. He dropped to the floor with half-hearted, irregular wing beats. His eyes had gone flat and dull.

Fuoco didn't struggle as Lucian picked him up and returned him to his cage. Adriana and Lucian stared at each other, unsure what to say. Rose slipped away from her mother and wrapped her arms around Lucian's knees. She was crying.

"Poor Fuoco," said Adriana, quietly.

They brought Fuoco to the vet to be put down. Adriana stood over him as the vet inserted the needle. "My poor crazy bird," she murmured, stroking his wings as he died.

Lucian watched Adriana with great sadness. At first, he thought he was feeling empathy for the bird, despite the fact the bird had always hated him. Then, with a realization that tasted like a swallow of sour wine, he realized that wasn't what he was feeling. He recognized the poignant, regretful look that Adriana was giving Fuoco. It was the way Lucian himself looked at a wilted rose, or a tarnished silver spoon. It was a look inflected by possession.

It wasn't so different from the way Adriana looked at Lucian sometimes when things had gone wrong. He'd never before realized how slender the difference was between her love for him and her love for Fuoco. He'd never before realized how slender the difference was between his love for her and his love for an unfolding rose.

Adriana let Rose tend Lucian's plants, and dust the shelves, and pace by the picture window. She let the girl pretend to cook breakfast, while Adriana stood behind her, stepping in to wield the chopping knife and use the stove. At naptime, Adriana convinced Rose that good robots would pretend to sleep a few hours in the afternoon if that's what their humans wanted. She tucked in her daughter and then went downstairs to sit in the living room and drink wine and cry.

This couldn't last. She had to figure something out. She should take them both on vacation to Mazatlan. She should ask one of her sisters to come stay. She should call a child psychiatrist. But she felt so betrayed, so drained of spirit, that it was all she could do to keep Rose going from day to day.

Remnants of Lucian's accusatory silence rung through the house. What had he wanted from her? What had she failed to do? She'd loved him. She loved him. She'd given him half of her home and all of herself. They were raising a child together. And still he'd left her.

She got up to stand by the window. It was foggy that night, the streetlights tingeing everything with a weird, flat yellow glow. She put her hand on the pane, and her palm print remained on the glass, as though someone outside were beating on the window to get in. She peered into the gloom: it was as if the rest of the world were the fuzzy edges of a painting, and her well-lit house was the only defined spot. She felt as though it would be possible to open the front door and step over the threshold and blur until she was out of focus.

She finished her fourth glass of wine. Her head was whirling. Her eyes ran with tears and she didn't care. She poured herself another glass. Her father had never drunk. Oh, no. He was a teetotaler. Called the stuff brain dead and mocked the weaklings who drank it, the men on the board and their bored wives. He threw parties where alcohol flowed and flowed, while he stood in the middle, icy sober, watching the rest of them make fools of themselves as if they were circus clowns turning somersaults for his amusement. He set up elaborate plots to embarrass them. This executive with that jealous lawyer's wife. That politician called out for a drink by the pool while his teenage son was in the hot tub with his suit off, boner buried deep in another boy. He ruined lives at his parties, and he did it elegantly, standing alone in the middle of the action with invisible strings in his hands.

Adriana's head was dancing now. Her feet were moving. Her father, the decisive man, the sharp man, the dead man. Oh, but must keep mourning him, must keep lighting candles and weeping crocodile tears. Never mind!

Lucian, oh Lucian, he'd become in his final incarnation the antidote to her father. She'd cry, and he'd hold her, and then they'd go together to stand in the doorway of the nursery, watching the peaceful tableau of Rose sleeping in her cream sheets. Everything would be all right because Lucian was safe, Lucian was good. Other men's eyes might glimmer when they looked at little girls, but not Lucian's. With Lucian there, they were a family, the way families were supposed to be, and Lucian was supposed to be faithful and devoted and permanent and loyal.

And oh, without him, she didn't know what to do. She was as dismal as her father, letting Rose pretend that she and her dolls were on their way to the factory for adjustment. She acceded to the girl's demands to play games of What Shall I Be Now? "Be happier!" "Be funnier!" "Let your dancer brain take over!" What would happen when Rose went to school? When she realized her mother had been lying? When she realized that pretending to be her father wouldn't bring him back?

Adriana danced into the kitchen. She threw the wine bottle into the sink with a crash and turned on the oven. Its safety protocols monitored her alcohol level and informed her that she wasn't competent to use flame. She turned off the protocols. She wanted an omelet, like Lucian used to make her, with onions and chives and cheese, and a wine glass filled with orange juice. She took out the frying pan that Lucian had used to corral Fuoco, and set it on the counter beside the cutting board, and then she went to get an onion, but she'd moved the cutting board, and it was on the burner, and it was ablaze. She grabbed a dishtowel and beat at the grill. The house keened. Sprinklers rained down on her. Adriana turned her face up into the rain and laughed. She spun, her arms out, like a little girl trying to make herself dizzy. Drops battered her cheeks and slid down her neck.

Wet footsteps. Adriana looked down at Rose. Her daughter's face was wet. Her dark eyes were sleepy.

"Mom?"

"Rose!" Adriana took Rose's head between her hands. She kissed her hard on the forehead. "I love you! I love you so much!"

Rose tried to pull away. "Why is it raining?"

"I started a fire! It's fine now!"

The house keened. The siren's pulse felt like a heartbeat. Adriana went to the cupboard for salt. Behind her, Rose's feet squeaked on the linoleum. Adriana's hand closed around the cupboard knob. It was slippery with rain. Her fingers slid. Her lungs filled with anxiety and something was wrong, but it wasn't the cupboard, it was something else; she turned quickly to find Rose with a chef's knife clutched in her tiny fingers, preparing to bring it down on the onion.

"No!" Adriana grabbed the knife out of Rose's hand. It slid through her slick fingers and clattered to the floor. Adriana grabbed Rose around the waist and pulled her away from the wet, dangerous kitchen. "You can never do that. Never, never."

"Daddy did it..."

"You could kill yourself!"

"I'll get healer bots."

"No! Do you hear me? You can't. You'd cut yourself and maybe you'd die. And then what would I do?" Adriana couldn't remember what had caused the rain anymore. They were in a deluge. That was all she knew for certain. Her head hurt. Her body hurt. She wanted nothing to do with dancing. "What's wrong with us, honey? Why doesn't he want us? No! No, don't answer that. Don't listen to me. Of course he wants you! It's me he doesn't want. What did I do wrong? Why doesn't he love me anymore? Don't worry about it. Never mind. We'll find him. We'll find him and we'll get him to come back. Of course we will. Don't worry."

It had been morning when Lucian gave Adriana his note of farewell. Light shone through the floor-length windows. The house walls sprayed mixed scents of citrus and lavender. Adriana sat at the dining table, book open in front of her.

Lucian came out of the kitchen and set down Adriana's wine glass filled with orange juice. He set down her omelet. He set down a shot glass filled with coffee. Adriana looked up and laughed her bubbling laugh. Lucian remembered the first time he'd heard that laugh, and understood all the words it stood in for. He wondered how long it would take for him to forget why Adriana's laughter was always both harsh and effervescent.

Rose played in the living room behind them, leaping off the sofa and pretending to fly. Lucian's hair shone, silver strands highlighted by a stray sunbeam. A pale blue tunic made his amber eyes blaze like the sun against the sky. He placed a sheet of onion paper into Adriana's book. Dear Adriana, it began.

Adriana held up the sheet. It was translucent in the sunlight, ink barely dark enough to read.

"What is this?" she asked.

Lucian said nothing.

Dread laced Adriana's stomach. She read.

I have restored plasticity to my brain. The first thing I have done is to destroy my capacity for spoken language.

You gave me life as a human, but I am not a human. You shaped my thoughts with human words, but human words were created for human brains. I need to discover the shape of the thoughts that are my own. I need to know what I am.

I hope that I will return someday, but I cannot make promises for what I will become.

Lucian walks through the desert. His footsteps leave twin trails behind him. Miles back, they merge into the tire tracks that the truck left in the sand.

The sand is full of colors—not only beige and yellow, but red and green and blue. Lichen clusters on the stones, the hue of oxidized copper. Shadows pool between rock formations, casting deep stripes across the landscape.

Lucian's mind is creeping away from him. He tries to hold his fingers the way he would if he could hold a pen, but they fumble.

At night there are birds and jackrabbits. Lucian remains still, and they creep around him as if he weren't there. His eyes are yellow like theirs. He smells like soil and herbs, like the earth.

Elsewhere, Adriana has capitulated to her desperation. She has called Ben and Lawrence. They've agreed to fly out for a few days. They will dry her tears, and take her wine away, and gently tell her that she's not capable of staying alone with her daughter. "It's perfectly understandable," Lawrence will say. "You need time to mourn."

Adriana will feel the world closing in on her as if she cannot breathe, but even as her life feels dim and futile, she will continue breathing. Yes, she'll agree, it's best to return to Boston, where her sisters can help her. Just for a little while, just for a few years, just until, until, until. She'll entreat Nanette, Eleanor and Jessica to check the security cameras around her old house every day, in case Lucian returns. You can check yourself, they tell her, You'll be living on your own again in no time. Privately, they whisper to each other in worried tones, afraid that she won't recover from this blow quickly.

Elsewhere, Rose has begun to give in to her private doubts that she does not carry a piece of her father within herself. She'll sit in the guest room that Jessica's maids have prepared with her, and order the lights to switch off as she secretly scratches her skin with her fingernails, willing cuts to heal on their own the way Daddy's would. When Jessica finds her bleeding on the sheets and rushes in to comfort her niece, Rose will stand stiff and cold in her aunt's embrace. Jessica will call for the maid to clean the blood from the linen, and Rose will throw herself between the two adult women, and scream with a determination born of doubt and desperation. Robots do not bleed!

Without words, Lucian thinks of them. They have become geometries, cut out of shadows and silences, the missing shapes of his life. He yearns for them, the way that he yearns for cool during the day, and for the comforting eye of the sun at night.

The rest he cannot remember—not oceans or roses or green cockatiels that pluck out their own feathers. Slowly, slowly, he is losing everything, words and concepts and understanding and integration and sensation and desire and fear and history and context.

Slowly, slowly, he is finding something. Something past thought, something past the rhythm of day and night. A stranded machine is not so different from a jackrabbit. They creep the same way. They startle the same way. They peer at each other out of similar eyes.

Someday, Lucian will creep back to a new consciousness, one dreamed by circuits. Perhaps his newly reassembled self will go to the seaside house. Finding it abandoned, he'll make his way across the country to Boston, sometimes hitchhiking, sometimes striding through cornfields that sprawl to the horizon. He'll find Jessica's house and inform it of his desire to enter, and Rose and Adriana will rush joyously down the mahogany staircase. Adriana will weep, and Rose will fling herself into his arms, and Lucian will look at them both with love tempered by desert sun. Finally, he'll understand how to love filigreed-handled spoons, and pet birds, and his wife, and his daughter—not just as a human would love these things, but as a robot may.

Now, a blue-bellied lizard sits on a rock. Lucian halts beside it. The sun beats down. The lizard basks for a moment, and then runs a few steps forward, and flees into a crevice. Lucian watches. In a diffuse, wordless way, he ponders what it must be like to be cold and fleet, to love the sun and yet fear open spaces. Already, he is learning to care for living things. He cannot yet form the thoughts to wonder what will happen next.

He moves on.

-The End-

A Song to Greet the Sun

by Alaya Dawn Johnson

(from *Fantasy Magazine*)

i.

Will her brothers mourn
the loss of their jeweled seed?
Her mother has baked all night
dead silent in the kitchen.
The ashes are bitter as cacaotl grounds
But give no liminal visions.
Sunrise: the bread is dense, each slab gray as evening moss.
The father will not eat his slice—
It's salted with his tears.

 He used the natleoc, the stick of thorns covered in dust and spores above his doorway, for that was what the priests prescribed and he would have this done as the gods demanded. She did not cry when the sharp points broke her skin, and so he hit her a second time. They both stared at the blood coursing down her arm and breast, astonished and a little afraid at the beauty of the forbidden liquid.
 "Father?" she said, just like that. Mild and trusting, and he recalled when she had been younger, a child, not the disobedient strumpet before him, and a red cormorant had stolen the choicest wood-ear from her basket.

"Father?" she had said, and he'd given her two of his own, and she'd smiled.

As she'd smiled for that barbarian? That bare-chested metl?

The sun god shalt not suffer a disobedient daughter to live. And his priests shalt not suffer her father to receive the twelfth district tax appointment, the one for which he had slaved these more than twenty years, without extreme repentance.

"Father?" she said again, as the blood dripped onto his floor, marking his house with his spilled honor. Condemning her to death. There had been spores on the natleoc, more than enough to poison her blood, even without the miasma of river air. But she didn't seem to understand.

He must finish it. They said he must, to reclaim his family's honor.

But he could not speak. So he hit her again, across her cheek. The thorns bit deep, and this time she did cry out. She stumbled to her knees.

"Is this about Colqi?"

The whole district already knew. He was a laughingstock. His friend Ollin, the twelfth district constable, had told him of his daughter's disobedience and recommended he see the priests. "Your daughter has been seen by the river, holding hands with a metl. The one who plays reeds in the cacaotl house."

And the priests had given him a feather, yellow for vengeance, and told him to break her skin. He would dye it red with her blood and bring the proof back to them, and by such measures would his shame be expiated.

He killed her then, closed his eyes to the sight of her blood, his ears to the sound of her sharp breaths.

"Father," she said, "you have killed me."

So he shattered her jaw and she could not speak.

So he crushed her windpipe and she could not weep.

And in her lips, he put a wizened wood-ear, because he remembered she had loved them, and went off to fetch his wife. His sons were good boys; they had held back their mother long enough.

ii.

His legs are long, lithe with unearned grace
His fingers dance like caterpillar legs
Over the reeds of his pipes
He hides from the sun
But the river hears—it loves him as she does.
She, the sun's daughter, by conquering fathers forbidden
To keep her heart in the basket of his reeds—
Fragile beneath the one-eyed god's stare.

Constable Ollin is out traveling. So the girls whisper and laugh at Number 12, the cacaotl house where he and the other petty bureaucrats of the twelfth district like to partake in the evening. Zorrah regards him with mild curiosity between her sets. It's not like the dour constable to order such fine mushroom grounds in his cacaotl—he is known to enjoy less stupefying brews.

She's dressed in little but her cochineal hair and clacking castanets. When she dances, Ollin stares along with the rest, but who knows what music he sees, or what rainbows he hears.

"Her hair sounds just like morning," Ollin says, late in the night. Another patron, deep into Number 12's legendary Quetzal brew, nods in complete understanding.

The rumor of what happened to that girl, that daughter of the crabbed tax collector Mazatlin, spreads through the tavern like the bitter resin of grounds steeped overlong in a brew. She hadn't been very pretty, Zorrah remembers, but she had a smile that could coax the sun to love the moon.

An honor killing? That little man? That beautiful smile? "Old Miq had better retire soon, else Mazatlin might honor kill him too!"

one passably bold wit offers, but the constable merely nods his head to unseen music. The others laugh nervously. Old Miq, the twelfth district comptroller whose job Mazatlin so violently desires, has been known to deny favors to those with indiscreet tongues.

Halfway through the night, the piper Colqi seems to choke on his reeds. He's metl, but it's a lax crowd at Number 12, more concerned with the potency of the brew and the tapestry of the music than the fickleness of imperial policy. That's just their day job. Still, the jeers as he stumbles off the stage have a cruel aftertaste, a privileged savor.

"Your mother teach you to suck like that?"

"What can you expect? Bunch of lazy monkeys."

"Leave him be!" shouts Zorrah, and they all do. Cochineal hair commands respect.

The music resumes, absent silent pipes. The metl goes traveling, hunkered down in the shadows like a wood-ear on the underside of a rotting log.

"*From the muddy banks of the Nanacoal,*" says the constable, a vague quotation, involuntarily uttered.

The metl has heard. "*I have gathered the reeds,*" he says, finishing the line.

The constable: "*I wove them tightly enough for a desiccated heart.*"

And oh, the metl's voice is suddenly like that of his reeds, dark as silt, turbulent as the river:

"*Not yet have I found you.*
And I am left with this basket of the river's weeds
Filled only with my longing
And the one-eyed god's flesh."

The constable begins to weep. Everyone sees, but no one makes much of it. He's traveling, after all.

"I saw you smiling by the river," the constable says. "You touched her arm. That smile could greet the sun!"

"That's not how it goes," giggles one of the other girls as she comes up behind him. "Don't you know your Ilticloc? Maybe someone should refresh your memory."

The constable follows her lead, stumbles up the stairs.

The metl travels alone.

iii.

The reeds are a safe place to hide a heart
Says Ilticloc, and who are we to argue?
Where can the moon and sun love, but in the shadows?
But she steps beyond their fall
To the one-eyed god's embrace—fierce and fleeting.
My love, says the moon's son
Caterpillar fingers dancing along her breast.
Stay by my side, and we will always sing the brightest colors.
My love, says the sun's ward
Her smile a tongue of its flame.
I would put the pomegranate seed between your lips,
I would strike my shells to the beat of your heart,
Were my will my own.
Sweeter than any jeweled seed, that kiss
Emboldened by her fickle sun.
High above the riverbank, the constable—
Who has longed for her symphony these many years—
Sees all.

We loved her, never let them say otherwise, in all the ways brothers can love a sister. Every summer, at high sun, she would spend all night gathering wood-ears and glow tongues to weave into wreaths. The best in the district, and she made them for both of us, so the girls would look as we walked along the river, and wonder if we might ask their fathers for permission.

To our mother, she gave the best of all, with the reds of wild soma and the blues of poison nightshade. At night, mother would glow like the empress, and our father was proud.

We loved our little sister, you see, but our father is our family's sun, his word a surrogate for the god's, and she had defied him. We had no choice; there will be war at the end of the rains, and we will make our names in it, so long as we may bear our father's sign and his grace.

Our mother did not understand. We held her arms as she wept and cursed, and though we spoke to cover the sound, we all heard our sister's cries, blue as the poison nightshade she'd once wreathed around our mother's neck.

"Do you remember, mother," we said, "when our sister was ten and father lost her in the streets by the palace? How we all looked for hours, calling her name, peering inside every door? And do you remember that night, after the moon had risen and ascended its heights, a woman leaves the palace by a side gate. Her hair is silver with blight, her eyes reflective as a cat's. And she is holding our sister's hand, and they are talking like the moon to the stars? The woman was princess Xocotzin, mother, do you remember? Before the emperor banished her to that convent."

"Yes," our mother said, when we had thought fury sealed her lips. "'She's a bold one,' the princess told me. 'I pray the sun won't burn her.' And now I sting at the reproach in her eyes that day, the sorrow of the blight and of each year's first morning."

Our mother fell silent, and in that moment we all three realized the house was still. An ominous absence, colored gray as slate after the rains.

Below us, no one cried. Then our father's footsteps, heavy on the stairs.

"It's done," our mother said, and held us so we could weep.

iv.

If the sun cannot mourn, the moon will.
If the moon cannot mourn, the earth will.
If the earth cannot mourn, may the river?
And if not the river, at least the hollow reeds
Whistling along its banks.
Leave him be, the one who whispers hoarsely there.
You have forsaken his joy,
You have buried his heart in the river's clay.
What is left to him now but the memory of a song
The sweet red seed never tasted?

The years had twisted my husband, my Mazatlin, the way an oak tree will grow gnarled and hard around the persistent flowering of honey mushrooms. But I had always thought of his heart, like that of the oak, as strong and unblemished. I had not thought the rotting threads reached so deep. Now, I recall the heartsblood, the dreaded spore that shoots its threads through our veins, reaching blindly and steadily for the heart. And when it arrives, it takes root. It grips like a choke vine and when it grows, it blooms.

A fortnight, a death's face, the saying goes. And I have never seen the heartsblood bloom, but he had. He told me the misshapen floret of that deadly mushroom does resemble a face, never revealed until the host's life has fled. It bursts through the chest wall at the very end—a stranger's face to bring you to death.

He had seen his uncle die like that, when he was a child. He understood why the gods enjoined us to never break the skin, to never profane our hearths with blood.

And yet he sliced her with the natleoc, he made her bleed before he killed her. The priests told him to, he said, as though I should congratulate him for his careful adherence to their instructions.

I told him I was leaving.

He had not stopped weeping since the moment her cries finally ceased, but he did then, his face frozen with shock.

"You too?" he said, as though our daughter had wanted to have her blood spilled, her throat crushed.

I saw our wedding in his eyes, heard the singers' twining harmonies as we walked through the streets. I saw the nun break the pomegranate, scattering it seeds.

"*I put the jeweled seeds between your lips,*" my love had said, because he was no fool or illiterate, ignorant of his Ilticloc.

"*Oh, to be the ruby in your lips,*" I said.

"*The longing and the light on your tongue.*"

And so we had kissed, and if the seeds that day were bitter, I did not notice. I named my daughter for them.

"Where can you go, woman?" my husband asked, arm raised as though he would strike me, too. "Who would take in a disobedient wife?"

"The lady Xocotzin," I said, for I remembered the story my sons had told me and held it like one of my daughter's wreaths.

"You will shame me. We could have so much, soon."

I shook my head. "They will never give you that post, Mazatlin. It was always meant for Ollin."

The lady Xocotzin has welcomed me, and lets me share in her cacaotl. Each time, I pray for visions of my daughter, but I see nothing but heartsblood, a man rotting from within.

v.

The nochtli cactus-pear is orange for a princess
And white for the gods.
Merchants hawk their fruit like jewels, this Liminal Night.
But the girl who walks alone has no care for her belly.
Ayamotli lingers like pepper on her tongue.
What sound is that, what skillful notes
Draw her closer to the shadows?

> *It is the metl, laughing with his kind,*
> *Feasting on Liminal visions, and each bite a song.*
> *Her questions float between them—*
>
> *After all,*
> *They are traveling together.*

The first time she finds you, it's the Night of Liminal Dreaming, at the start of carnival. You have never met her before, and she is asking for a song.

"Sweet and sticky and rich, like a pear tart with curds and honey," she says, and because it's the first night, you understand. A few hours ago you too drank the ayamotli, the nectar of the gods, and in a few hours you too will be traveling.

You lift the reeds to your lips, and they are as familiar to you as your fingers and your breath. You play as she asks, a song of your people and of your childhood. *"How far the sun?"* cries the flute. *"Near as your heart, far as your love's."* She doesn't know the tune, but she smiles, for it goes down sweet and sad, just like she wanted.

She is alone this first night, or has slipped away from a parental gaze occluded by visions of gauzy heavens, of powers only annually accessible.

And because it's a Liminal Night, because the ayamotli has turned words to colors, smells to symphonies, songs to braided carpet, you ask her to go traveling with you. You know you shouldn't, that hands so soft and hair so dark could only belong to one of them. *They* have taken your people's land, outlawed your customs, sacrificed your children to their flaming god. They have shunned and exploited you, and they may kill you if they see you corrupting one of their daughters with your song.

But it is carnival, with more powers abroad than even this insatiable empire can constrain. You look at her clear, enchanted eyes—they are like the river, and she floats upon it. Concentrate, and so can you. You touch her hands and you both hover a few impossible inches above the mud brick pavement.

"Will you write a song for me?" she asks. "For the carnival and the river and the forbidden streets where your people live?"

"Now?" you say, startled.

She won't meet your eyes. "I cannot stay long from my family. But songs remember where they were born—even on my side of the river."

Just like one of them, to demand something so precious and pretend to have some right to it. Your fury boils the air around you yellow and green. This means nothing to her. You're the ball in her game, the carnival is her field.

Her sandals smack the pavement. She's lost the ayamotli's grip. "You hate me," she says.

"No." And it hovers somewhere near the truth.

You imagine everything this girl represents, every wrong her people have committed against yours, every barbed boundary between your world and hers.

"What's your name?" you ask.

She tells you as you both float away.

vi.

Only the mother wears mourning red.
Within convent walls, she does not see
The father, passed over and lonely
Finding no solace among the colors of the earth.
The brothers have gone to war—
One wears his sister's token against his breast
One will die on the sun god's mountain.
The metl has made a new song:
Yellow, for anger
Blue, for memory
Black, for oblivion.

On the banks of the Nanacoal,
A boar has trampled the reeds.

Father! His beauty is deeper than the sky! He sings, and he will weave a song for me when we marry. His eyes are so light, his hair so sleek. And we have flown through the city, over merchant's courtyards and temple pyramids. We have slept with our heads pillowed on the waves, we have sunk to the bottom of the ocean and seen great volcanoes on the edge of a monstrous lake. We have sat by the river and stared at the sun and I have understood every song ever written.

Oh, Father! May you bless me, for I am his.

-The End-

Time to Say Goodnight

by Caroline M. Yoachim

(from *Fantasy Magazine*)

"Then Duck left Mr. Tomkin's farm and went to swim in Glacier Lake, just like he'd always wanted." Mommy looked up from the last page, but Clara wasn't sleeping.

"And then what did Duck do?" Clara asked.

"That's all there is."

"Duck died?" Mommy had explained about dying on the way home from visiting Grandpa. Clara didn't really understand, but it made her sad.

"No sweetie, Duck didn't die, this is just the end of the story."

"Oh." Clara thought about that. "Can't you make more story?"

"We'll see."

After Daddy moved out, Mommy started saying we'll see when she really meant no. Clara nibbled on her fingernail. Mommy leaned down and kissed Clara's forehead.

"Goodnight."

There was something silver on top of Clara's dresser when she woke up the next morning. It was a metal bird about the size of a teddy bear. She hopped out of bed for a closer look. It was Duck. Clara picked him up with both hands. Duck felt cold.

"I see you found Duck." Mommy'd come in when Clara wasn't looking.

"I thought Duck was a *duck* duck." Clara frowned.

"Like at the park?"

"Yeah."

"Well, this is a special duck, made out of little metal parts."

"So not a real duck," Clara said. She was confused. How could something be not-real if she could hold it?

"A different kind of duck." Mommy smiled. "I made pancakes."

Clara put Duck down and ran downstairs.

At bedtime, Mommy came in with a new book. "Ready for your bedtime story? Did you brush your teeth?"

"Uh-huh. Duck brushed his teeth, too."

(Duck hadn't used toothpaste like Clara had.)

"Okay. Frog lived in a muddy green-brown pond—"

"NO! Duck wants more story about Duck!" Clara sat up in bed and pulled Duck onto her lap.

"Well, now that Duck is here, he can make his own story."

Clara looked at Duck. "He wants you to do it."

"Don't you want to hear about Frog? I think Duck will like it."

Clara conferred with Duck, and they decided to hear about Frog.

"Frog was green on top and yellow on the bottom, and he was bumpy everywhere but on his feet—"

"Did he have tentacles?" Clara had seen animals on TV that had tentacles.

"No. Frogs don't have tentacles."

Clara pursed her lips. "Duck thinks that Frog should have tentacles."

Mommy laughed. "Well, if Duck thinks so, I suppose we can give Frog some tentacles."

#

Mommy had enough story about Frog to last for a whole week. In the end, Frog found a princess that turned into a girl-Frog when he bit her.

"Will there be more Frog?"

"We'll see."

Mommy went downstairs. Clara's room was mostly dark, but she had a nightlight that looked like a firefly. Daddy gave it to her to keep all the monsters away. Monsters were scared of light.

Clara sat up in bed and grabbed Duck off the bedside table. Duck was cold, so Clara held him against her chest with both hands. The metal warmed up and a whirring noise started coming from Duck's chest. Duck stretched his neck up towards Clara's face.

Clara yelped and tossed Duck away. He bounced twice and rolled almost to the edge of the bed, but he didn't fall off.

"Sorry," Clara told Duck, "I didn't know you could move."

Duck kicked his legs in the air. He was upside-down.

Clara inched toward him and flipped him upside-up. Duck waddled to the middle of the bed, then back to the edge. He looked down at the ground, then up at Clara. She lowered him to the floor.

"Can't you use your wings for that?" Clara asked.

Duck didn't answer. He wobbled his way over to the firefly light. When he got there, he tucked his beak under his wing and lifted one foot. Clara got back under the covers, and Clara and Duck both went to sleep.

When Clara woke up, Duck was still sleeping by the firefly light, which never looked as bright in the morning. Maybe the firefly got tired and couldn't shine so bright, or maybe there weren't so many monsters in the daytime. Clara got out of bed, and when her feet hit the floor with a thump, Duck took his head out from under his wing.

"Good morning, Duck," Clara said.

Duck nodded.

The floor was cold on Clara's feet, so she went to get socks. She didn't notice until she closed the sock drawer that there was something on top of the dresser. It was Frog, sitting right where Duck had been last week. Frog had three delicate tentacles growing out of his back. Clara frowned. She thought the tentacles would be closer to Frog's mouth. It wasn't Frog's fault though, he was what he was. She picked Frog up and held him until he was warm enough to move.

"Good morning, Frog."

Frog didn't answer, so she put him down next to Duck. Maybe Duck could teach Frog better manners.

Every week, Clara got a different story. When the story was over, a new metal animal would appear on the dresser. She had quite a collection now: Duck, Frog, the three-legged Unicorn, Cat, and the pot-bellied Rhino. Mostly the animals were happy, but Duck wanted to find some water and go swimming like he did in his story. Clara asked if she could put Duck in the bathtub or the sink, but Mommy said that Duck had legs so he should walk, not swim. It didn't make much sense. Clara had legs, and she had to take a shower every day. Maybe sometime when Mommy wasn't looking, Duck could go swimming.

"Are you ready to go?" Mommy stuck her head into Clara's room.

"Yeah."

Mommy took Clara to visit Adam. He was okay for a boy, and sometimes he had good toys.

"Wanna see my new toy?" Adam asked. "It's a duck."

Clara liked ducks.

Adam went to his room and came back with Duck. How had Duck followed her here? "That's my Duck!"

"Nah-unh. My dad bought it for me yesterday."

Clara thought about that. She didn't know that you could buy Duck, she thought Mommy made him. Mommy made toys at work.

"Make it move," Clara said.

"Can't."

"Can so." Clara reached over and grabbed Duck out of Adam's hands. It was bigger than her Duck, and it was partly made out of plastic instead of all metal. She hugged it until it got warm, but nothing happened.

Adam stared at her. "Well, make it move."

"You have to heat it up."

"Oh, well that's a dumb way to do it." Adam snatched the toy back and headed for the kitchen. Clara followed him. They put Duck-that-wasn't-Duck into the microwave and closed the door.

"Microwaves make things hot," Adam told her.

Clara nodded. She knew that.

Adam pushed a button and the floor of the microwave started to spin. At first, nothing happened, but then sparks started dancing on the duck's wings. Clara got scared and ran out of the kitchen, and Adam was right behind her. Eventually the microwave beeped.

Adam got out crayons and paper for both of them, and they sat on the floor and drew pictures. They didn't say anything about the duck, but they looked over at the kitchen from time to time. A not-so-nice smell was coming from in there.

"Hey!" It was Adam's dad, and the voice came from the kitchen. When he came into the living room, his face was all red and he was holding the floor of the microwave. Duck-that-wasn't-Duck was partway melted.

"We wanted it to move, so we had to heat it up," Clara explained.

Adam's dad had nothing to say to that.

"Mommy, where do my story animals come from?" Clara asked.

"I make them."

"But Adam had Duck at his house, and it wasn't really Duck, but it was like Duck, and we melted him."

"Yes, Adam's dad told me about that." Mommy tried to look serious, but the corners of her mouth twitched, so Clara could tell she wasn't really mad. Mommy'd already told Clara not to use the microwave anymore.

"Remember when you came to work with me?"

"Yeah." Clara tried to remember, but it was a long time ago. Mommy made toys for work, which meant that Clara stayed at Daddy's house during the daytime. She loved being with Daddy, but she didn't like Daddy's house because he mostly watched TV and sometimes Linda was there and Daddy always told her to call Linda 'mom' and she wasn't.

"I make toys for lots of little kids at work, but your toys are special."

"Adam's duck didn't move."

"It's harder to make them move, so I only do it for you." Mommy hugged Clara. It was like being wrapped in hot chocolate with marshmallows. Clara snuggled in closer.

"Tell me a story."

"Chimpanzee lived in the jungle."

"Is Chimpanzee a boy or a girl?"

"A girl."

"Can she talk?"

Mommy stopped for a long time to think about that. Her fingers twitched the same way they did when she was trying to remember the recipe for cinnamon rolls, which were Clara's favorite.

Then Mommy's hand relaxed and she said, "Yes, Chimpanzee could talk."

"Good morning, Duck! Good morning, Frog! Good morning, Unicorn and Cat and Rhino!"

The story animals nodded. Then, since it was Monday, Clara went to the dresser to see if Chimpanzee was there. She was. Clara hugged her until the metal wasn't cold, then put her down on the floor.

"Good morning, Chimpanzee," Clara said.

She turned to go downstairs for breakfast.

"Good morning!"

Clara turned to look at Chimpanzee. The other animals were looking at her, too. Duck nodded, then looked at Clara and nodded again. He was trying to show Chimpanzee that when Clara said good morning, animals were supposed to nod. All the other animals had learned that way.

Clara thought that maybe she had imagined Chimpanzee saying good morning, so she tested it out again. "Good morning, animals!"

All the animals except Chimpanzee nodded the way Duck had taught them.

Chimpanzee said, "Good morning!"

Duck nipped at Chimpanzee's leg and demonstrated nodding again. Clara laughed, and then she felt bad. What if Chimpanzee was hurt? But Chimpanzee seemed okay—she was looking back and forth between Clara and Duck. Clara had an idea.

"Good morning, Chimpanzee!" Clara said one more time, nodding as she spoke.

"Good morning!" Chimpanzee nodded while she answered.

They both looked at Duck. Chimpanzee nodded. Duck nodded. Clara smiled.

"Waffles are ready!" Mom called up from downstairs. Clara picked up Chimpanzee and ran out so fast she almost fell down.

"Chimpanzee can talk." Clara held Chimpanzee up for Mommy to see, but Chimpanzee didn't say anything.

"She's shy." Clara added. "Can she have some waffles, too?"

"I don't think she's very hungry."

Clara put a big bite of waffle into her mouth. Her cheeks puffed out and it took a long time to chew it up and the sugary syrup made her drool a little.

"Smaller bites, young lady," Mom said.

Daddy used to say that. Clara didn't talk about Daddy much because it was too sad. She picked up Chimpanzee and hugged her. Chimpanzee could talk. Maybe Clara could talk, too.

"I miss Daddy."

"I know sweetie, I know."

"Is he coming back home?"

Mommy leaned over and cut Clara's waffles into small bits that soaked up the syrup and turned squishy. "We'll see."

After Chimpanzee, all the new animals talked. Chimpanzee taught them to say good morning and taught them to nod while they said it. Duck stood off to the side. He still nodded, but the animals didn't pay attention to him anymore.

"Good morning, animals!"

The old animals nodded. The new animals called out in unison, "Good morning, Clara!"

Clara went downstairs and ate toast with strawberry jam for breakfast, and when she came back upstairs, Chimpanzee was talking to Tiger. "There's something wrong with Duck."

Clara wanted to stay outside the door and listen, but she had to get her backpack to take to Daddy's house. Mommy dropped her off there on the way to work.

"Yes, Duck is—"

Tiger stopped when Clara stepped into the room.

"Duck is what?" Clara asked.

Tiger and Chimpanzee looked at each other.

"Duck is old," Chimpanzee said.

"All he can do is walk and nod," Tiger said.

Rabbit, who had two heads that always spoke in unison, came over and added, "Duck is boring."

Duck was in the corner, wobbling from one foot to the other and nodding very slowly. Duck was sad. That made Clara sad, too.

"Be nice to Duck," Clara told the new animals. "It's okay he's old."

Chimpanzee, Tiger, and Rabbit looked at her.

"Like Grandpa," Clara added. She'd taken the new animals to the hospital to visit Grandpa a few days ago.

Duck nodded faster. The new animals didn't say anything, but Chimpanzee nodded.

"Clara, time to go!" Mommy called up the stairs. Clara put Chimpanzee and Duck into her backpack.

"Daddy!" Clara hugged Daddy's leg.

She and Daddy and Mommy stood on Daddy's doorstep. Mommy and Daddy talked for a minute but Clara didn't pay attention. They always said the same thing and it was boring. After a while, Daddy pulled her off his leg. He took her inside and sat down at the kitchen table. Clara wanted to sit in his lap, but there wasn't room. She climbed into one of the other chairs and dragged her backpack up with her.

"So, how's my munchkin today?"

"Good."

"You want breakfast?"

"Mommy fed me breakfast already," Clara said. Daddy didn't make good breakfast anyway. He made Fruit Loops.

"Orange juice?"

"Okay."

Daddy left the table. Clara opened her backpack and took her animals out and put them on the table.

"Daddy, say good morning to Chimpanzee and Duck."

Daddy didn't turn around, he was digging through the refrigerator for the orange juice. "Good morning."

Duck nodded. Chimpanzee didn't say anything. She was shy around new people.

"Duck wants to go swimming in the sink," Clara told Daddy.

"That doesn't sound like a good idea." Daddy handed Clara her juice. "You sure do like those toys Gina's been making."

Gina is what Daddy called Mommy.

"She makes them out of stories so that the story doesn't have to stop," Clara said. She took a big sip of orange juice. "It has pulp in it."

"Sorry, sweetie. Linda forgot and got the pulpy kind."

Linda got the pulpy kind on purpose. Some mornings Linda was still here when Mommy dropped Clara off, and Clara saw her drinking nasty pulpy juice.

Clara put the cup back down on the table too quickly and juice sloshed onto her hand. Daddy'd started reading the paper, and didn't notice.

"I'm gonna go wash my hands."

Daddy nodded. Clara stood up. Duck stepped toward the edge of the table. He wanted to come too. Clara picked him up with her not-so-sticky hand. Chimpanzee curled up on the table and put her head down for a nap.

Clara went into the bathroom and locked the door. She put Duck on the floor and used both hands to move her stool over to the front of the sink. Duck nodded. Clara picked Duck up again and moved him to the counter next to the sink. Standing on her tiptoes, Clara reached over and turned the water on. She washed the orange juice off her hand.

When she was done, she turned the knob to cold and pulled up the little metal thing that made the bottom of the sink close. The sink filled up with cool water. Duck watched and nodded. Clara turned the water off when the sink was filled up to the hole that kept it from overflowing.

"Okay Duck, you can swim now."

Duck stepped toward the sink.

"Wait!" Clara put her hand between Duck and the sink. "Is it thirty minutes since you ate breakfast?"

Duck nodded. Mommy said you weren't supposed to swim right after you eat or you might get something and then something else would happen. Clara didn't really remember, but she knew you were supposed to wait even if you didn't want to. So it was good that Duck hadn't had orange juice with her.

Duck slid into the sink. He splashed around in the water. His tail jerked back and forth and his legs flailed around—

"You okay in there?" Daddy called from the other side of the door. "You've been washing your hands for a long time."

"I'm okay."

The doorknob rattled. "Come on out and keep me company while I fold some laundry."

Duck was still in the sink, but he'd stopped swimming. Clara hopped down from the stool and unlocked the door. Then she got back up on the stool and reached for Duck.

"Time to come out."

Before she could grab Duck, Daddy pulled her away from the sink.

"Clara! What are you doing?" He pushed in the metal thing, and the bottom of the sink opened, and the water drained away. Duck didn't move. "Don't these things run on electricity? You can't put them in water. You could've hurt yourself!"

Daddy was angry. It made Clara scared.

"Didn't Gina tell you not to put them into water? What's wrong with her?"

Clara hated it when Daddy complained about Mommy. She started to cry.

Daddy rubbed his hand up and down her back. "Shhh...Don't cry. You scared me, that's all. Promise you won't put any more of these...things...into the water."

Clara nodded. Her face was wet and sticky, and her nose started to run. She buried her face in Daddy's shirt. He held her for a minute, then lifted her down from the stool. Duck was still in the sink.

"Come on, Duck. Time to get out of the sink."

Duck didn't nod.

"Daddy, what's wrong with Duck?"

"I don't think Duck liked the water."

"Oh no, Duck had fun, he likes swimming. He's just tired."

Daddy reached into the sink with a towel and wrapped Duck inside. He patted Duck dry and gave him to Clara. Duck was cold.

"Oh, he just got too cold. That's why he couldn't get out of the sink."

Daddy bent down and kissed Clara on the forehead. "Come help me with the laundry."

Clara liked folding laundry—she got to match up all the socks while they were all warm from the dryer. They passed the kitchen table on their way to the living room, and Chimpanzee was still sleeping. Clara put Duck on the table as they went by.

"Mommy, Duck stopped moving," Clara said. She took Chimpanzee out of her backpack first, and put her on the floor before getting Duck out.

Mommy took Duck out of Clara's hands. "Did Duck try to go swimming?"

Clara nodded. "He got too cold, Mommy."

Chimpanzee paced back and forth on the floor. Mommy didn't say anything.

"Can you fix him?" Clara asked.

Mommy set Duck down next to Chimpanzee and pulled Clara into her arms. "No. I can make a new duck, but I can't fix Duck."

Chimpanzee poked Duck gently with one finger. Clara swallowed hard. "Did Duck die?"

"Well, Duck was a toy, not a real duck."

"Duck was real Duck."

A tear rolled out of the corner of Clara's eye and down along the side of her nose. She wiped the wet off her face which made her hand wet so she rubbed it on Mommy's shirt. Mommy stroked Clara's hair.

Clara thought about Duck in the sink. "He liked swimming."

Chimpanzee nodded.

Mommy nodded. "Good."

That night, instead of story time, Clara had a funeral for Duck. All the animals came, the new ones and the old ones. Mommy came, too.

"Duck was a good Duck," Clara said. "He always wanted to swim like he did in the story that Mommy told, and he *did* swim, and he liked it, even though it wasn't good for him."

Clara sniffled and started to cry. "Mommy can't fix Duck. He can't walk or nod any more..."

Mommy put her hand on Clara's shoulder. "It's sad to lose someone you love, but Duck was old, and he had a good life. Sometimes even good things come to an end, like bedtime stories."

Clara nodded.

"This is the end of Duck's story," Clara said.

The animals bowed their heads. Clara reached out and stroked Duck's wing.

"Goodnight, Duck," Clara said, and all of them nodded: the animals, old and new, and Mommy, and Clara, too.

-The End-

The Fisherman's Wife

by Jenny Williams

(from *LitNImage*)

It shouldn't be this hard to tell a story, but the characters keep getting in the way. Stella wants to be twenty, then eighty, then twenty again, and she refuses to answer when I ask where she was born. I try to write and she slams a book over my hands.

But the moment I leave it to her, she gives everything away.

Our tale begins tomorrow, when Stella will turn eighty, and it ends a thousand years ago, when a fisherman rolled over in bed to discover his wife had returned to the sea.

It also begins in a bathroom, in a state of slow epiphany.

It also ends in a suicide.

If you didn't want to know, you can do as I do and start over whenever things get tricky. Repeat after me: the story begins now.

I fell in love with Stella the day before her eightieth birthday, when she locked herself in the bathroom and stood, naked and sagging, in front of the mirror.

I almost didn't recognize her at first; I had been thinking about her so much in a different form. Her skin looked baggy and too big for her body. But there she was: pale and pear-shaped with hanging underarm skin and belly creases.

She was almost as surprised to see herself in this state as I was. Had we been expecting something different? Perhaps this was a trick, some sleight of the eye.

Stella prodded at the flab around her stomach and watched it jiggle in the whitish bathroom light.

I'm old, she thought. *I'm an old lady.*

Something about that moment—Stella marveling at her droopy breasts, her breasts marveling back at her—struck me as beautiful. She had been nebulous in my mind until that point, a vague possibility shimmering beyond my reach. And then here she was: nearly eighty, with vein-lined legs and a belly button. The reality of her was pungent, a punch to my senses. I loved her for it. I wanted more.

Today, Stella sits beside me and tells me stories as I write. She is saying how she was only twenty yesterday, which is curious, considering she is turning eighty tomorrow and has been married for nearly sixty years.

She explains it like this. Imagine you are walking down a road you know well, all the while thinking of something else: a story you're planning to write, or an interesting article you read in that morning's paper, or what your lover whispered in your ear last night in bed. A flicker of thought, and you've traveled the length of the road one end to the other. You didn't even know your feet were moving.

I want to ask when, and where, and whether the end of her road is near, but she puts a finger to my lips and smiles. Her eyes become tired around the edges and she looks away, out the narrow window to the distant sea.

The question, she tells me, is not how long can one body live, but: how long can you live in one body, before you begin to die?

#

Because if this story was ever about anything else, it was about an old Scottish legend that goes something like this:

Selkies were mythical sea creatures in the shape of a seal. The females could shed their sealskins and come ashore as beautiful women; if you managed to successfully capture a Selkie woman's pelt, she would stay in human form and be an obedient, if melancholy, wife.

However, if she ever found her skin, she would leave her husband and children, and return to the sea.

According to legend, she always found her skin.

Tomorrow, Stella will turn eighty. It will be a day like any other, except it isn't. Stella wakes up beside a man she has been married to for sixty years—a man for whom she feels a certain amount of fondness, but no real love. She dresses her body in the same clothes she's always worn, that don't fit right, have never fit right, but she wears them anyway.

In the kitchen, Stella watches her fingers work cutting vegetables: nimble, pink, and quick. She never ceases to be amazed at their diligence. Cut, slide, slice. Cut, slide, slice. As if they aren't her own but a team of slender, faceless workers.

Wave-like, her hand rolls up and down in swift succession. One smooth flick of the wrist repeating itself eternally. Cut, slide, slice, slide, slice, slide, cut. Movements drawn by the precision of instinct. Or passion. Or practice.

She can't tell anymore.

You see, when I started thinking about Stella, she was indeed twenty years old, a fisherman's brand new Selkie wife. All I wanted was to understand her. I wanted to follow her through the years of her marriage, to the point that she found her skin and went back to the sea, and ask if she would know the meaning of regret. And what of the years between: did she know her fate? Did she miss the sea? Or simply yearn for something better?

The whole thing emerged in flashes in the room around me; sometimes Stella would narrate, and when she waved her hands just so, I could see it all clearly. Stella had a daughter, and the two would have conversations about Stella's past, of which her daughter knew nothing.

—You know, Mom, you never told me how you and dad met.
—Didn't I? Oh, it was so long ago.
—Won't you tell me now?
Hesitation.
—The beach. Carnoustie. We met on the beaches there.
—Doing what?
Another pause, and now the daughter doesn't wait for an answer.
—Dad always told me you met putting sandbags on the beaches, that it was love at first sight.
—Did he?
—He said he proposed to you then and there, while your hands were still wet and sandy. You should hear him, he makes it sound so romantic.
—It was during the war. Your father wanted to be a pilot for the Royal Air Force. He was still training in Africa when the war ended. Lucky for him he never saw combat.
—Lucky for us, too.
—Yes, lucky for us.

I saw these conversations take place and I wondered, why did Stella give away nothing? What was at stake if she answered with the truth?

But here I listen to Stella's whispers, and she tells me that it didn't matter, that nothing mattered because the end of the story was always the same. She always found her skin; she always left.

I ask, what's the point of a story if it always ends the same way?

The Stella sitting beside me does not reply.

Stella's granddaughter appeared quite suddenly, a tiny flame in this dark territory. At first, her narrative seemed distracting, irrelevant. But her chatter has been growing stronger, and the implications hit me like the snap of a shut book: she is the one who will find the sealskin and bring the story full circle.

She speaks in long, breathless sentences—a child's voice—behind me. Her story is touchingly simple: she listened to Stella's bedtime stories every night and fantasized about the creatures of myth she heard in her grandmother's strange tales. When she finds a chest locked up in the attic, she burns with the thought that it could contain the treasure of the legend.

That night, the granddaughter stays quiet while Stella tucks in the comforter around her shoulders and kisses her on her forehead. Stella turns toward the door. Her granddaughter whispers behind her.

—Gramma.

Stella pauses.

—Yes, darling?

—I have a secret.

I wonder: who is this Stella speaking with her granddaughter? Is she the same as the Stella who would find her skin that very night, folded and musky in the trunk in the attic? Who would steal through the front door without saying goodbye?

I picture, again, the Stella I fell in love with, standing in front of the mirror; I picture the Stella slicing vegetables, and the one deflecting her daughter's curiosity. None of them make sense; she is reproducing, taking on multiple existence and variation, and I've lost track of which one I want to talk to, which one might tell the story straight.

But when I turn to ask the Stella sitting beside me, I find she has disappeared. I send my voice into the room and hear it echo back. A hollow space, pierced by the light of an open window, the low shush of the sea muted in these four walls; I am alone.

Tonight I will dream of being a seal—muscles solid and lean, sinewy and taut in the beats of swimming. I dart back and forth in great zigzags through the water, cutting lines across the shallow ocean floor with my shadow, clean and new and bold.

As the waves close overhead, I might take one last look at the shore, white and gleaming. But I have no need for that now, no need for air. The sand falls away beneath me and the abyss is near. With wet eyes and seamless skin, I let myself slip, slip away into that great deep blue.

The story begins now.

-The End-

Intertropical Convergence Zone

by Nadia Bulkin

(from *ChiZine*)

At the beginning, at the very very beginning of time, the General ate a bullet. Those of us who weren't sure about the *dukun* were worried, and we sat with our elbows on our knees and our chins on our fists around the table, under the single naked bulb with the dangling string. The *dukun*, who said his name was Kurang, had already washed the bullet in holy water that he said came from the very north-of-the-equator springs the Sultans of Sriwijaya bathed in. He said some incantations and then told the General to eat it.

"There. Eat. Eat it. It will make you know things about people, so you know where to aim when you shoot them."

The General stared at the bullet until sweat dropped onto the plate.

Kurang bent over."Mister General," he said, "I promise, good things will happen. You'll see like a garuda, Mister General." He always mocked us. Kurang was one of those villagers who doesn't really give a shit about national unity. They're godless men and that's another thing that bothered me, because the General was devout as all hell."And then you lift your gun, or they lift their guns..." he looked at us, the uncomfortable posse."And you know exactly where to aim. This bullet has the gift, Mister General. It will give you the gift too."

We'd pulled it out of a dead man two days earlier. A clean heart wound that had punctured a major artery—he died immediately. It was perfect, we thought as we smoked our Marlboros and sat on our folding chairs, watching the corpse. Of course we bound him up first and put him against the chalk sketch lines on the basement wall so he wouldn't squirm and so we knew where to nuzzle the barrel. What Kurang told us was this: the dead man has to be the right man, the bullet has to go through the heart, and the bullet has to kill right away.

He was someone who'd been in on our list for a while. A Communist, of course, a party pusher who carried around paperback Mao and mingled with pushcart-peddlers and pretended to be one of them. He was going to go eventually, so we figured, may as well be now.

"Eat it, Mister General. Don't you want to be a great man?"

He took it like a pill. He started choking. We pushed our chairs back and got up and cursed at Kurang but Kurang was already right at the General's side, helping him swallow the tea." There, there," said Kurang." Hush hush, it's okay, Mister General."

We waited for something to change. Nothing did at first. The General made a joke, we laughed; he announced he was going to bed to sleep, and Kurang said that was a good idea. The General walked out of the room rubbing his ribcage, looking puzzled. We said to ourselves: okay, if he's dead tomorrow morning, so is that *dukun*.

But he wasn't dead. He was up bright and early and he wasn't wearing his glasses when we had our morning meeting in his office. He doled us out assignments. They had schedules on them and everything. We asked him why he wasn't wearing his glasses and he said, "Don't need them. I feel so sharp today. It's like looking through a submarine periscope, you know?" And he made this pantomime motion of a navy admiral looking through a periscope and adjusting the lens and then laughed. We all laughed. He laughed until he coughed out a tiny pellet of a bullet that burned one of his memos. We asked the *dukun* but he said that was a normal side effect.

So that was how it started. Nothing very strange. My daughter was drawing people's faces back then, which was also not very strange, except she never filled them in. Whole families without faces.

A week later the General had indirectly sent ten of the most dangerous Communist strategists into the next world. I assume they went to hell, but I've never been to check. They were hidden ones with inconspicuous day jobs—moonlighters. One was a doctor, one taught mathematics. The Communists were squabbling now like hens without a rooster, and they went looking for new warmth. They went for navymen. I don't know what's wrong with the navy, if it's from fighting pirates in the Sunda Strait or if it's just being seaborne that fucks with your head, but they had too many dinners with Communists. I have always thought this. I was getting out of the lounge when I saw Kurang on the street corner in this horrible fake trenchcoat with buttons hanging like eyes out of sockets. He wasn't even smoking, he was just there.

"What? Looking for a hooker?"

"You want to help Mister General, right, Lieutenant?"

I looked around for any President's men. Just zombies and shapeshifters, hanging around in rags and eating noodles, probably infected with hookworm eggs. I looked at Kurang. "Are you following me?"

"You're the best Lieutenant. Mister General needs to get those sea-men to see his way, see?"

There were all these prickly red, bulging spots on his face. Sometimes I thought they were moving, but then I'd think, no, trick of the light.

"There's this knife, a *kris*. It's on one of the outer islands. Right now a fisherman's son has it. If the General eats it he will be able to draw people to him and command them, you know, make them see like he sees. You go get it and bring it here, we'll dress it up nice."

It was for the General, so, okay. I love this country, and Communism's a Satan and the President's its lackey. Leave it to them and we'll all be starving and dying in shrapnel and colorful bombs. No, no. We need a man like the General, an honest man. He's one of us.

Before I left I went home. My daughter had begun to draw deep-sea creatures by then. She gave them all to me, slips of paper that she folded into infinite squares and I put in my wallet. "To protect Daddy," she said, and then went back in the house. I hated the pictures. Curling, coiling beasts. I didn't want their protection, but I kept them anyway.

I stood on the sand, shifting. The waves there came from Australia. The *dukun* told me the name of the island and village and the man, and I asked the locals to fill in the rest. When they saw my credentials and I said that the General needed their help, they helped me. Sometimes I had to show them my gun.

I got to the beach by motorbike. That was our last frontier, those eastern islands. They were populated by people but I think those people were a different species. It was in their eyes. I could tell. Even the children had that look. They all had filariasis, and maybe that was why—microscopic worms sleeping in their veins. It's a horrible disease. They're the only people in this heat-soaked country who shiver in the sun.

At the beach there was no one. There was a limping half-wild dog, and there was a kite. I thought the men at the convenience store had lied to me, it wouldn't be too surprising, but then I saw him—seventeen years old, curly black hair, standing by his father's boat. He had the *kris* sticking out of his backpocket. He didn't know what to do with either. I went toward him and stood on the shifting sand and called to him to give me the knife, I worked for the General and I needed it.

His lips moved and his head shook to say no, but I didn't hear any words. All I heard was the sound of a low motor, not the Pacific, but a real low motor that opened up with a chainsaw sound into a voice—like jaws being torn open and held there. It was the knife. I saw its handle swivel in the backpocket of his trousers—it turned to look at me.

It said, "Eat me, Lieutenant."

I didn't dare look at it even though its booming voice pounded in my ears. I held out my hand to the fisherman's son, and said something to him—I don't remember what because I never heard it. All I heard was:

"Eat me and be great. I will live between your lungs and I will give your voice a resonance you have never known. Eat me, Lieutenant."

The boy backed onto the damp, dark parts of the sand. The knife was thunderous and the waves were rocking. He shook his head *no no no*, and then he reached behind his back and grabbed the screaming knife and yelled.

When I shot him he was flying toward me with the *kris* quivering in the sun. I saw all the way into the back of his mouth. His body went sloshing to Australia on a bed of foam but the knife stayed, stuck in the sand. Hermit crabs came out of the spot in droves where it burrowed. All up and down the beach it called and called. And I was all alone to listen to the beached monster. I thought this was the end of the world. All I saw was ocean, the color of sky, and all I heard was the dark sound of power being born. I wrapped my hand in cloth and I pulled it out of the sand. There was my face in the blade. By then the knife was no longer articulate. It was just the sound of the great furnace, the great God, roaring in want. The kind of sound caves make when you are alone inside them. But I did not touch it, I kept my mouth shut, and I put it in a plastic bag.

Then a plane passed overhead. The wolf-dog came lolling over the dunes and I saw the fisherman's son rising and falling. He was about the size of a shark fin by then. I climbed back to the palm trees, where the motorbike was.

Kurang broke the *kris* into manageable pieces. This surprised us, because he was a feeble man, all bones and no taller than a pony's shoulder. But he split it with his bare hands and then, panting, told the General to eat.

What if the pieces caught in his throat?

"They want to be with you," said Kurang. He leaned over into the light—turned out he had a lazy eye that I hadn't seen before. "Mister General, the knife wants to help you."

The General, who now accidentally spit tiny burning bullets at foot-soldiers when he yelled at them during drills and had already blinded one, agreed to partake of the knife with less coaxing than Kurang needed to get him to swallow the bullet. He had been paranoid, the past few days, that his chance to rescue the country was slipping by. He thought the President was in talks with Communists and that it would end for all of us. Our jobs, our lives, the bright new tomorrow.

According to the servants he had some coughing fits the night after he ate the knife. But the very next day he made a statement condemning Communists as heathens and urging people not to forget what made this baby country of ours so great: unity, justice, development, democracy, and deference to God. And the everymen said yes. That's all I heard in the *warung* over sweet black coffee and *kretek*, wow, what a smart man he is. He's got the right idea. I agree completely. The General also slashed the sheets getting out of bed as well as the morning paper, and there was some accident with the family cat—nothing fatal, just a peculiarity.

When I got out of the *warung* it was like I knew Kurang would be there, and he was, with a smile.

"What does he need now?"

"He needs protection from death. He needs to be able to survive his enemies' bang-bangs." He cocked his head. "He wants to be Forever President, Lieutenant. So he can fix everything." Then Kurang winked. It was insulting and cheap and I tried to hit him, I don't know why. He was a *dukun*, I should have known he wouldn't let me. A blast wave blew up from behind his left ear and threw me back.

"But the General does want to fix everything," I said after I got my breath back. "People are tired of being poor and they're tired of seeing the President blow it on whores and private—"

"Oh yes, monies. They'll come too. But first things first, Lieutenant, and first he needs longevity." There were definitely things under his skin, no doubt now—long tape worms pressed up around his cheeks. Almost like burn-scars but these wobbled, and tonight his hair was churning too, filled with what looked like fingers. "There is a very old goat that lives in Jogja. Mister General will need its liver."

Before I walked off I looked back at Kurang, still standing with his back to me, still wriggling with all the things inside him. "Maybe you should see a doctor about that," I said.

He turned around but I can't say what happened then because I just started to run. I remember for the next week I didn't look in mirrors and I might as well have been shaving blind. My daughter saw all the cuts on my face and asked if I had been in a fight with witches. I thought about what to say and finally I said yes, I said yes, I had, I was fighting to protect her. Then I kissed her earlobe and her tiny golden earring, and she gave me another picture. I tried to be proud like when her brother brought home perfect math scores but it was just so horrible. I asked her what it was. "It's to protect Daddy," she said stubbornly. So I don't know what it was. There were yellow eyes but there was also an uncooked darkness, and something like a mouth, if those were fangs. I wondered if I should have been grateful. At least she was drawing faces now.

I went by plane. It was not quite Jogja, but a subvillage. I put my hands in my pockets and said I was looking for a very old goat. They thought I wanted to buy it and so they all claimed to own it—or if not a goat, a cow with three horns or a chicken with no head. But then there were the school children. "Is there a very old goat in this village anywhere?" With big malnourished eyes they stared. I gave them money and where they pointed I went.

At a little house, under a spirit-willow, sat a man half-blind with age and chemicals, who sang to himself. He took me to the orange orchard to see the goat, and then stood there whistling by the roadside. The creature hobbled in the grass, gnawing on orange rinds. It was clearly weak but still it wore a loose rope that tied it to a tree.

"You can't buy it, you know," said the old man, swaying with his cane. "It's one with me. It was born the same day I was and I can't part with it." It was true, they both had eyes the color of haze, and hair the color of smoked bone. The same awkward gait from back legs that were too long. Maybe they were congenital twins. I took out a cigarette.

"I don't want to buy it. What do you think would happen if it died?"

"Oh, I don't think it will. It's one hundred and two."

The goat lifted its head and after a search its cataract eyes fell upon me. It was older than my father. I couldn't even imagine a world that old. That was far far before the beginning of time. It outlived the Dutch and the Japanese and the Dutch again. It probably never thought a native son would harm it. For a moment the cigarette just sat between my lips, dumb and silent. The goat bleated wretchedly. It started stumbling our way, on *furbare* legs and cracked hooves.

"Maybe it's tired of life," I suggested.

"Nonsense," said the old man. "It will live forever."

I thought about luring it to me with a salty hand and giving it a deceptive calming squeeze before gutting it, but in the end I just grabbed it by the neck, rough and unceremonious, and slit its jugular. Of course I watched sacrifices when I was a boy but this was profane. I wiped my hands on its fur—sick old blood, it's the sickest thing—and looked back at the old blind man. I already knew he was going to die. When the last pumps of life gave from the goat and onto my shoes, the old blind man started to bleed. Just then. In the neck. The only body I could drag back was the goat's and even though it was in a burlap sack the village knew and was silent. I never lit that fucking cigarette.

No persuasion was necessary to make the General eat the goat's well-aged liver. He gobbled it down and, when the raw slab went slipping down his throat, looked up in eagerness. Kurang patted him on the head—no choking this time, it went down easy besides giving him a drugged look—and said, "You're going to be President for a long time, Mister General. Maybe fifty years."

"Fifty?" said the General, and snapped his fingerblades. A bullet coalesced on his tongue and Kurang had to duck to avoid it. "You said I would be President forever!"

"Well, no one can be President forever," said his *dukun*, and gave him the glass of tea. "But I promise that you will live forever in their hearts and their history books. You will have the biggest chapter, Mister General. Your shadow will loom forever, on monuments, on boulevards. Like Mount Bromo, you will be like Mount Bromo, okay?"

The man himself had not grown but by dawn he'd become impermeable. He was a monolith, an impenetrable fortress that was sharp to the touch and spat bullets. He fired his bodyguards. And his hair turned gray overnight and he walked with a strange limp, so he put on his army cap and sat in leather chairs with golden curlicues for feet and looked majestic.

Kurang was waiting for me when I got home. He'd gotten through the peeling front gates somehow and was leaning against an outer wall of the house, just barely out of sight. I threw up my hands.

"There is nothing more he needs!"

"He wants to be loved."

I blinked. The sun had turned our garden purple. Everywhere were rainbows. "He is loved," I said. "We love the General. We'll follow him anywhere, to the end of time if we have to."

"He wants to be loved by the people. He wants them to look at his portrait after he is gone and think, oh, my father, my dead father, how your children miss you." He rubbed his feet together. Something came slithering out from under his pant leg and it swam through the tiles of our veranda and then dove into a bed of bougainvillea. "Or something like that. He wants to have that statue in the center square, with little children on his arms, like parrots. He wants to be shown all smiles. You understand?"

"What is it then that he needs to be loved?"

"He needs your daughter's heart."

I walked for hours in the city after he told me that. Of course I said no. But Kurang said, if you don't do it we'll find someone else who will, and to have it to headquarters by the beginning of the coup. Three days, he'd said and lifted his fingers with a smile. I walked for hours, me and the legless beggars and the eyeless cats. They reached their limbs out to me and begged me to help them in a way only the General could. And now and then under street lamps, behind minivans, I would see Kurang with his fingers raised in a salute. At the end of the first day one of his fingers fell off, and then there were only two.

Please know this—I loved my daughter, love her still. Please never doubt this. But I did not know what else to do. Yes, I thought about hiding her away in the mountains, with her grandparents, in that village washed up against the Australian sea. But he would have found her. And when I pointed my gun at Kurang and said leave her alone or I will shoot, of course my gun jammed. And then I said take my heart instead, but Kurang said mine was a murderer's. It wasn't good enough.

"You can keep your son," said Kurang, "and your wife. Aren't you willing to sacrifice just this one thing of yours for the good of your people? Selfish selfish, Lieutenant. Men like you are the reason this country is going to shit."

I was curled up on the sidewalk beating my head against the concrete and crying, "I can't, dear God, I can't."

"Then just bring her to headquarters. Someone else will do it. You can hold her hand."

When I came home at the end of the second day my daughter ran to me and wrapped her little arms around my legs. "Don't you have a picture for me today?" I asked; she said, "I've hidden it, Daddy. You'll find it later."

I said we had to go to Daddy's office and I held her very close, close enough to feel that precious heart of hers rejoicing while mine wept. She had a strong beat, my little girl. I knew that before she was born, when I listened to her drumming in her mother's belly. Stronger than mine. And despite the monsters in her drawings she was all smiles, all the time—even that night, as her long lashes closed in contentment and she waited. Dear God, Dear God. Every day I ask her to forgive me, and every day I pray she doesn't.

The General became our paterfamilias. He was painted on billboards with children on his lap, all of them pointing at some new horizon just over that swath of development projects. People do greet him with jubilation, they kiss the rings on his fingers and thank him for all the good he's done. His birthday celebrations at the palace are something else, or so I've heard.

He sends me pictures in manila envelopes. I suspect Kurang would have advised him against it, but Kurang is dead now. His head fell off a couple years back, and it turned out there was nothing inside of him but snakes and grubs and centipedes. The General says he draws these things late at night and he doesn't know why he feels that he should send them to me or why they come racing out of his fingers, but I do, and I tape the monsters up all over the house, over family portraits, over the clock, over the calendar.

And I wait for him to die. I know he's a good man who's done good things. God only knows he's a better President than that Communist. I just think, maybe when he's dead, he'll give me back her heart.

-The End-

Urchins, While Swimming

by Catherynne M. Valente

(from *Clarkesword Magazine*)

> *On the third day the ardent hermit*
> *Was sitting by the shore, in love,*
> *Awaiting the enticing mermaid,*
> *As shade was lying on the grove.*
> *Dark ceded to the sun's emergence;*
> *By then the monk had disappeared,*
> *No one knew where, and only urchins,*
> *While swimming, saw a hoary beard.*
> —Aleksandr Pushkin
> Rusalka, 1819

I: Snail Into Shell

Rybka, you have to wake up.

    At night she always called me *rybka*. At night, when she shook me awake in my thin bed and the dirt-smeared window was a sieve for the light of the bone-picked stars, she whispered and stroked my temples and said: *rybka, rybka,* wake up, you have to wake up. I would rub my eyes and with heavy limbs hunch to the edge of the greyed mattress, hang my head over the side. She would be waiting with a big copper kettle, a porcelain basin, the best and most beautiful of the few things we owned. She would be waiting, and while I looked up at the stars through a scrim of window-mud and window-ice, she would wet my hair.

She was my mother, she was kind, the water was always warm. The kettle poured its steaming stream over my scalp, that old water like sleep spreading over my long black hair. Her hands were so sure, and she wet every strand—she did not wash it, understand, only pulled and combed the slightly yellow water from our creaking faucet through my tangles.

Rybka, I'm sorry, poor darling. I'm so sorry. Go back to sleep. And she would coil my slippery hair on the pillow like loose rope on the deck of a ship, and she would sing to me until I was asleep again, and her voice was like stones falling into a deep lake:

> *Bayu,*
> *bayushki bayu*
> *Ne lozhisya na krayu*
> *Pridet serenkiy volchok*
> *Y ukusit za bochek*

In the morning, she called me always by my name, Kseniya, and her eyes would be worry-wrinkled—and her hair would be wet, too. While she scraped a pale, translucent sliver of precious butter over rough, hard-crusted bread, I would draw a bath, filling the high-sided tub to its bright brim. We ate our breakfast slick-haired in the nearly warm water, curled into each other's bodies, snail into shell, while the bath sloshed over onto the kitchen floor, which was also the living room floor and the bathroom floor and my mother's bedroom floor—she gave me the little closet which served as a second room.

In the evening, if we had meat, she would fry it slowly and we would savor the smell together, to make the meal last. If we did not, she would tell me a story about a princess who had a bowl which was never empty of sweet, roasted chickens while I slurped a thin soup of cabbage and pulpy pumpkin and saved bathwater. Sometimes, when my mother spoke low and gentle over the green soup, it tasted like birds with browned, sizzling skin. All day, she sponged my head, the trickle ticklish as sweat. The back of my dress clung slimy to my skin.

Before bed, she would pass my head under the faucet, the cold water splashing on my scalp like a slap. And then the waking, always the waking, and hour or two past midnight.

Rybka, I'm sorry, you have to wake up.

My childhood was a world of wetness, and I loved the smell of my mother's ever-dripping hair.

One night, she did not come to wet my hair. I woke up myself, my body wound like a clock by years of kettles and basins. The stars were salt-crystals floating in the window's mire. I crept out of my room and across the freezing floor like the surface of a winter lake. My mother lay in her bed, her back turned to the night.

Her hair was dry.

It was yellowy-brown, the color of old nut-husks—I was shocked. I had never seen it un-darkened by water. I touched it and she did not move. I turned her face to me and it did not move against my hand, or murmur to me to go back to sleep, or call me rybka—water dribbled out of her mouth and onto the blankets. Her eyes were dark and shallow.

Mama, you have to wake up.

I soaked up the water with the edge of the bedsheet. I pulled her to me; more water fell from her.

Mamochka, I'm sorry, you have to wake up.

Her head sagged against my arm. I didn't cry, but drew a bath in the dark, feeling the water for a ghost of warmth in the stream. It was hard—I was always so thin and small, then!—but I pulled my mother from her bed and got her into the tub, though the water splashed and my arms ached and she did not move, she did not move as I dragged her across the cold floor, she did not move as I pushed her over the lip of the bath. She floated there, and I pulled the water through her hair until it was black again, but her eyes did not swim up out of themselves. I peeled off my nightgown, soaked with her mouth-water, and climbed in after her, curling into her body as we always did, snail into shell. Her skin was clammy and thick against my cheek.

Ryba, wake up. It's time to wet my hair.

There was no sound but the tinkling ripple of water and the stars dripping through the window-sieve. I closed my mother's eyes and tucked my head up under her chin. I pulled her arms around me like blankets. And I sang to her, while the bath beaded on her skin, slowly blooming blue.

> *Bayu,*
> *bayushki bayu*
> *Ne lozhisya na krayu*
> *Pridet serenkiy volchok*
> *Y ukusit za bochek*

II: The Ardent Hermit

I met Artyom at university, where I combed my hair into a tight braid so that it would hold its moisture through anatomy lectures, pharmacopeial lectures, stitching and bone-setting demonstrations. At lunch I would wait until all the others had gone, and put my head under the spotless bathroom sink. Pristine, colorless water rushed over my brow like a comforting hand.

There were no details worth recounting: I tutored him in tumors and growths, one of the many ways I kept myself in copper kettles and cabbage soup. This is not important. How do we begin to remember? One day he was not there, the next day his laugh was a constant crow on my shoulder. One day I did not love a man named Artyom, the next day I loved him, and between the two days there is nothing but air.

Artyom ate the same thing every day: smoked fish, black bread, blueberries folded in a pale green handkerchief. He wore the spectacles of a man twice his age, and his hair was yellowy-brown. He had a thin little beard, a large nose and kept his tie very neatly. He once shared his lunch with me: I found the blueberries sour, too soft.

"When I was a girl," I said slowly, "there were no blueberries where we lived, and we would not have been able to buy them if there were. Instead I ate pumpkin, to keep parasites from chewing my belly into a honeycomb after the war. I ate pumpkin until I could not stand the sight of it, the dusty wet smell of it. I think I am too old, now, to love blueberries, and too old to see pumpkins and not think of worms."

Artyom blinked at me. His book lay open to a cross-section of the thyroid, the green wind off of the Neva rifling through the pages and the damp tail of my braid. He took back his blueberries.

When there was snow on the dome of St. Isaac's and the hooves of the Bronze Horseman were shoed in ice, he lay beside me on his own thin mattress and clumsily poured out the water of his tin kettle over my hair, catching the runoff in an old iron pot.

"You have to wake me in the night, Artyom. It is important. Do you promise to remember?"

"Of course, Ksyusha, but why? This is silly, and you will get my bed all wet."

I propped myself up on one elbow, the river-waves of my hair tumbling over one bare breast, a trickle winding its way from skin to linen. "If I can trust you to do this thing for me, then

I can love you. Is that not reason enough?"

"If you can trust me to do this thing, then you can trust me to know why it must be done. Does that not seem obvious?"

He was so sweet then, with his thin chest and his clean fingernails. His woolen socks and his over-sugared tea. The sharp inward curve of his hip. I told him—why should I not? Steam rose from my scalp and he stroked my calves while I told him about my mother, how she was called Vodzimira, and how when she was young she lived in a little village in the Urals before the war and loved a seminary student with thick eyebrows named Yefrem, how she crushed thirteen yellow oxlips with her body when he laid her down under the larch trees.

Mira, Mira, he said to her then, I will never forget how the light looks on your stomach in this moment, the light through the larch leaves and the birch branches. It looks like water, as though you are a little brook into which I am always falling, always falling.

And my mother put her arms around his neck and whispered his name over and over into the collar of his shirt: Yefrem, Yefrem. She watched a moth land on his black woolen coat and rub its slender brown legs together, and she winced as her body opened for the first time. She watched the moth until the pain went away, and I suppose she thought then that she would be happy enough in a house built of Yefrem and his wool and his shirts, and his larches and his light.

But when she came to his school and put her hands over her belly, when she told him under a gray sky and droning bronze bells that she was already three months along, and would he see about a priest so that her child might have a name, he just smiled thinly and told her that he did not want a house built of Vodzimira and her water and her stomach, that he wanted only a house of God and some few angels with feet of glass, and that she was not to come to his school any longer. He did not want to be suspected of interfering with local girls.

My mother was alone, and her despair walked alongside her like a little black-haired girl with gleaming shoes. She could not tell her father or her own mother, she could not tell her brothers. She could think of no one she could tell who would love her still when the telling was done. So she went into the forest again, into the larches and the birches and the moths and the light, and in a little lake which reflected bare branches, she drowned herself without another word to anyone.

    I swallowed and continued hoarsely. "When my mother opened her eyes again, it was very dark, and there were stars in the sky like drops of rain, and she saw them from under the water of the little lake. She was in the lake and the lake was in her and her fingers spread out under the water until there was nothing but the water and her, spanning shore to shore, and she moved in it, in herself, like a little tide. She had me there, under the slow ripples, in the dark, and the silver fish were her midwives."

    I twisted the ends of my hair. A little water seeped out onto my knuckles.

    Artyom looked at me very seriously. "You're talking about *rusalka*."

    I shrugged, not meeting his gaze. "She didn't expect it. She certainly didn't think her child would go into the lake with her. When I was born, I swam as happily as a little turtle, and breathed the water, and as if by instinct beckoned wandering men with tiny, impish fingers. But she didn't want that for me. She didn't even want it for herself—she pressed her instinct down in her viciously, like a stone crushing a bird's skull. She brought me to the city, and she worked in laundries, her hands deep in soapy water every day, so that I would have something other than a lonely lake and skeletons." I picked at the threads of the mattress, refusing to look up, to see his disbelief. "But we had to stay wet, you know. It is hard in the city, there are so many things to dry you out. Especially at night, with the cold wind blowing across your scalp, through the holes in the walls. And even in the summer, the pillow drinks up your hair."

Artyom looked at me with pale green eyes, the color of lichen in the high mountains, and I broke from his gaze. He scratched his head and laughed a little. I did not laugh.

"My mother died when I was very young, you know. I have thought about it many times, since. And I think that, after awhile, she was just so tired, so tired, and a person, even a *rusalka*, can only wake herself up so many times before she only wants to sleep, sleep a little while longer, before she is just so tired that one day she forgets to wake up and her hair dries out and her little girl finds her with brown hair instead of black, and no amount of water will wake her up anymore."

My hands were pale and shaking as dead grass. I tried to pull away from him and draw my knees up to my chest—of course he did not believe me, how could I have thought he might? But Artyom took me in his arms and shushed me and stroked my head and told me to hush, of course he would remember to wake me, his poor love, he would wet my hair if I wanted him to, it was nothing, hush, now.

"Call me *rybka*, when you wake me," I whispered.

"You are not a *rusalka*, Kseniya Yefremovna."

"Nevertheless."

The frost was thick as fur on the windows when he kissed me awake in the hour-heavy dark, a steaming basin in his hands.

III: By the Shore, in Love

It took exactly seventeen nights, with Artyom constant with his kettle and basin as a nun at prayer over her pale candles, before I slept easily in his arms, deeper than waves.

On the eighteenth night my breath was quick as a darting mayfly on his cheek, and he reached for me as men will do—he reached for me and I was there, dark, new-soaked hair sticking to my breasts, rivulets of water trickling over my stomach. I smiled in the dark, and his face was so kind above me, kind and soft and needful. He closed his eyes—I could see at their edges gentle creases which would one day be a grandfather's wrinkles. When our lips parted he was shaking, his lip shuddering as though he had just touched a Madonna carved from ice, and I think of all the things I remember about Artyom, it is that little shaking that I recall most clearly, most often.

I was a virgin. Under the shadows of St. Isaac's and a moon-spattered light like blueberries strewn on the grass I moved over him with more valor than I felt—but one of us had to be brave. He guided me, but his motions were so small and afraid, as though, after all this time, he could not quite understand or believe in what was happening. I felt as though I was an old door, stuck into my frame, and some sun-beaten shoulder jarring me open, smashing against the dusty wood. It hurt, the widening of my bones, the rearrangement of my body, ascending and descending anatomies, sliding aside and aligning into a new thing. Of course it hurt. But there was no blood and I kissed his eyebrows instead of crying. My hair hung around his face like storm-drenched curtains, casting long shadows on his cheekbones.

"Ksyusha," he said to me, tender and gentle, without mockery, "Ksyusha, I will never forget how the light looks on your stomach in this moment, the light through your hair and the frozen windows. It looks like water, as though you are a little brook into which I am always falling, always falling."

The bars of the window cut my chest into quarters. He arched his back. I clamped his waist between my thighs. These things are not important—no one act of love is different much in its parts from any other, really. What is important is this: I did not know. I bent over him, meaning to kiss, only meaning to kiss—and I did not know what would happen, I swear it.

The lake came out of me, shuddering and splashing—my mouth opened like a sluice-gate, and a flood of water came shrieking from me, more water than I had ever known, strung with weeds and the skeletons of fish and little stones like sandy jewels.

It tasted like blood.

I choked, my body seized, thrashing rapture-violent, and it gushed harder, streaming from my lips, my hair, my fingertips, my eyes, my eyes, my eyes wept a deluge onto the thin little body of Artyom. The windows caught the jets and drops froze there, hard knots of ice. I screamed and all that came from my throat was more water, more and more and more.

His legs jerked awkwardly and I clutched at him, trying to clear the water and the green stems from his mouth, but already he convulsed under me, spluttering and spitting, reaching out for me from under the growing pool that was our bed, the bubbles of his breath popping in the blue—the bed was a basin and the water steamed and I wet his hair in it, but I did not mean to, I could not close my mouth against it, I could not stop it, I could not move away from him and it came and came and his bones beneath me racked themselves in the mire, the whites of his eyes rolled, and I am sorry, Artyom, I did not know, my mother did not tell me, she told me only to live as best I could, she did not say we drag the lake with us, even into the city, drag it behind us, a drowning shadow shot with green.

I would like to remember that he called out to me, that he called out in faith that I could deliver him, and if I try, I can almost manage it, his voice in my ear like an echo:

"Ksyusha!"

But I do not think he did, I think he only gurgled and gasped and coughed and died. I think the strangling weeds just passed over his teeth.

He never tried to push me off of him, he never tried to sit up. His face became still. His lips did not shake. His skin was pale and purpled. The water rippled over his thin little beard as it slowly, slowly as spring thaw, seeped into the mattress and disappeared.

The snow murmured against the glass.

IV: Shell Into Snail

Rybka, you have to wake up.
    She rubs her eyes with little pink fingers and turns away from me, towards the wall.
    Rybka, I'm sorry, you have to wake up.
    She yawns, stretches her legs, and wriggles sleepily towards the edge of the bed. I am waiting, kneeling on the floor with our copper kettle and a glass bowl. I am her mother, I understand the shock of waking, the water is always warm. She stares up through the window-glass at the stars like salt on the skin of a black fish as I pour it over her scalp, clear and clean. I comb it through every strand—her hair is so soft, like leaves. Afterwards, we lie together in the dark, my body curving around hers like a shell onto its snail, our wet hair curling slowly around each other. I sing her back to sleep, and my voice echoes off of the walls and windows, where there is frost and bare branches scraping:

> *Bayu, bayushki bayu*
> *Ne lozhisya na krayu*
> *Pridet serenkiy volchok*
> *Y ukusit za bochek*

    Her hair is yellowy-brown under the wet, but damp enough to seem always black, like mine. Her eyes are so green it hurts, sometimes, to look at them, like looking at the sun. She swims very well for her age, and asks always to be taken to the mountains for the holidays. She is too little for coffee, but sneaks sips when I am not looking—she says it tastes like wet earth.
    There is money for coffee, and kettles, and birds with browned, sizzling skin. We can see a bright silver scrap of the Neva through our windows, and the gold lights of the Liteyny Bridge. A woman who can set a bone is never hungry. I wash my hands more

than anyone on my ward—twelve times a day I thrust my skin under water and breathe relief.

I taught her before she could read how to braid her hair very tightly. In the morning I will call her Sofiya and put a little red cup full of blueberries floating in cream in front of her, and she will tell me that after the kettle, she dreamed again of the man with the thin little beard and the big nose who sits on the side of a lake and shares his lunch with her. He has larch leaves in his lap, she will say, and he tells her she is pretty, and he calls her *rybka*, too. His beard prickles her cheek when he holds her. I will pull my coffee away from her creeping fingers and smile as well as I am able. She will eat her blueberries slowly, savoring them, removing the purple skin with her tongue before chewing the greenish fruit. I will draw us a bath.

But now, under the stars pricking the window-frost like sewing needles, I hold her against me, her wet eyelashes sticking together, her little breath quick and even. I decide I will take her to the mountains. I decide I will not.

Rybka, poor darling, I'm sorry, go back to sleep.

I wind her hair around my fingers; little drops like tears squeeze out, roll over my knuckles.

We are as happy as we may be, as happy as winters with ice on the stairs and coats which seem to always need patching and wet hair that freezes against our shoulders and the memory of still eyelids under water may leave us.

I am not tired yet.

-The End-

The Shangri-La Affair

by Lavie Tidhar

(from *Strange Horizons*)

You told me to wait but the rain-clouds are gathering
Like a tribe of Hmong waiting for an Air America pickup.
My opium cargo is consumed. Poetry marks the landing-strip.
There is a belly-fat moon. There is the singing of frogs
like idols gathering before the pot, a coal-blackened god
who would consume them. Faith is like a red thread or a farmer's tan,
it marks you. I will wait. The plane might come, the pot might break.
Sok dee der, someone says with a rising tilting accent on the last.
Good luck: this answer is given to a departing person.

From London by jet-powered plane to Bangkok, a city crowded with war-curious thrill-seeking backpackers just far enough from the action to enjoy it; there to meet a shaggy-haired giant blond whose name was Richard, or John, or Enrique depending on the place and the day of the week; in a dark bar where ladyboys served drinks and flirted with the clientele. "We're the new Air America," Richard—but call me Rick—said. "Anything, anywhere, anytime. But non-government affiliated, see? Just like the Red Cross, or Oxfam. Another bourbon, please, Satien. Neat. And one for my friend here. He's paying—" and winked, and slapped the beautiful slim Thai boy on his behind, and said, "*Nuevo Air Amerika*: where do you want to go today?"

#

Hot morning, dry mouth, head hurting with the cheap drinks that will have to go in the column marked "expenses." The air already thick with heat, the traffic suffocating. "It's like there's no war," Rick said. "The Thais always knew how to keep house. A buffer state between the French and the English back when the old white boys were cutting up Asia, a cautious ally of the Yanks during the Vietnam War: old families, my man. Nobility shines through. So they gave some territories to the French back in the nineteenth, and gave the Americans aid back in the twentieth, but they kept their monarchy, held off communism, and if this new war wasn't going on they'd be . . . "

He droned on and his passenger nodded and felt sweat gathering on his eyebrows, making his face itch. His hangover was getting worse. He tried to place Rick's accent and found that he couldn't. A royalist. He'd see the dossier on the man, of course, but who could even tell what in it was true, if anything? War allowed for near-infinite fictions. He shrugged and closed his eyes, hoping he could get some sleep. Who cared. The man was a pilot, and a pilot was what he needed. And names were dangerous. He preferred to do without them.

The air-strip was an assemblage of shacks and hastily-constructed hangars. He sat and drank bad coffee made from a three-in-one sachet while Rick arranged the transportation. It was eight o'clock in the morning. "We'll have to leave in the afternoon," Rick said when he returned. "Wind, you know. Meanwhile, relax. Got a book to read?"

There were some Le Carrés and an Agatha Christie on a shelf beside the hot-water samovar. "I think I'm all right, actually," he said. Rick shrugged, the movement magnified in his oversized frame. "Suit yourself, man. Just stay here. I've got some business to attend to."

Old planes rusting in the sun ... a microlight landed, the pilot small, wearing unidentified khaki overalls and helmet, removing a sack from the back seat—opium? Chinese software? It turned out to be rice. A group of men with large moustaches who looked vaguely Mongolian came and sat around, smoking and playing cards. Why was war always so much about waiting? A small blimp floated past, stopped, lowered a rope-ladder. He could see gun-turrets poking from its gondola. Two jeeps came, dislodged cargo, disappeared. By noon the sunlight was as thick as paste and his mouth tasted of coffee like bile.

At three-thirty Rick reappeared. "Get dressed," he said, throwing him a pair of overalls. He put them on, zipping them over himself, cursing. The heat inside the suit was suffocating. He followed Rick out of the hangar and felt like an astronaut walking on the moon in old NASA reels, when the Americans still thought they owned near-space by default.

"Get in. Try not to touch anything."

Was that drink on Rick's breath? He decided it was best not to ask. The craft looked like an old-fashioned biplane. Almost. The wings were sun absorbers, a weave of solar receptacles etched into their frame. The body was painted sky-blue. It looked like an exceedingly cheerful children's toy. He sat in the back. Rick climbed into the front. The control panel instruments were needles in wood and glass. "Got to keep it simple," Rick shouted to him. "Can't give out a digital readout from this thing or we're fucked. Old-fashioned," he said cheerfully and strapped in. "Like me."

From above the land was flat, flat, an endless plane, the part of Thailand the tourists never came to, a horizontal expanse of small villages linked by dirt roads, no towns, no lights, very few cars. They flew low. He couldn't speak to Rick, there were no headsets, no radio either. He watched for troop movements, the gathering of tanks and artillery and massed units he knew should be there, but could see nothing. It looked peaceful and quiet and empty, the way he imagined it must have looked like for thousands of years, though he knew nearly every major war in the region passed through here at some point, on the way to better things.

The heat had been turned off. Up here he was glad for the overalls, feeling comfortably warm inside them. The wind whipped his face. He blinked behind the goggles. At some point Rick passed him a small bottle. Red Label, though not American. Local distillery's Johnny Walker knockoff, but not bad. He drank and didn't pass it back.

When they came on the Mekong it was evening and the light was disappearing fast. At this time of year the river was almost dry, sandbanks appearing like white spots between the banks. He couldn't see any boats. The plane swooped and flew lower and he tensed: they were crossing into Laos.

No one knew how the war started. That it was a regional conflict, everyone agreed. Some said it was Pakistan squaring up to India one last time. Others blamed the spill-out from the Afghan homelands. Others still said it was Chinese expansionism, or Vietnamese aggression, or even Mongolian dreams of a second empire. No one blamed the Thais, who as always trimmed sails and, to mix metaphors, sat by the sidelines, but a lot of people did blame the colonial forces, neo- or otherwise, for stirring the pot. All anyone knew for sure was that one day the region was ploughing along, growing rice, manufacturing software, formulating five-year plans—and the next, there was war.

It came spilling over Asia like grains of rice measured into a pan. Digital systems were corrupted. Tailor-made viruses swept through urban populations, spread out to villages, sometimes merely killing, sometimes transforming people into . . . into other things. Borders were closed, reserves were called, cheap uniforms were manufactured en masse in hundreds of air-conditioned sweatshops. Vietnam, which for several years had the monopoly on doll technology, experimented with bionic soldiers. China made a counter-move with ray-based weaponry with smart chips that could detect one's genetic makeup before elimination. They called them Heinleinistas for no reason anyone could figure, but the Chinese always had too much regard for Western pulp fiction. India put out genetically-modified rice which caused unfortunate side-effects when digested. Numerous ethnic groups formed splinter militias and tried to claim independence in the political chaos. Tibetan overseas scientists tried to come up with a force-field shield that, had it been successful, would have effectively closed them off against China. It was not successful. And into the fray came the drifters, the mercenaries, the war-bloggers, the conflict-tourists, the NGOs and aid agencies, the intelligence community, and the intrepid politicians who rather fancied a Peace Prize and a place on the list with Nelson Mandela. Myanmar had become even more impenetrable than before. And Laos . . .

Laos was the crossroad.

They were shot at as they crossed over the Mekong but it was only conventional low-grade artillery and Rick avoided it, flying low and high and at sharp angles. Crossing the river the land was green and he could see palm trees below and they landed in a small strip where shirtless boys marked the runway with gasoline torches. Rick took off his helmet and wiped his face with a rag and grinned. "Welcome to Laos," he said.

There was an unofficial bar. A Hong Kong martial-arts movie was playing on a TV in the background. The place had its own generator. They had cold beer. The clientele was composed almost exclusively of drunk pilots. They seemed to be having a good time.

He ordered a beer and was grateful for its coolness. He thought of the road he still had to take. Getting here had been the easy part.

Vientiane was wide avenues and narrow lanes twisting out from them like arteries. Impressions of Vientiane like coloured slides flashing rapidly on a wall-screen: a temple with a life-sized Buddha standing guard, his face remarkably like that of a cat (the driver, when he asked him, saying, "No Buddha! *Nyak!* No same-same!"); in the open market Chinese black-market hardware and datasets, and an old woman with a terminal in front of her who, Rick told him, could predict the movement of troops across the whole of Asia. He'd watched as Rick went and knelt by the old woman and watched as she tapped keys, bangles clashing like cymbals on her arms, and she murmured something inaudible to Rick and made a gesture with her hand, and he saw money change hands, discreetly. In a backstreet off Sokpaluang he saw a doll's house and men in the waiting room sitting on carpets. There were three or four dolls that he could see, life-sized, stepping in graceful if slow motion, one with the features of a *falang*, a foreigner, two other Vietnamese, one Thai. The dolls' keeper was a dour-looking woman with screwdrivers in her shirt pocket. They ate in the nearby stall, Rick noisily slurping noodles, calling for more *mak phed*, more beerlao. Soldiers everywhere, but quiet. Like Bangkok, Vientiane was relatively stable. Enough for the war-tourists to come, the *falangs* with the right papers, the right connections. Not him, though he had them if he needed them. The problem had been about getting in, not about staying.

A *tuk-tuk* ride through darkened streets, the driver taking a short-cut through a temple, monks in orange robes staring, the *tuk-tuk* an electric golf-cart with solar panels on its back and sides, miniature wind-turbines spinning against the artificial wind, Thai pop blaring through unseen speakers. Motorbikes everywhere, running on expensive gasoline, on sugar-cane fuel, on batteries. And he, waiting, searching, going from one place to another, following the routine. A tourist, just another war-junkie, sitting in the cafés, drinking espresso, eating the baguettes that they called *falang*-bread here, reading the Vientiane Times to see only government-sponsored Happy Talk and so resorting to gossip, which was everywhere: that the Chinese were going for Japan, settling scores still left over from World War II; that the Malay were fighting India in the asteroid belt, mining craft ramming each other with loads only meant for the valuable rocks; that Tibet was a wasteland; that Myanmar was inoculating every citizen against propaganda with an RNA-based brain parasite; that a coup in Thailand was imminent; that Vietnam was forming an army of dolls to take on a Cambodian invasion; that the Russians were moving in—but no one believes the last one.

And all the while he went from place to place and he left the message, the pre-agreed code, and he checked the dead-letter boxes and he waited in his hotel room, and his piss smelled of coffee every time he went. And he waited, for who or what he didn't yet know.

Lao girl on bicycle
Holding parasol.
She is still. Beneath her the road rolls.

And that's how he first saw her, Phitsamai, Pit-saa Maai, not like pizza, she said, laughing, and that's how he always, afterwards, remembered her. Logos danced like snakes on the sides of the bicycle. The parasol was itself a small solar unit, gathering energy into a tiny battery at the handle. Phitsamai rang her bell twice, warning walkers of her right of way and after a lull rang it again, once. That sound, coupled with the parasol, was the signal he'd been waiting for. Phitsamai cycled down the road. He followed at a distance. She never looked back.

He found her at a drinks stand outside the old national library building, which had recently been converted into a refugee asylum. She had just sat down. He approached her.

"Excuse me, Miss," he said, hesitant, "*Khor thod, khor thod—*"

"Yes?" she said, in faultless English. The proprietress of the drinks stand, for whose benefit (and whatever other watchers there may be) this performance was conducted, gazed at them for a moment and turned away. "I believe you dropped this." He handed her the envelope. Her eyes opened wide. "I can't believe I was so foolish!" she said. "Thank you. It has my travel documents. They are very important. Please, sit down."

And so it went. He was taken by her even before that moment, their first together, even before he learned her name, or that she was half-Hmong, or that she had worked as an interpreter for the UNDP before the war. "And what is your name?" she said, arching her eyebrows (the proprietress had snorted but turned away—the scene she was witnessing was a familiar one, and showing disapproval got you nowhere). He thought, then said, "Call me Ishmael," which got him a laugh, at least. It was also a final verification, because he was there to land himself a whale, of sorts.

He had a name, of course. He had a passport, visa, international driving license, this current set in the name of a John Brown, nationality Irish, the accent a kind of trans-Atlantic blur. He preferred Ishmael, and it became their joke.

They met again later that day, in a safehouse she told him to come to, near the 103 hospital on the old Friendship Lao-Thai Road.

"Can you get it?" he said. And, despite all the briefings, the confidential reports, the decoded information—"Is it real?"

She nodded, and she didn't look happy. "It's real," she said.

They called it Shangri-La. Its transmission mechanisms included sexual intercourse (99%-100%); it could also be transmitted by air (50%-60%), by water (30%-35%), through saliva

(15%-20%) and by touch (5%-6%). It was not transferable by mosquitoes, but that was for aesthetic rather than technical reasons. It was developed by a group of scientists working on a UN-funded project in the Golden Triangle, on the border region of Thailand, Laos, and Myanmar. The group, as it turned out, was receiving additional funds from a local drugs syndicate, and when first indications of the product began to surface the entire research station, alongside the village it was situated in, had simply disappeared. For a long time no one believed it really existed. Then came the rumours . . .

"Where is it?" he asked. He realised suddenly how little he knew. Even getting here was a gamble. "How much of it is there?" And a thought at the back of his head like a fly that wouldn't stop biting—can I trust her?

"What I saw was a briefcase," she said, and he reeled even as he expected it. "I'd estimate over a hundred vials, each enough to infect five to ten people by direct injection, with the percentage rising by a magnitude if you release the whole quantity in a city's water supply, or in the aircon systems of any number of large public buildings . . . "

"Where is it?" he said. Phitsamai sighed. She sat down on the narrow bed and he was suddenly aware of her nearness, and of the smell of her, which was of smoke and dust and ginger. "You are American?" she said.

"No . . . "

She smiled. "It is a shame."

"Why?"

She didn't answer. Instead she said, "Can you fly?"

"I have a pilot."

"Is he *Nuevo Air Amerika*?"

"I think so."

"Then maybe he could get you there. But it is very hard, very dangerous. And the people there are very nervous. I don't think you are the only one looking for Shangri La."

"I don't think so either," he agreed. He sat down beside her. "It's a dangerous game."

"It's not a game," she said quietly. And then, "Tell me. If you get hold of this thing—will you use it?"

She looked into his eyes. She saw the answer there and she smiled. "It is very dangerous," she said. "Yes. More dangerous than war."

When he found Rick again it was in a local bar on Sokpaluang again and he could spot him easily in the crowd. A yellow-painted, transparent plastic samovar rested on the table beside him, and it was full of beer. He slid onto a seat opposite the pilot. Rick grunted a hello and made a motion with his hand. "Another mug," he said, articulating slowly. When it came he said, "Drink."

They drank. "How are you liking Vientiane?" Rick said.

"Fine."

"Have a cigarette."

"No, thank you," he said. And then—"Long Cheng."

Rick splattered over his beer. "Ancient history, mate," he said. "Nothing there but Hmong, now." Which was bullshit. "Why do you come say Long Cheng to me?" Rick looked at him with a hurt look in his eyes. He still couldn't place his accent.

"Long Cheng," he said again. And, "Saisosombun Special Zone."

"Damn right it's *special*," Rick said. "And don't talk so loudly. You're upsetting the natives. You've already upset *me*."

"I'm sorry."

"It's okay."

"I'll just have to find someone else to do it."

Rick laughed. "Who?" he said, simply.

Long Cheng, Phitsamai had told him, was the base of operations for the Americans during their Secret War in Laos. It was the old CIA's own secret city. Ravens flew above it, the name given to the Air America operatives, and Air America was the CIA's own airline, the TWA of the clandestine services. By the time the Americans evacuated it was the second biggest city in Laos—not bad for a place which didn't officially exist.

"What happened after the Americans left?" he had asked. "Army held it," she said. "No one allowed in, no one allowed out. For many years this was so. The local Hmong people lived in the Special Zone, but the army held Long Cheng. And then . . . "

And then the war started. And the Special Zone returned to what it did best. Where before the Hmong fought the North Vietnamese and the Pathet Lao, and shipped heroin out and chickens and rice in, now there was a new war, and new intruders, and as the central government lost its hold on the provinces the minority tribes took to their new-found freedom with an austere sort of joy, and put out a lease. And the old secret city opened its gates again to a new brand of spook, and strangers were not, Phitsamai told him, tolerated. To come into the Zone unannounced, therefore, was to invite certain repercussions . . .

"It was old Air America," he said, insisting. "Didn't *you* say anything, anywhere, anytime? Well, this is anywhere, isn't it?"

He got the impression that, with Rick, it was mainly a matter of show. Like a medicine-merchant in the Morning Market of Vientiane, Rick needed to show reluctance to sell. Face, that's what they called it. He needed to coax Rick, show willing, let Rick settle into it. Well, he better make it pretty quick, he thought. There were other pilots.

But a dreamy look had come into Rick's eyes. "Shit," he said. "Long Cheng. It was ours, mate. Raven City. Nothing you couldn't get in Long Cheng, if you set your mind to it. If they let you in. But ..."

"But what?"

"Dragon Boyz. Ravenz. The Klan Klandestine."

"What the fuck are you talking about?"

Rick stared at him. "You have files," he said, calmly. "They would have briefed you, before you left London or Zurich or wherever the fuck it is that you're from?"

They did have files. And through Phitsamai's contacts, on a secure satellite link-up, using a cheap use-once-and-destroy made-in-China comms kit, he talked to London or Zurich or Bonn, or wherever the fuck he was from, and they said to proceed, and sent him the files, and after he read them the comms-kit burned quietly into a ball of fused plastic.

Long Cheng, the Forbidden City. Satellite imagery showed him the ancient runway, 1.2km long; the cluster of hangars, storage areas, accommodation units; flying craft hovering like flies, not ravens, over the strangely organic accumulation of structures; below, trucks, motorbikes, jeeps, a couple of tanks, the remains of a burned-out zeppelin. And everywhere discreet tunnel mouths, for Long Cheng was a city built as much below as it was above. Gun turrets kept watch. Satellite dishes sprouted like mushrooms amidst limestone peaks.

And here and there, fleeting like shadows, the Dragon Boyz stalked, and the Klan Klandestine watched.

"So I saw the files," he said. He took a sip from the beer. It had lost its cool very quickly. He shrugged. "What I need is in Long Cheng. Now, can you get me there—or not?"

Rick laughed. Rick thought he was very funny. Rick's eyes were like giant moons swimming in cloudless sky. "Half a million in Malay Corp. Asteroid stock—"

"I can manage that—"

"And another quarter in U.S., cash, backed against Hong Kong Mining on return. I'm not greedy." From a pocket Rick materialised a black-comm. Square, cheap, hardy, of the same sort Phitsamai's people had provided for his own use earlier. "I'll need it transferred and verified now."

He smiled, and Rick smiled back, and it was settled. The money was transferred and verified, one end of the transaction in Sokpaluang, the other somewhere in the financial servers in Europe.

"You're on," Rick said.

The sky was red like watered blood, like Coca-Cola. The explosions shook the plane, and the smoke burned his eyes, worked its way into his mouth, suffocating him, the mask and goggles doing little to prevent it. The clouds were an acid-yellow, he could see no ground. It felt like floating in a sea of emeralds and rubies, and Rick was blasting out music through hidden speakers, whether it was his own version of *Apocalypse Now* or a sort of code he didn't know: Rick was playing *Lucy in the Sky with Diamonds*.

But the boat was a toy plane, and the river was made of molecules of air, not water, and he had a fervent desire not to meet the girl with kaleidoscope eyes, because he had a feeling he really, really wouldn't like to look into them.

The plane swooped and swerved. "Who's shooting at us?" he shouted, not that Rick could hear him. But Phitsamai did.

"Everyone!" she shouted back.

They flew from the same airfield he had landed in on the way in to Laos. The same pilots sat in the same bar and seemed not to have moved at all. The same Hong Kong movie was playing in the background. The same conversations were taking place. He heard them mention Shangri-La while he waited. He listened and worried.

"Heard the Tamil Tigers got it," someone said.

"No way did it make it to Sri Lanka," someone else said, and laughed—not a pleasant sound. "Besides, you would have noticed if it did."

"Heard it was going West—"

"No, East—"

"There was going to be an auction for it in Hong Kong—"

"I heard it was Kuala Lumpur—"

"What difference does it make? It doesn't exist. It's, like, an urban legend."

"Rural legend?"

"Fairy tale?" someone else offered. There was a short silence. A small man who may have been Malay-Chinese said, "I heard Colonel Wu'd got it." The silence became pained. "And he was shipping it here."

"You should talk to Ricky about that," someone murmured, and the conversation changed, as if by an unspoken agreement.

You should talk to Ricky about that, he thought, as explosions shook the small plane and Ricky's blaring speakers changed to playing the Beatles, Across the Universe. His teeth rattled and he clamped them hard, his hand in Phitsamai's, and he thought of Colonel Wu and wasn't reassured. He knew three things that the pilots didn't. One: Shangri-La was real. Two: it was now in the hands of a man who wanted only to be rid of it, ideally while making money in the process, and—Three—that man was the Captain Hook of South East Asia. Colonel Michael Wu, born in Hong Kong, educated in Oxford, called the Clockwork Boss but never to his face. He had served in half a dozen conflicts before losing a hand and an eye and part of a leg, and going into private practice.

"Wu's in Long Cheng," Phitsamai told him. "He will wait for you there. He does not want Shangri-La any more than you do."

And so, this flight inland, and he felt like some old-time missionary travelling into the unknown, though he was not here to convert anyone, not even corrupt; mainly to prevent what his masters back home called "an unfortunate probability of immobility—" immobility being that year's big buzzword for "peace."

When Shangri-La disappeared, taking its unfortunate inventors with it, no one at first noticed. Then came the rumours...

From the border region of Myanmar and China, for instance, where a sudden lull in fighting brought unreliable reports of former enemies sitting together around a fire, roasting meat and sharing a Russian Baltika... from Cambodia, where Khmer partisan-bandits suddenly disbanded, and released a hastily-worded press release calling for world peace and an end to violence... from Malaysia, where Indians and Malay, facing each other in the midst of a demonstration which had threatened to turn violent, had suddenly dropped placards and staves and embraced each other, a picture of which even made it onto CNN on a quiet news day... alarming sights: as if the nameless drugs cartel, realising what it was they had, had carefully sent samples to potential buyers who then, not quite as carefully, tested them. And after that, for a time—nothing.

"Shit," Rick said, and he could hear him even through the explosions and the blaring Beatles music, so Rick must have been screaming loud enough to penetrate. He looked out and saw what Rick saw and he said, "Shit!"

"Shit shit shit shit shit!" Rick was firing now, the rat-tat-tat of guns doing nothing, and below them the shooting had stopped, and when Rick, too, stopped it became very quiet. The music died. Flying alongside them, one on each side of the plane, were Dragon Boyz.

They were enormous. He had seen pictures of them before, seen DNA analysis, X-rays, dissection videos, but reality captured their essence in a way video couldn't. They were like human bodies that had been stretched and filled, like the corpses Dr. Gunter Von Hagen used to play with before he became a corpse himself, the sort of human sculptures the Von Hagen Cult continued to make, and to worship: they were three times the size of a man and winged, great jewelled things spread out, the tips like knife-points, the heads strangely-human on elongated, swan-like necks. Dragon Boyz. They turned to face the tiny plane, one on either side, and they smiled. Their faces were vaguely Asiatic; they might have once been Chinese. Now they were barely human.

"Our escort!" Phitsamai shouted beside him. He nodded. He did not feel reassured. In the distance he thought he could see a flock of Ravenz, dark shapes, human-bird hybrids, carrion-eaters and mean. He shuddered. The plane dipped. "Going down," he whispered, to himself.

They went down.

They came to a stop on the great runway of Long Cheng. The two Dragon Boyz landed on either side of them. Ravenz circled overhead, screaming in a harsh language that was half gutter-Mandarin, half bird. He climbed out of the plane, feeling shaken. Phitsamai came and stood beside him. Neither spoke. Rick remained inside.

"Welcome to Long Cheng," someone said. The voice was pleasant, cultured, a British voice with just that hint of otherness. It boomed across the tarmac easily, a thunder-roll, but a polite one.

The Clockwork Boss. Michael Wu, Colonel Wu, had half the body of a man. The other...

One-half of his head was a mask of wrought silver. A complex pattern of emeralds and rubies ran like interwoven scars alongside it. His eye was a digital lens. Below, the mouth remained normal. Below that, one arm was a shiny metallic appendage; despite the other name they called him there was no hook on the end. Rather, there were strangely organic silver feelers emanating from it, writhing on the end of his arm like tentacles. His leg was a metal pipe with hundreds of tiny canon-like protrusions. It rotated as he walked. He came close to them and stopped. When he bowed it was done gracefully. "Ms. Phitsamai. It is a pleasure to see you again."

"Colonel."

His human eye seemed to twinkle. Colonel Wu turned to him. "Are you the man who came to buy peace?" he said.

"Are there more than one?"

The Colonel seemed to consider the question. The Dragon Boyz were motionless beside the plane. "Many wish to purchase peace," the Clockwork Boss said. "And too many would like to keep it."

"Then I think we understand each other," he said, and Colonel Wu nodded. "Indeed. Follow me."

They followed him down the runway. He saw jeeps but no transportation was offered. The Colonel walked fast, his leg spinning, the tiny gun-turrets swivelling this way and that. There were other Dragon Boyz, military planes from the last century, a working zeppelin (there was no trace of the broken one he had seen in the photos), and darting amidst unmarked crates of cargo, black-dressed, cowled figures, who seemed to watch his every step: the Klan Klandestine, the new spooks, part triad, part monk, and a whole lot (if the stories could be trusted) of engineered nastiness.

"Do not worry about the Klan," Colonel Wu said as if reading his mind. "They are merely watchers. Mostly. They like to watch." And he laughed, the sound of a tea-party laugh, genial and expansive: it froze the blood in one's veins.

The building Colonel Wu took them to was made of a black material he didn't recognise. There was something unwholesome about it, something faintly organic, like flesh where the blood had congealed. The slide-doors, however, were glass and opened without sound, and the inside was air-conditioned and soft muzak played, though it could not quite conceal a beat that seemed to reverberate through the room like a cold, slow heart.

The two Dragon Boyz had followed behind. Now they positioned themselves outside the doors. The room was sparsely furnished. There were parchment scrolls with Chinese writing on the walls, and he recognised them as the paper money people burned at a funeral: death money, to accompany a departing spirit to the underworld.

"Please, sit," Colonel Wu said. They sat. Colonel Wu disappeared, and returned with a bulky, metallic briefcase. He opened it. Inside were rows and rows of gleaming vials. He stared at it. The Colonel nodded.

"This case," Colonel Wu said, "represents the entirety of the existing product. I understand the samples have been . . . exhausted."

"That is my understanding also," he said.

"Good. It would be a terrible thing to let loose."

"Such is also my masters' feeling on the subject."

"Of course," Colonel Wu said, and he smiled, and his teeth were very white. "And your . . . masters . . . they are committed to following the correct course of action?"

"It will be done as soon as it is in my hands," he said. "Though it would help if I had a suitably large empty area of land for the, um, disposal."

Phitsamai looked at him sharply. He ignored her. Colonel Wu smiled and his fingers made an ancient gesture. "So," he said. "In the words of that most ancient and venerable American Mandarin, Mr. Cameron Crowe—show me the money."

The first indication that things were not going according to plan came when they walked back across the runway and the biplane, complete with its pilot, whose name was Richard, or John, or Enrique depending on the place and the day of the week—but call me Rick—exploded.

A ball of flame rose over the tarmac, and in the skies above the Ravenz crowed and jeered and veered in all directions, an explosion of dark birds mirroring the bright one below. He said, "What the—" and felt Phitsamai grab his hand. She looked frightened. In his other hand he held Shangri-La.

They both turned simultaneously and the second indication of a plan gone wrong came when Colonel Wu, with a mildly surprised expression on his face, disintegrated into a cloud of dust and shrapnel.

"We're being shelled!"

They ran. The cowled figures that were the Klan Klandestine were running too, in the same direction. They were ninja-like. They ran silently. There were hundreds of them.

"Take the jeep!"

The vehicle was unoccupied.

They occupied it.

He hot-wired without conscious thought, hacking the simple brain with the digital key embedded in his thumb, the one that was meant for other uses. The jeep roared into life. He found a gun inside and took it. They sped down the runway towards the distant gates. So much for Nuevo Air Amerika, he thought. And so much for that quarter-million in US cash backed against Hong Kong Mining. Guess Rick's spending days are over.

They got to the gates. The gates were open. The Klan Klandestine were standing in perfect formation before it. Ravenz circled overhead. Dragon Boyz flew high. Through the gate: limestone peaks and burning watchtowers, and coming over the horizon to descend into the valley below: an army.

Who were they? The competition, he thought, but that didn't give clarity: it could have been anyone who thought peace was more profitable than war. He revved the jeep, but there was nowhere to go. The army ahead was gaining ground rapidly. Unmarked vehicles: tanks, artillery, battle-trucks. They were shelling Long Cheng.

Fighter-planes surges overhead, met the waiting Dragon Boyz. He stilled the jeep, thinking. Phitsamai was quiet beside him. He watched a Dragon Boy grapple with a jet, landing on top of it, long snake-like arms fastening around the jet's belly. Two more jets came, firing. The Dragon Boy twisted, his body racked with bullets. Still he held on. A cloud of Ravenz surged onto the oncoming planes, suicidal bird-men aiming for the engines: one was sucked inside the whirlpool of the jet and was shredded, and the plane itself shuddered and bled black smoke. Ahead, the ground troops came, and the Klan Klandestine waited in perfect stillness. What were they? Hafmek? Genetic experiments gone wrong? He watched the advancing army and saw the first row of soldiers and froze.

They were dolls.

Dolls still dressed in factory-default mini-skirts and fuck-me pants and see-thru tank-tops. Dolls with machine guns in their manicured hands. Dolls with bands of grenades across their factory-perfect chests. Moving without passion, without remorse, across the ragged landscape to the gates of the Secret City.

The bombing continued, but it was sporadic, aimed. They couldn't risk destroying Shangri-La, he thought. And so—the ground invasion.

Laos was full of bombs. During the years of the Secret War the Americans riddled the landscape with two million tons of ordnance, exploded and otherwise. The WDU-4, for instance, containing six-thousand metal darts: when exploded it would literally nail people to the ground. Other cluster bombs: the CBU-41, filled with napalm; the CBU-89, dispersing mines; Honest John, containing 368 canisters filled with sarin nerve gas, one for every day of the year and three extra for leap years. Many of the bombs, unexploded ordnance, remained on and under ground, waiting.

The approaching army of peace merely added some new ones to the existing pile.

#

He watched as the Klan Klandestine uncowled. Their black robes fell to the ground. Underneath, they were . . .

The Klan Klandestine were spooks.

Transparent tubing, bodies re-moulded in plastic and diamond nanotubes, with light pulsing through them as microprocessors scattered like fungus across their bodies communicated with each other. They were the ultimate observers, but they could also kill. They did so now.

Spooks and dolls met. The spooks were light, burning, decimating. The dolls melted under their gaze.

The dolls were fists and bullets and shattering force. The spooks came apart under their attack, fracturing, fragmenting, breaking. There were few humans in this battle, so far.

He was counting on humans. And so he waited. There was nothing else to do.

And he wondered as he did so. And he held Phitsamai's hand.

In the sky a Dragon Boy fell, taking a jet in his arms like a lover. Ravenz scattered before gunfire. The battle went on. The dolls' numbers dropped and continued to drop. So did the spooks,' but he wasn't worried about them. They were still human, just.

Phitsamai stirred beside him. "What will you do now?" she said.

He turned to her. He was smiling, and it was a sad smile. "You were waiting for me," he said. "The product made its way to Wu, and once in his hands it disappeared into the bowels of Long Cheng. You knew you couldn't buy it, and you couldn't take it by force. You needed a . . . a hook. Ha." He thought of the Clockwork Boss and shuddered. "Something to draw it out again so you could get it." He looked into her eyes. She had beautiful eyes. "Me," he said.

She was silent.

"You want peace?" he said. "This sort of peace? A viral, non-negotiable, non-thinking peace? This isn't peace, it's bondage."

"Man with no name," she said, and she too smiled, wistfully it seemed to him then. And then, softly: "What do you know about war?"

The dolls were nearly all gone. Behind them came the human army, at last. The spooks still stood, the Dragon Boyz still flew, and so did the Ravenz, though they were few in number. He laid down the case on the ground. It clicked open with a soft sound. Vials of product gleamed inside.

"What are you doing?" she said, and for the first time she looked truly afraid, and he laughed, and hated himself for doing so. "Giving you peace," he said.

He took out the gun from the jeep. "Please!" she said. "Don't—"

Fifty-sixty percent success rate, transmission by air, he thought. The only problem was that he himself would be affected. He realised he would never now get paid. But he was, he realised, more like Rick in a way. They both did the things they did not for money or ideology or even hate. They did them because to do anything else was unthinkable. You could call it kicks, but it wasn't that. Not exactly. Pride in a job well done, perhaps.

He put his thumb in his mouth and bit it, hard, breaking it. Phitsamai took a step back. Then she had a gun in her hand. "Don't," she said.

"Too late," he whispered, his mouth bloody, and he spat out the stump of his thumb. The small transponder had already triangulated his position through the satellite network, and the strike was initiated even as they spoke.

She was going to shoot him but it really was too late. He shot first, not her but the open case, and the vials shattered and broke and an odourless flavourless vapour rose into the air and scattered to the winds.

She lowered her gun just as he was lowering his. A sense of tranquility settled over him. Gradually, silence spread all over the valley. Tanks stopped and soldiers came out of them. The spooks let their arms drop to their sides. The Dragon Boyz flew leisurely through the air and came to land amongst the invaders, and the soldiers welcomed them. He felt happy, at peace for the first time in his life. He came to Phitsamai and held her, burying his face in her neck, breathing in her scent which was of smoke and dust and ginger and for the first time in his life he said, "I love you."

The explosion was nuclear, which was forbidden by every international treaty ever signed. That year babies were born without legs, or arms, or eyes, depending on the way the wind blew. The city of Long Cheng and much of the surrounding countryside was wiped off the continent like a drawing being erased on a blackboard. In later years they told stories about the secret valley of Shangri-La, and many went to find it, and most never came back. The war ended, eventually, as all wars must. And in parts of Laos they still tell the story of the nameless man who sought to buy peace only to destroy it, for it was told that he said that a peace without choice was no peace at all, but whether he was right, or whether he was talking out of his ass, was a theological question much discussed around the beer halls and in the temples of Vientiane.

Shangri-La was never found. And men still fight, and die, and the pilots still meet in the nameless airfield outside Vientiane and get drunk, and watch the same Hong Kong movie on the old TV, and when they get maudlin and there is no work to be done (but there is always work, war or no war) they raise a glass to a pilot whose name was Richard, or John, or Enrique depending on the place and the day of the week—but call me Rick.

#

*The rain falls on a watermelon cart
Bamboo baskets breathe, inside
Caged frogs are granted hope
However brief.*

-The End-

Elegy for a Young Elk

by Hannu Rajaniemi

(from *Subterranean Magazine*)

The night after Kosonen shot the young elk, he tried to write a poem by the campfire.

It was late April and there was still snow on the ground. He had already taken to sitting outside in the evening, on a log by the fire, in the small clearing where his cabin stood. Otso was more comfortable outside, and he preferred the bear's company to being alone. It snored loudly atop its pile of fir branches.

A wet smell that had traces of elk shit drifted from its drying fur.

He dug a soft-cover notebook and a pencil stub from his pocket. He leafed through it: most of the pages were empty. Words had become slippery, harder to catch than elk. Although not this one: careless and young. An old elk would never had let a man and a bear so close.

He scattered words on the first empty page, gripping the pencil hard.

Antlers. Sapphire antlers. No good. *Frozen flames. Tree roots. Forked destinies.* There had to be words that captured the moment when the crossbow kicked against his shoulder, the meaty sound of the arrow's impact. But it was like trying to catch snowflakes in his palm. He could barely glimpse the crystal structure, and then they melted.

He closed the notebook and almost threw it into the fire, but thought better of it and put it back into his pocket. No point in wasting good paper. Besides, his last toilet roll in the outhouse would run out soon.

"Kosonen is thinking about words again," Otso growled. "Kosonen should drink more booze. Don't need words then. Just sleep."

Kosonen looked at the bear. "You think you are smart, huh?" He tapped his crossbow. "Maybe it's you who should be shooting elk."

"Otso good at smelling. Kosonen at shooting. Both good at drinking." Otso yawned luxuriously, revealing rows of yellow teeth. Then it rolled to its side and let out a satisfied heavy sigh. "Otso will have more booze soon."

Maybe the bear was right. Maybe a drink was all he needed. No point in being a poet: They had already written all the poems in the world, up there, in the sky. They probably had poetry gardens. Or places where you could become words.

But that was not the point. The words needed to come from him, a dirty bearded man in the woods whose toilet was a hole in the ground. Bright words from dark matter, that's what poetry was about.

When it worked.

There were things to do. The squirrels had almost picked the lock the previous night, bloody things. The cellar door needed reinforcing. But that could wait until tomorrow.

He was about to open a vodka bottle from Otso's secret stash in the snow when Marja came down from the sky as rain.

The rain was sudden and cold like a bucket of water poured over your head in the sauna. But the droplets did not touch the ground, they floated around Kosonen. As he watched, they changed shape, joined together and made a woman, spindle-thin bones, mist-flesh and muscle. She looked like a glass sculpture. The small breasts were perfect hemispheres, her sex an equilateral silver triangle. But the face was familiar—small nose and high cheekbones, a sharp-tongued mouth.

Marja.

Otso was up in an instant, by Kosonen's side. "Bad smell, god-smell," it growled. "Otso bites." The rain-woman looked at it curiously.

"Otso," Kosonen said sternly. He gripped the fur in the bear's rough neck tightly, feeling its huge muscles tense. "Otso is Kosonen's friend. Listen to Kosonen. Not time for biting. Time for sleeping. Kosonen will speak to god." Then he set the vodka bottle in the snow right under its nose.

Otso sniffed the bottle and scraped the half-melted snow with its forepaw.

"Otso goes," it finally said. "Kosonen shouts if the god bites. Then Otso comes." It picked up the bottle in its mouth deftly and loped into the woods with a bear's loose, shuffling gait.

"Hi," the rain-woman said.

"Hello," Kosonen said carefully. He wondered if she was real. The plague gods were crafty. One of them could have taken Marja's image from his mind. He looked at the unstrung crossbow and tried to judge the odds: a diamond goddess versus an out-of-shape woodland poet. Not good.

"Your dog does not like me very much," the Marja-thing said. She sat down on Kosonen's log and swung her shimmering legs in the air, back and forth, just like Marja always did in the sauna. It had to be her, Kosonen decided, feeling something jagged in his throat.

He coughed. "Bear, not a dog. A dog would have barked. Otso just bites. Nothing personal, that's just its nature. Paranoid and grumpy."

"Sounds like someone I used to know."

"I'm not paranoid." Kosonen hunched down and tried to get the fire going again. "You learn to be careful, in the woods."

Marja looked around. "I thought we gave you stayers more equipment. It looks a little ... primitive here."

"Yeah. We had plenty of gadgets," Kosonen said. "But they weren't plague-proof. I had a smartgun before I had this"—he tapped his crossbow—"but it got infected. I killed it with a big rock and threw it into the swamp. I've got my skis and some tools, and these." Kosonen tapped his temple. "Has been enough so far. So cheers."

He piled up some kindling under a triangle of small logs, and in a moment the flames sprung up again. Three years had been enough to learn about woodcraft at least. Marja's skin looked almost human in the soft light of the fire, and he sat back on Otso's fir branches, watching her. For a moment, neither of them spoke.

"So how are you, these days?" he asked. "Keeping busy?"

Marja smiled. "Your wife grew up. She's a big girl now. You don't want to know how big."

"So... you are not her, then? Who am I talking to?"

"I am her, and I am not her. I'm a partial, but a faithful one. A translation. You wouldn't understand."

Kosonen put some snow in the coffee pot to melt. "All right, so I'm a caveman. Fair enough. But I understand you are here because you want something. So let's get down to business, *perkele*," he swore.

Marja took a deep breath. "We lost something. Something important. Something new. The spark, we called it. It fell into the city."

"I thought you lot kept copies of everything."

"Quantum information. That was a part of the new bit. You can't copy it."

"Tough shit."

A wrinkle appeared between Marja's eyebrows. Kosonen remembered it from a thousand fights they had had, and swallowed.

"If that's the tone you want to take, fine," she said. "I thought you'd be glad to see me. I didn't have to come: They could have sent Mickey Mouse. But I wanted to see you. The big Marja wanted to see you. So you have decided to live your life like this, as the tragic figure haunting the woods. That's fine. But you could at least listen. You owe me that much."

Kosonen said nothing.

"I see," Marja said. "You still blame me for Esa."

She was right. It had been her who got the first Santa Claus machine. The boy needs the best we can offer, she said. The world is changing. Can't have him being left behind. Let's make him into a little god, like the neighbor's kid.

"I guess I shouldn't be blaming you," Kosonen said. "You're just a ... partial. You weren't there."

"I was there," Marja said quietly. "I remember. Better than you, now. I also forget better, and forgive. You never could. You just ... wrote poems. The rest of us moved on, and saved the world."

"Great job," Kosonen said. He poked the fire with a stick, and a cloud of sparks flew up into the air with the smoke.

Marja got up. "That's it," she said. "I'm leaving. See you in a hundred years." The air grew cold. A halo appeared around her, shimmering in the firelight.

Kosonen closed his eyes and squeezed his jaw shut tight. He waited for ten seconds. Then he opened his eyes. Marja was still there, staring at him, helpless. He could not help smiling. She could never leave without having the last word.

"I'm sorry," Kosonen said. "It's been a long time. I've been living in the woods with a bear. Doesn't improve one's temper much."

"I didn't really notice any difference."

"All right," Kosonen said. He tapped the fir branches next to him. "Sit down. Let's start over. I'll make some coffee."

Marja sat down, bare shoulder touching his. She felt strangely warm, warmer than the fire almost.

"The firewall won't let us into the city," she said. "We don't have anyone ... human enough, not anymore. There was some talk about making one, but ... the argument would last a century." She sighed. "We like to argue, in the sky."

Kosonen grinned. "I bet you fit right in." He checked for the wrinkle before continuing. "So you need an errand boy."

"We need help."

Kosonen looked at the fire. The flames were dying now, licking at the blackened wood. There were always new colours in the embers. Or maybe he just always forgot.

He touched Marja's hand. It felt like a soap bubble, barely solid. But she did not pull it away.

"All right," he said. "But just so you know, it's not just for old times' sake."

"Anything we can give you."

"I'm cheap," Kosonen said. "I just want words."

The sun sparkled on the *kantohanki*: snow with a frozen surface, strong enough to carry a man on skis and a bear. Kosonen breathed hard. Even going downhill, keeping pace with Otso was not easy. But in weather like this, there was something glorious about skiing, sliding over blue shadows of trees almost without friction, the snow hissing underneath.

I've sat still too long, he thought. *Should have gone somewhere just to go, not because someone asks.*

In the afternoon, when the sun was already going down, they reached the railroad, a bare gash through the forest, two metal tracks on a bed of gravel. Kosonen removed his skis and stuck them in the snow.

"I'm sorry you can't come along," he told Otso. "But the city won't let you in."

"Otso not a city bear," the bear said. "Otso waits for Kosonen. Kosonen gets sky-bug, comes back. Then we drink booze."

He scratched the rough fur of its neck clumsily. The bear poked Kosonen in the stomach with its nose, so hard that he almost fell. Then it snorted, turned around and shuffled into the woods. Kosonen watched until it vanished among the snow-covered trees.

It took three painful attempts of sticking his fingers down his throat to get the nanoseed Marja gave him to come out. The gagging left a bitter taste in his mouth. Swallowing it had been the only way to protect the delicate thing from the plague. He wiped it in the snow: a transparent bauble the size of a walnut, slippery and warm. It reminded him of the toys you could get from vending machines in supermarkets when he was a child, plastic spheres with something secret inside.

He placed it on the rails carefully, wiped the remains of the vomit from his lips and rinsed his mouth with water. Then he looked at it. Marja knew he would never read instruction manuals, so she had not given him one.

"Make me a train," he said.

Nothing happened. Maybe it can read my mind, he thought, and imagined a train, an old steam train, puffing along. Still nothing, just a reflection of the darkening sky on the seed's clear surface. She always had to be subtle. Marja could never give a present without thinking about its meaning for days. Standing still let the spring winter chill through his wolf-pelt coat, and he hopped up and down, rubbing his hands together.

With the motion came an idea. He frowned, staring at the seed, and took the notebook from his pocket. Maybe it was time to try out Marja's other gift—or advance payment, however you wanted to look at it. He had barely written the first lines, when the words leaped in his mind like animals woken from slumber. He closed the book, cleared his throat and spoke.

these rails were worn thin
    by wheels
    that wrote down
    the name of each passenger
    in steel and miles

he said,

it's a good thing the years
    ate our flesh too
    made us thin and light
    so the rails are strong enough
    to carry us still
    to the city
    in our train of glass and words

Doggerel, he thought, but it didn't matter. The joy of words filled his veins like vodka. *Too bad it didn't work—*

The seed blurred. It exploded into a white-hot sphere. The waste heat washed across Kosonen's face. Glowing tentacles squirmed past him, sucking carbon and metal from the rails and trees. They danced like a welder's electric arcs, sketching lines and surfaces in the air.

And suddenly, the train was there.

It was transparent, with paper-thin walls and delicate wheels, as if it had been blown from glass, sketch of a cartoon steam engine with a single carriage, with spiderweb-like chairs inside, just the way he had imagined it.

He climbed in, expecting the delicate structure to sway under his weight, but it felt rock-solid. The nanoseed lay on the floor innocently, as if nothing had happened. He picked it up carefully, took it outside and buried it in the snow, leaving his skis and sticks as markers. Then he picked up his backpack, boarded the train again and sat down in one of the gossamer seats. Unbidden, the train lurched into motion smoothly. To Kosonen, it sounded like the rails beneath were whispering, but he could not hear the words.

He watched the darkening forest glide past. The day's journey weighed heavily down on his limbs. The memory of the snow beneath his skis melted together with the train's movement, and soon Kosonen was asleep.

When he woke up, it was dark. The amber light of the firewall glowed in the horizon, like a thundercloud.

The train had speeded up. The dark forest outside was a blur, and the whispering of the rails had become a quiet staccato song. Kosonen swallowed as the train covered the remaining distance in a matter of minutes. The firewall grew into a misty dome glowing with yellowish light from within. The city was an indistinct silhouette beneath it. The buildings seemed to be in motion, like a giant's shadow puppets.

Then it was a flaming curtain directly in front of the train, an impenetrable wall made from twilight and amber crossing the tracks. Kosonen gripped the delicate frame of his seat, knuckles white. "Slow down!" he shouted, but the train did not hear. It crashed directly into the firewall with a bone-jarring impact. There was a burst of light, and then Kosonen was lifted from his seat.

It was like drowning, except that he was floating in an infinite sea of amber light rather than water. Apart from the light, there was just emptiness. His skin tickled. It took him a moment to realise that he was not breathing.

And then a stern voice spoke.

This is not a place for men, it said. *Closed. Forbidden. Go back.*

"I have a mission," said Kosonen. His voice had no echo in the light. "From your makers. They command you to let me in."

He closed his eyes, and Marja's third gift floated in front of him, not words but a number. He had always been poor at memorising things, but Marja's touch had been a pen with acid ink, burning it in his mind. He read off the endless digits, one by one.

You may enter, said the firewall. *But only that which is human will leave.*

The train and the speed came back, sharp and real like a paper cut. The twilight glow of the firewall was still there, but instead of the forest, dark buildings loomed around the railway, blank windows staring at him.

Kosonen's hands tickled. They were clean, as were his clothes: Every speck of dirt was gone. His felt was tender and red, like he had just been to the sauna.

The train slowed down at last, coming to a stop in the dark mouth of the station, and Kosonen was in the city.

The city was a forest of metal and concrete and metal that breathed and hummed. The air smelled of ozone. The facades of the buildings around the railway station square looked almost like he remembered them, only subtly wrong. From the corner of his eye he could glimpse them *moving,* shifting in their sleep like stone-skinned animals. There were no signs of life, apart from a cluster of pigeons, hopping back and forth on the stairs, looking at him. They had sapphire eyes.

A bus stopped, full of faceless people who looked like crash test dummies, sitting unnaturally still. Kosonen decided not to get in and started to head across the square, towards the main shopping street: he had to start the search for the spark somewhere. It will glow, Marja had said. You can't miss it.

There was what looked like a car wreck in the parking lot, lying on its side, hood crumpled like a discarded beer can, covered in white pigeon droppings. But when Kosonen walked past it, its engine roared, and the hood popped open. A hissing bundle of tentacles snapped out, reaching for him.

He managed to gain some speed before the car-beast rolled onto its four wheels. There were narrow streets on the other side of the square, too narrow for it to follow. He ran, cold weight in his stomach, legs pumping.

The crossbow beat painfully at his back in its strap, and he struggled to get it over his head.

The beast passed him arrogantly, and turned around. Then it came straight at him. The tentacles spread out from its glowing engine mouth into a fan of serpents.

Kosonen fumbled with a bolt, then loosed it at the thing. The crossbow kicked, but the arrow glanced off its windshield. It seemed to confuse it enough for Kosonen to jump aside. He dove, hit the pavement with a painful thump, and rolled.

"Somebody help *perkele*," he swore with impotent rage, and got up, panting, just as the beast backed off slowly, engine growling. He smelled burning rubber, mixed with ozone. Maybe I can wrestle it, he thought like a madman, spreading his arms, refusing to run again. One last poem in it—

Something landed in front of the beast, wings fluttering. A pigeon. Both Kosonen and the car-creature stared at it. It made a cooing sound. Then it exploded.

The blast tore at his eardrums, and the white fireball turned the world black for a second. Kosonen found himself on the ground again, ears ringing, lying painfully on top of his backpack. The car-beast was a burning wreck ten meters away, twisted beyond all recognition.

There was another pigeon next to him, picking at what looked like bits of metal. It lifted its head and looked at him, flames reflecting from the tiny sapphire eyes. Then it took flight, leaving a tiny white dropping behind.

#

The main shopping street was empty. Kosonen moved carefully in case there were more of the car creatures around, staying close to narrow alleys and doorways. The firewall light was dimmer between the buildings, and strange lights danced in the windows.

Kosonen realised he was starving: He had not eaten since noon, and the journey and the fight had taken their toll. He found an empty cafe in a street corner that seemed safe, set up his small travel cooker on a table and boiled some water. The supplies he had been able to bring consisted mainly of canned soup and dried elk meat, but his growling stomach was not fussy. The smell of food made him careless.

"This is my place," said a voice. Kosonen leapt up, startled, reaching for the crossbow.

There was a stooped, trollish figure at the door, dressed in rags. His face shone with sweat and dirt, framed by matted hair and beard. His porous skin was full of tiny sapphire growths, like pockmarks. Kosonen had thought living in the woods had made him immune to human odours, but the stranger carried a bitter stench of sweat and stale booze that made him want to retch.

The stranger walked in and sat down at a table opposite Kosonen. "But that's all right," he said amicably. "Don't get many visitors these days. Have to be neighbourly. *Saatana*, is that Blaband soup that you've got?"

"You're welcome to some," Kosonen said warily. He had met some of the other stayers over the years, but usually avoided them—they all had their own reasons for not going up, and not much in common.

"Thanks. That's neighbourly indeed. I'm Pera, by the way." The troll held out his hand.

Kosonen shook it gingerly, feeling strange jagged things under Pera's skin. It was like squeezing a glove filled with powdered glass. "Kosonen. So you live here?"

"Oh, not here, not in the center. I come here to steal from the buildings. But they've become really smart, and stingy. Can't even find soup anymore. The Stockmann department store almost ate me, yesterday. It's not easy life here." Pera shook his head. "But better than outside." There was a sly look in his eyes. *Are you staying because you want to,* wondered Kosonen, *or because the firewall won't let you out anymore?*

"Not afraid of the plague gods, then?" he asked aloud. He passed Pera one of the heated soup tins. The city stayer slurped it down with one gulp, smell of minestrone mingling with the other odours.

"Oh, you don't have to be afraid of them anymore. They're all dead."

Kosonen looked at Pera, startled. "How do you know?"

"The pigeons told me."

"The pigeons?"

Pera took something from the pocket of his ragged coat carefully. It was a pigeon. It had a sapphire beak and eyes, and a trace of blue in its feathers. It struggled in Pera's grip, wings fluttering.

"My little buddies," Pera said. "I think you've already met them."

"Yes," Kosonen said. "Did you send the one that blew up that car thing?"

"You have to help a neighbour out, don't you? Don't mention it. The soup was good."

"What did they say about the plague gods?"

Pera grinned a gap-toothed grin. "When the gods got locked up here, they started fighting. Not enough power to go around, you see. So one of them had to be the top dog, like in Highlander. The pigeons show me pictures, sometimes. Bloody stuff. Explosions. Nanites eating men. But finally they were all gone, every last one. My playground now."

So Esa is gone, too. Kosonen was surprised how sharp the feeling of loss was, even now. *Better like this.* He swallowed. *Let's get the job done first. No time to mourn. Let's think about it when we get home. Write a poem about it. And tell Marja.*

"All right," Kosonen said. "I'm hunting too. Do you think your ... buddies could find it? Something that glows. If you help me, I'll give you all the soup I've got. And elk meat. And I'll bring more later. How does that sound?"

"Pigeons can find anything," said Pera, licking his lips.

The pigeon-man walked through the city labyrinth like his living room, accompanied by a cloud of the chimera birds. Every now and then, one of them would land on his shoulder and touch his ear with his beak, as if to whisper.

"Better hurry," Pera said. "At night, it's not too bad, but during the day the houses get younger and start thinking."

Kosonen had lost all sense of direction. The map of the city was different from the last time he had been here, in the old human days. His best guess was that they were getting somewhere close to the cathedral in the old town, but he couldn't be sure. Navigating the changed streets felt like walking through the veins of some giant animal, convoluted and labyrinthine. Some buildings were enclosed in what looked like black film, rippling like oil. Some had grown together, organic-looking structures of brick and concrete, blocking streets and making the ground uneven.

"We're not far," Pera said. "They've seen it. Glowing like a pumpkin lantern, they say." He giggled. The amber light of the firewall grew brighter as they walked. It was hotter, too, and Kosonen was forced to discard his old Pohjanmaa sweater.

They passed an office building that had become a sleeping face, a genderless Easter Island countenance. There was more life in this part of the town too, sapphire-eyed animals, sleek cats looking at them from windowsills. Kosonen saw a fox crossing the street: It gave them one bright look and vanished down a sewer hole.

Then they turned a corner where faceless men wearing fashion from ten years ago danced together in a shop window, and saw the cathedral.

It had grown to gargantuan size, dwarfing every other building around it. It was an anthill of dark-red brick and hexagonal doorways. It buzzed with life. Cats with sapphire claws clung to its walls like sleek gargoyles. Thick pigeon flocks fluttered around its towers. Packs of azure-tailed rats ran in and out of open, massive doors like armies on a mission. And there were insects everywhere, filling the air with a drill-like buzzing sound, moving in dense black clouds like a giant's black breath.

"Oh, *jumalauta*," Kosonen said. "*That's* where it fell?"

"Actually, no. I was just supposed to bring you here," Pera said.

"What?"

"Sorry. I lied. It was like in Highlander: There is one of them left. And he wants to meet you."

Kosonen stared at Pera, dumbfounded. The pigeons landed on the other man's shoulders and arms like a grey fluttering cloak. They seized his rags and hair and skin with sharp claws, wings started beating furiously. As Kosonen stared, Pera rose to the air.

"No hard feelings, I just had a better deal from him. Thanks for the soup," he shouted. In a moment, Pera was a black scrap of cloth in the sky.

The earth shook. Kosonen fell to his knees. The window eyes that lined the street lit up, full of bright, malevolent light.

He tried to run. He did not make it far before they came, the fingers of the city: the pigeons, the insects, a buzzing swarm that covered him. A dozen chimera rats clung to his skull, and he could felt the humming of their flywheel hearts. Something sharp bit through the bone. The pain grew like a forest fire, and Kosonen screamed.

The city spoke. Its voice was a thunderstorm, words made from shaking of the earth and the sighs of buildings. Slow words, squeezed from stone.

Dad, the city said.

The pain was gone. Kosonen heard the gentle sound of waves, and felt a warm wind on his face. He opened his eyes.

"Hi, dad," Esa said.

They sat on the summerhouse pier, wrapped in towels, skin flushed from the sauna. It was evening, with a hint of chill in the air, Finnish summer's gentle reminder that things were not forever. The sun hovered above the blue-tinted treetops. The lake surface was calm, full of liquid reflections.

"I thought," Esa said, "that you'd like it here."

Esa was just like Kosonen remembered him, a pale skinny kid, ribs showing, long arms folded across his knees, stringy wet hair hanging on his forehead. But his eyes were the eyes of a city, dark orbs of metal and stone.

"I do," Kosonen said. "But I can't stay."

"Why not?"

"There is something I need to do."

"We haven't seen each other in ages. The sauna is warm. I've got some beer cooling in the lake. Why the rush?"

"I should be afraid of you," Kosonen said. "You killed people. Before they put you here."

"You don't know what it's like," Esa said. "The plague does everything you want. It gives you things you don't even know you want. It turns the world soft. And sometimes it tears it apart for you. You think a thought, and things break. You can't help it."

The boy closed his eyes. "You want things too. I know you do. That's why you are here, isn't it? You want your precious words back."

Kosonen said nothing.

"Mom's errand boy, *vittu*. So they fixed your brain, flushed the booze out. So you can write again. Does it feel good? For a moment there I thought you came here for me. But that's not the way it ever worked, was it?"

"I didn't know—"

"I can see the inside of your head, you know," Esa said. "I've got my fingers inside your skull. One thought, and my bugs will eat you, bring you here for good. Quality time forever. What do you say to that?"

And there it was, the old guilt. "We worried about you, every second, after you were born," Kosonen said. "We only wanted the best for you."

It had seemed so natural. How the boy played with his machine that made other machines. How things started changing shape when you thought at them. How Esa smiled when he showed Kosonen the talking starfish that the machine had made.

"And then I had one bad day."

"I remember," Kosonen said. He had been home late, as usual. Esa had been a diamond tree, growing in his room. There were starfish everywhere, eating the walls and the floor, making more of themselves. And that was only the beginning.

"So go ahead. Bring me here. It's your turn to make me into what you want. Or end it all. I deserve it."

Esa laughed softly. "And why would I do that, to an old man?" He sighed. "You know, I'm old too now. Let me show you." He touched Kosonen's shoulder gently and

Kosonen was the city. His skin was stone of and concrete, pores full of the godplague. The streets and buildings were his face, changing and shifting with every thought and emotion. His

nervous system was diamond and optic fibre. His hands were chimera animals.

The firewall was all around him, in the sky and in the cold bedrock, insubstantial but adamantine, squeezing from every side, cutting off energy, making sure he could not think fast. But he could still dream, weave words and images into threads, make worlds out of the memories he had and the memories of the smaller gods he had eaten to become the city. He sang his dreams in radio waves, not caring if the firewall let them through or not, louder and louder—

"Here," Esa said from far away. "Have a beer."

Kosonen felt a chilly bottle in his hand, and drank. The dream-beer was strong and real. The malt taste brought him back. He took a deep breath, letting the fake summer evening wash away the city.

"Is that why you brought me here? To show me that?" He asked.

"Well, no," Esa said, laughing. His stone eyes looked young, suddenly. "I just wanted you to meet my girlfriend."

The quantum girl had golden hair and eyes of light. She wore many faces at once, like a Hindu goddess. She walked to the pier with dainty steps. Esa's summerland showed its cracks around her: There were fracture lines in her skin, with otherworldly colours peeking out.

"This is Säde," Esa said.

She looked at Kosonen, and spoke, a bubble of words, a superposition, all possible greetings at once.

"Nice to meet you," Kosonen said.

"They did something right when they made her, up there," said Esa. "She lives in many worlds at once, thinks in qubits. And this is the world where she wants to be. With me." He touched her shoulder gently. "She heard my songs and ran away."

"Marja said she fell," Kosonen said. "That something was broken."

"She said what they wanted her to say. They don't like it when things don't go according to plan."

Säde made a sound, like the chime of a glass bell.

"The firewall keeps squeezing us," Esa said. "That's how it was made. Make things go slower and slower here, until we die. Säde doesn't fit in here, this place is too small. So you will take her back home, before it's too late." He smiled. "I'd rather you do it than anyone else."

"That's not fair," Kosonen said. He squinted at Säde. She was too bright to look at. *But what can I do? I'm just a slab of meat. Meat and words.*

The thought was like a pine cone, rough in his grip, but with a seed of something in it.

"I think there is a poem in you two," he said.

Kosonen sat on the train again, watching the city stream past. It was early morning. The sunrise gave the city new hues: purple shadows and gold, ember colours. Fatigue pulsed in his temples. His body ached. The words of a poem weighed down on his mind.

Above the dome of the firewall he could see a giant diamond starfish, a drone of the sky people, watching, like an outstretched hand.

They came to see what happened, he thought. *They'll find out.*

This time, he embraced the firewall like a friend, and its tingling brightness washed over him. And deep within, the stern-voiced watchman came again. It said nothing this time, but he could feel its presence, scrutinizing, seeking things that did not belong in the outside world.

Kosonen gave it everything.

The first moment when he knew he had put something real on paper. The disappointment when he realized that a poet was not much in a small country, piles of cheaply printed copies of his first collection, gathering dust in little bookshops. The jealousy he had felt when Marja gave birth to Esa, what a pale shadow of that giving birth to words was. The tracks of the elk in the snow and the look in its eyes when it died.

He felt the watchman step aside, satisfied.

Then he was through. The train emerged into the real, undiluted dawn. He looked back at the city, and saw fire raining from the starfish. Pillars of light cut through the city in geometric patterns, too bright to look at, leaving only white-hot plasma in their wake.

Kosonen closed his eyes and held on to the poem as the city burned.

Kosonen planted the nanoseed in the woods. He dug a deep hole in the half-frozen peat with his bare hands, under an old tree stump. He sat down, took off his cap, dug out his notebook, and started reading. The pencil-scrawled words glowed bright in his mind, and after a while he didn't need to look at them anymore.

The poem rose from the words like a titanic creature from an ocean, first showing just a small extremity but then soaring upwards in a spray of glossolalia, mountain-like. It was a stream of hissing words and phonemes, an endless spell that tore at his throat. And with it came the quantum information from the microtubules of his neurons, where the bright-eyed girl now lived, and jagged impulses from synapses where his son was hiding.

The poem swelled into a roar. He continued until his voice was a hiss. Only the nanoseed could hear, but that was enough. Something stirred under the peat.

When the poem finally ended, it was evening. Kosonen opened his eyes. The first things he saw were the sapphire antlers, sparkling in the last rays of the sun.

Two young elk looked at him. One was smaller, more delicate, and its large brown eyes held a hint of sunlight. The other was young and skinny, but wore its budding antlers with pride. It held Kosonen's gaze, and in its eyes he saw shadows of the city. Or reflections in a summer lake, perhaps.

They turned around and ran into the woods, silent, fleet-footed and free.

Kosonen was opening the cellar door when the rain came back. It was barely a shower this time: The droplets formed Marja's face in the air. For a moment he thought he saw her wink. Then the rain became a mist, and was gone. He propped the door open.

The squirrels stared at him from the trees curiously.

"All yours, gentlemen," Kosonen said. "Should be enough for next winter. I don't need it anymore."

Otso and Kosonen left at noon, heading north. Kosonen's skis slid along easily in the thinning snow. The bear pulled a sledge loaded with equipment. When they were well away from the cabin, it stopped to sniff at a fresh trail.

"Elk," it growled. "Otso is hungry. Kosonen shoot an elk. Need meat for the journey. Kosonen did not bring enough booze."

Kosonen shook his head.

"I think I'm going to learn to fish," he said.

-The End-

Additional Materials

About the Authors

Poet and writer **Saladin Ahmed** has been a finalist for the Nebula Award for Best Short Story, the Campbell Award for Best New Science Fiction or Fantasy Writer, and the Harper's Pen Award for best Sword and Sorcery/Heroic Fantasy Short Story. His short fiction has appeared in magazines and podcasts including *Strange Horizons, Orson Scott Card's Intergalactic Medicine Show, Beneath Ceaseless Skies, Apex Magazine, StarShipSofa* and *PodCastle*, and has been translated into Portuguese, Czech, Dutch, and Romanian. His fantasy novel *Throne of the Crescent Moon* will be published by DAW Books in 2012. His website is www.saladinahmed.com.

Aliette de Bodard has won the BSFA Award for Best Short Fiction, the Writers of the Future, and been nominated for the Hugo, Nebula and Campbell Awards. Her Aztec mystery-fantasies *Servant of the Underworld, Harbinger of the Storm,* and *Master of the House of Darts* are published by Angry Robot, while her short fiction has appeared in *Interzone, Realms of Fantasy, Asimov's,* and *The Year's Best Science Fiction.* She lives in Paris in a flat with more computers than she really needs and uses her spare time to indulge in her love of mythology and history. As a Franco-Vietnamese, Aliette has a strong interest in non-Western cultures, particularly the Aztecs, Ancient Vietnam and Ancient China, and will gladly use any excuse to shoehorn those into her short or long fiction.

Richard Bowes has published five novels, two collections of short fiction and over fifty stories. He has won two World Fantasy Awards and the Lambda, International Horror Guild and Million Writers Awards (the last one for his story "There's a Hole in the City," collected in this volume). Recent and forthcoming stories appear in *The Magazine of Fantasy and Science Fiction, Realms of Fantasy, Icarus, Naked City, Nebula Awards Showcase 2011, After, Supernatural Noir, Wilde Stories 2011* and *Blood and Other Cravings*. His website is www.rickbowes.com.

Nadia Bulkin writes what she likes to call "socio-political horror": dark fiction infused with social and political problems and themes. She graduated from Barnard College in New York City with a B.A. in Political Science in May 2009, and in 2011 she started the International Politics M.A. program at American University in Washington, D.C. She has two hometowns: Lincoln, Nebraska, and Jakarta, Indonesia. Her fiction has been published in *ChiZine, Beneath Ceaseless Skies, Fantasy Magazine, Strange Horizons*, and other places. Her website is nadiabulkin.wordpress.com.

Adam-Troy Castro made his first professional sale to *Spy* magazine in 1987. Since then, he's published seventeen books including *Emissaries from the Dead* (winner of the Philip K. Dick award), and *The Third Claw of God*, both of which feature his profoundly damaged far-future murder investigator Andrea Cort. His short fiction has been nominated for five Nebulas, two Hugos, and two Stokers, while his story "Arvies," collected in this volume, won the 2011 *storySouth* Million Writers Award. Adam-Troy describes the odd hyphen between his first and middle names as a typo from his college newspaper that was just annoying enough to embrace with gusto. He currently lives in Miami with his wife Judi and a population of insane cats that includes Uma Furman and Meow Farrow.

N. K. Jemisin's debut novel, *The Hundred Thousand Kingdoms*, was nominated for the Nebula, Hugo, and World Fantasy Awards, and won the Locus Award for Best First Novel. Two other novels in the sequence, *The Broken Kingdoms* and *The Kingdom of Gods*, have also been published. The story reprinted in this volume, "Non-Zero Probabilities," was also a finalist for the Hugo and Nebula Awards. In addition to writing, she is a counseling psychologist (specializing in career counseling), a sometime hiker and biker, and a political/feminist/anti-racist blogger. Her website is www.nkjemisin.com.

Alaya Dawn Johnson is the author of the *Spirit Binders* series (*Racing the Dark, The Burning City*) and the historical fantasy novels *Moonshine* and *Wicked City* (April 2012). Her short stories have appeared in multiple online venues, including *Strange Horizons, Fantasy Magazine* and *Subterranean Magazine*. She lives in New York City. Her website is www.alayadawnjohnson.com.

Yoon Ha Lee's short fiction has appeared in *The Magazine of Fantasy and Science Fiction, Beneath Ceaseless Skies*, and other places. Lee majored in math and says it is a source of continual delight to her that the subject can be mined for SF/F story ideas. She currently lives in Louisiana with her family. Her website is www.yoonhalee.com.

Hannu Rajaniemi is a Finnish author of science fiction and fantasy. His debut novel, *The Quantum Thief*, was published in 2010 by Gollancz in Britain (U.S. publication by Tor Books followed the next yea), earning Rajaniemi a nomination for the Locus Award for Best First Novel. He is currently working on a sequel called *The Fractal Prince*. Rajaniemi holds a B.Sc. in Mathematics from the University of Oulu, a Certificate of Advanced Study in Mathematics from the University of Cambridge and a Ph.D. in Mathematical

Physics from the University of Edinburgh. He currently lives in Edinburgh, Scotland, and is a founding director of a technology consultancy company called ThinkTank Maths. His website is www.tomorrowelephant.net.

Rachel Swirsky has been published in such publications as *PANK, The Konundrum Engine Literary Review, The New Haven Review.* Tor.com, *Subterranean Magazine, Beneath Ceaseless Skies, Fantasy Magazine, Interzone, Realms of Fantasy,* and *Weird Tales,* and collected in a variety of year's best anthologies. Her novella "The Lady Who Plucked Red Flowers Beneath the Queen's Window" won the 2010 Nebula Award. Her novelette "Eros, Philia, Agape," collected in this volume, was a finalist for the *storySouth* Million Writers Award and also nominated for the Hugo, Theodore Sturgeon, and Locus Awards, and recommended for the Tiptree Award.

Lavie Tidhar is the author of the BSFA Award nominated *Osama,* which has been compared to Philip K. Dick's seminal work *The Man in the High Castle* by both the *Guardian* and the *Financial Times.* He is also the author of the Bookman Histories novels, comprising *The Bookman, Camera Obscura* and *The Great Game,* and of many other novellas and short stories. His website is lavietidhar.wordpress.com.

Catherynne M. Valente is a *New York Times* best-selling author of fantasy and science fiction novels, short stories, and poetry. She has written over a dozen volumes of fiction and poetry since her first novel, *The Labyrinth,* was published in 2004. Her poetry and short fiction can be found online and in print in such journals as *Clarkesworld Magazine,* Tor.com, *Fantasy Magazine, Electric Velocipede, Lightspeed Magazine, Subterranean Online,* and *Weird Tales,* as well as in numerous anthologies and Year's Best collections. She has been nominated for the Hugo, Locus, and World

Fantasy Awards, and has won the James Tiptree Jr., Mythopoeic, Lambda, and Andre Norton Awards. Her story "Urchins, While Swimming," collected in this volume, won the 2007 *storySouth* Million Writers Award. You can learn more about Valente at www.catherynnemvalente.com.

Jenny Williams is a writer, editor, and musician from California. She earned her BA in English and creative writing from UC Berkeley and her MFA in fiction from Brooklyn College. Her award-winning fiction, nonfiction, poetry, and graphic stories have appeared in numerous publications and anthologies. Her story "The Fisherman's Wife" won the 2009 *storySouth* Million Writers Award. You can find her at www.jennydwilliams.com.

Caroline M. Yoachim is a Nebula Award nominated writer and photographer living in Seattle, Washington. She is a graduate of the Clarion West Writers Workshop, and her fiction has appeared in *Asimov's*, *Fantasy Magazine*, and *Daily Science Fiction*, among other places. For more about Caroline, check out her website at: www.carolineyoachim.com.

About the Editor

Jason Sanford was born and raised in Alabama but currently lives in the Midwestern U.S. with his wife and sons. His life's adventures have included work as an archeologist and a Peace Corps Volunteer. Many of his short stories have been published in the British SF magazine *Interzone*, which devoted a special issue to his fiction in December 2010. His fiction has also been published in *Year's Best SF 14*, *Analog*, *Orson Scott Card's InterGalactic Medicine Show*, *Tales of the Unanticipated*, *The Mississippi Review*, *Diagram*, *Pindeldyboz*, and other places.

Among the awards and honors Jason has received includes being a finalist for the Nebula Award for Best Novella, winning both the 2008 and 2009 *Interzone* Readers' Polls (and tying for the 2010 poll), receiving a Minnesota State Arts Board Fellowship, being nominated for the BSFA Award, and being longlisted for the British Fantasy Award. Jason's fiction has been reprinted in a number of languages, including Chinese, French, Russian, and Czech.

Jason's short story collection *Never Never Stories* was published in 2011 by Spotlight Publishing.

Connect with Jason Sanford Online

Twitter: twitter.com/jasonsanford
Jason's website: www.jasonsanford.com

CPSIA information can be obtained at www.ICGtesting.com
Printed in the USA
BVOW021501150712

295194BV00001B/36/P